...ne has
... *Baksheesh*
...ing on the success
...been published in eight

Also available from Bitter Lemon Press
by Esmahan Aykol:

*Hotel Bosphorus*

# BAKSHEESH

## Esmahan Aykol

Translated by Ruth Whitehouse

**BITTER LEMON PRESS**
**LONDON**

BITTER LEMON PRESS

First published in the United Kingdom in 2013 by
Bitter Lemon Press, 37 Arundel Gardens, London W11 2LW

www.bitterlemonpress.com

First published in Turkish as *Kelepir Ev*
by Everest Yayinlari, Istanbul, 2003

Bitter Lemon Press gratefully acknowledges the financial
assistance of the Arts Council of England and of the TEDA Project
of the Ministry of Culture and Tourism of the Republic of Turkey

A CIP record for this book is available from the British Library
ISBN 978-1-908524-04-1

Typeset by Tetragon
Printed and bound by CPI Group (UK) Ltd, Croydon, CR0 4YY

*Once again, for him...*

# 1

"I'll get the Chinese mafia to bump them off," she said, stirring her barley cappuccino with an elegance that was totally at odds with her even thinking about doing away with somebody.

"The local mafia are cheap and do a clean job. Why the Chinese?"

"If only they were both still here in Istanbul. But they're not, sweetie. Çetin's gone back to New York to get a divorce, and his mother's gone too, with her darling son, her precious little lamb," she said. "The New York Chinese would take care of them," she added, sternly.

With my index and middle fingers, I was massaging the skin beneath my chin where it had started to sag slightly – a habit I'd recently developed.

"So, men are right to fear female vengeance. You're thinking of killing off the poor man *and* his mother," I said.

"Actually, it's the other way round. The mother-in-law is my real target, not my ex."

Involuntarily, I pulled a face.

"I know you think it's just normal rivalry between wife and mother-in-law. But believe me, it's not," she said, putting her hand over my right hand. The left was still busy working on the massage.

Over the next half-hour, I had plenty of time to practise my chin massage as I listened to Özlem talking about her relationship with her estranged husband and mother-in-law.

Actually, I was in no fit state to be bothering about my friends' problems at that time. I had plenty of my own, and they were increasing daily. The discovery that my chin had begun to sag was the least of them.

So think how bad the others were.

Approaching her mid-forties, but looking no more than thirty-five, with a great job... Or put another way: what could be missing in the life of a woman who loves reading detective stories and has a shop specializing in crime fiction that provides her with enough to live on, who lives in a city she adores and has a lover she finds attractive, despite his slight paunch – in fact, precisely because of that slight paunch? I kept asking myself this, but each time I ended up feeling worse than ever. As Fatma Hanım would say: only in Turkey!

If you were wondering what that means, dear reader, you don't know enough about Turkey. Actually, having trekked around a number of different countries, I no longer think so badly of people who know nothing about places outside the country they live in. In fact, I can't bear to spend more than five minutes reading about events in the country I live in, let alone the town. Anyway, you've already met the person best placed to explain the meaning of "only in Turkey".

"Only in Turkey", where rents were paid in US dollars or euros, where becoming a tenant entailed providing the owner with an "undertaking to vacate" document that had been certified by a notary. With this document, as its name indicates, you guaranteed that after a certain period of time you would vacate the apartment you were about to inhabit as a tenant. On the day of departure – and even having a lawyer as a lover could not spare you this – you had to leave the home where you had spent bittersweet days, crying, laughing and making love.

Actually, there was another option, which was to pay the rent increase demanded by the landlord. This at least meant getting out of having to move and leaving behind memories of morning coffees on the balcony, the flush that didn't work properly, the chipped enamel on the kitchen sink, and the doors in the sitting room that didn't shut completely. Most importantly, it avoided being thrown out into the unknown.

If you, dear reader, had a childhood anything like mine, spent moving from city to city and country to country, then you will know very well what I mean. You know deep down that the cost of moving cannot be counted in financial terms. You understand that no one chooses to move for the sake of a couple of euros.

But that was the problem. It wasn't just a couple of euros. My poverty-stricken, dried-up old bag of a landlady suddenly wanted an increase of 150 euros. Can you imagine what that meant for this honest, hard-working proprietor of a small bookshop?

It meant a lot of money.

Anyway, the long and the short of it was that I either had to give in and pay the extra 150 euros, or find somewhere else to live.

I decided to find somewhere else – if I could, of course.

I couldn't do anything until Özlem had finished explaining her monstrous plans, so I used up three precious hours on matters quite unrelated to house-hunting. However, before paying the bill, I used my mobile phone to call an estate agent in Akarsu Road.

You may have noticed in that previous sentence – because I know you're very smart, dear readers – that I, too, now had a mobile phone. I'd given in about six months before. It wasn't a new or expensive model, and it was pay-as-you-go. People looked disparagingly at me when I gave them my number or if they saw me talking on my mobile, because Turks in my circle were always exchanging their mobiles and cars for new models. But as you know, I'm not the sort of woman who bothers about that sort of thing. And that's fine with me.

Before you read any further, I should tell you about something else that was new in my life: I'd dyed my hair. It was previously deep auburn, but for the last ten days it had been orange. I'm not exaggerating – really orange.

Selim, Lale and Yılmaz loved the new colour, and I couldn't have cared less whether Fofo liked it or not. Anyway, he hadn't seen it – neither me nor my new hair.

For anyone interested who has not read the previous book, I should explain that Fofo was my housemate and even my closest friend, until he found a lover and left me. He's a Spaniard who left his partner, friends and city to chase after a few men. His real name is Juan Antonio. Is any of this important? Maybe not. But it just goes to show that novelties in my life amounted to no more than a mobile phone and a new hair colour. As for disasters – they were all related to house-hunting.

I loathed the high heels that had been all the rage since spring. I mean the contorted, shapeless ones. It was already far from easy walking along the uneven streets of Istanbul, but it had become sheer torture because of these weird heels. However, I was never one to make concessions when it came to keeping up with new fashions, so, despite looking like a lame duck, I wore them to make the arduous walk around Taksim Square, down Sıraselviler Road to Cihangir, where I called in at Rüstem Real Estate, 26 Akarsu Road.

By then, the mere words "real estate" or "estate agent" made me shudder. For two weeks I'd been trailing around from dawn to dusk, as if on overtime shifts. No wonder I'd dyed my hair! Every woman going through a crisis changes either the style or colour of her hair, doesn't she? Don't turn your nose up at clichés – they are only reflections of the truth. No one knows better than I do that we Germans are stingy, tiresome and prescriptive, with a reverence for authority and hostility towards anyone different from ourselves.

Rüstem, the estate agent, sprang to his feet as soon as I entered, which was only natural given that, if I were to rent any of the dilapidated apartments he'd shown me, he would get a handsome twelve-per-cent commission. You're no doubt expecting me to rant about people taking commission for real estate or about parasites making money from doing sweet nothing, but I'd said all I had to say about this to my lover and friends, so now I'll just say that I was feeling on edge.

I left the shop with Rüstem's assistant, Musa, who was to show me a two-bedroomed apartment in Özoğul Street.

"It has a marvellous view, madam, but needs a bit of work," he said. I nodded in reply.

I wasn't afraid of a bit of DIY. Despite fourteen years of living and even going native in Istanbul, I was still German enough to cut costs by doing my own decorating. The fact that this apartment was much smaller than where I was currently living was no problem. I would just chuck stuff out.

What did worry me was the reputation that Özoğul Street had acquired in Cihangir. It was a cul-de-sac with a good view, linked by steps down to Fındıklı at sea level. However, its reputation was not for the view, but for the frequent muggings that happened there. For years, I'd heard stories of women being dragged along the ground when they fought back against muggers stealing their bags. I knew that women couldn't walk home alone there at night and that taxi drivers were reluctant to go down it because it was a cul-de-sac.

So you see, the fact that I knew Cihangir inside out, to the extent that I had an almost physical connection with it, was a hindrance rather than a help in finding an apartment. Had

I been living in one of the matchbox apartments in those horrid bourgeois blocks on the Asian side, where your head practically touches the ceiling when you stand up, I would probably have fallen for Özoğul Street the moment I set foot in it. Not probably, definitely. However, the moment we entered the street, I found myself looking around anxiously, imagining how muggers would use the steps down to Fındıklı as a getaway route.

I returned to Kuledibi and my beloved shop deep in thought. My friends and Selim had been trying to convince me that there were other areas of Istanbul apart from Cihangir, and that I needed to broaden my horizons. But the one thing I was absolutely adamant about was the district I lived in. If I'd been in Berlin instead of Istanbul I wouldn't have lived in the smart, leafy district of Zehlendorf or fashionable Prenzlauer Berg. I'd have been very happy living in Kreuzberg, mingling in the side streets with the heavy-browed Turkish adolescents who pull faces and spit on the ground from their fashionable cars.

I didn't live in Cihangir because everything about it was wonderful. What did it have that was so special anyway? Members of the Turkish intelligentsia boasting about being Bach lovers? Why would anyone with no links to Christianity endure the public self-punishment of sitting on a wooden bench in a Protestant church listening to music, when they could be reclining on a comfortable sofa in a sitting room overlooking the Bosphorus without a care in the world? If they were indeed really listening and enjoying a bit of discomfort, was that anything to boast about? Listening to Bach? Taking pleasure from the pain, despite not being Protestant?

The truth was that I had no alternative but to live in Cihangir. Where else could I live? Nişantaşı – where women with blonde-streaked hair trailed around the streets all day shopping? Moda – said to be the first place an earthquake would strike? The Bosphorus waterfront – beyond my wildest dreams on my small budget? Also, I needed to be near my shop. I was no longer a fit young thing, so the more time I spent walking instead of driving in the mornings the better. Furthermore, scientists were claiming that walking on an empty stomach in the mornings helped to burn off free fatty acids.

As I said, I returned to the shop deep in thought at the disappointing prospect of never again finding a place to live where I'd feel happy. Pelin, my assistant, was sitting at her desk as usual. She'd had a sullen look on her face for three days, ever since a big row with her boyfriend that had involved some hurling of dishes. Whatever I did seemed to infuriate her, so I said nothing, to avoid upsetting her.

I made some herbal tea. We both thought it smelled disgusting. The idea that aroma matters less than colour simply isn't true. Never mind, herbal tea is good for you.

I sat down in the rocking chair with my cup of tea, rocking back and forth, my eyes fixed on a point above the shop window. Rocking back and forth and drinking tea, while Pelin sat at her desk, also drinking tea.

That was the situation at the shop when she appeared in the doorway.

She was wearing black trousers, a T-shirt and a pair of very smart thick-heeled shoes. They were undoubtedly very easy to walk in, unlike the shoes in fashion that year. When she turned around, I noticed she had "young at heart" written on the back of her T-shirt.

*

13

It was my friend Candan. She owned a large bookshop in Beyoğlu, and it was she who had suggested I took on Pelin, one of her former employees.

"What brings you here?" I asked. She hadn't set foot in the shop since my opening cocktail party four years earlier. But I didn't mention that.

"I'm looking for a book by Barbara Vine and I thought you might have it," she said.

She was joking of course. The thought of Candan going out looking for a book was ridiculous. I laughed.

"You do know that Barbara Vine is Ruth Rendell's pen name, don't you?"

No, it wasn't me who said that, it was Candan's former employee Pelin. She fell silent as soon as she saw my icy stare.

However, Candan just smiled and we exchanged a few polite pleasantries. Have I ever mentioned how much I love the cool-headedness of a true businesswoman?

We went out to the Café Geneviz, just on the other side of Kuledibi Square, so that we could be alone, away from that priggish Pelin, and have a decent cup of tea. We discussed everything under the sun before I got onto my house-hunting disaster. It's never easy explaining to a rich person that you're forced to move to avoid paying an extra 150 euros a month.

This is how it goes:

First, the friend listens to me without saying a word, probably worried about saying the wrong thing. Then, unable to hold out any longer, she blurts out:

"Why don't you buy an apartment?"

How? Where would I find the money to buy an apartment? I was moving because I couldn't afford a rent increase. Was she teasing me?

You can say anything about fiction, newspaper articles, people or politicians to friends with similar tastes, but money is a subject that divides people. While one person is trying to manage by stretching every cent, another is giving their hairdresser a tip of 150 euros. The very sum that was causing me problems.

"Buy an apartment on the cheap," Candan said, hastily changing tack when she saw the look on my face and sensed what it was that I was unable to put into words.

Despite everything, I didn't reproach her, but merely responded, "I don't want to move away from this area. I want an apartment close to my work."

"Yes, I'm talking about a cheap way of buying an apartment round here. You know the building where I live in Cihangir? Well, it belongs to a minorities' charity that has a number of places to let or for sale in Kuledibi and Cihangir. Someone I know at this charity told me they have places to rent out near here and I've come to have a look at one of them." Laughing, she took my arm and added, "Maybe I'll open a rival bookshop in Kuledibi."

"Does this charity want to sell any apartments?" I asked, ignoring her previous remark.

"Perhaps I didn't make myself clear. As well as buildings to rent, the charity has apartments that are put up for sale once they're handed over to the Treasury."

"Just a minute," I said, "explain this slowly, in a way I can understand."

She did.

The situation was this: if members of minorities emigrated from Turkey, leaving behind unoccupied immovable property, after a certain period of time that property could be deemed ownerless by a court ruling and turned over to the Treasury. The Treasury could then either let this ownerless property or sell it. It usually took the second of these options, meaning that the property could be sold off at public auction at considerably less than its market value, and that the proceeds of the sale could be registered as Treasury revenue. All you needed to know was where these apartments were located and the dates of the auction. That meant finding someone at the National Real Estate Bureau, a process referred to as "finding a man", and handing money over to him. Candan didn't yet know how much money, but claimed she could find someone working at the Bureau who would take me to see some apartments that were to be sold.

For the first time in a long while, I fell asleep the moment my head touched the pillow that night.

I spent the weekend waiting impatiently for Monday to come, unable to enjoy either my Saturday morning rendezvous with Yılmaz or the sushi I ate with Selim on Sunday afternoon.

# 2

As I walked to the shop on Monday morning, I found myself carefully scrutinizing the buildings along the way with the eye of a buyer. To be honest, until then, I'd never taken any interest in the past residents of Çukurcuma, an area of junk shops trying to look like antique shops, or of Kuledibi, where cosmopolitan confusion reigned, or indeed in the people who had built the lovely old buildings.

All I knew was that Kuledibi had been a district where impoverished Jews lived until the 1950s and that, after the state of Israel was created, a lot of the Jews emigrated, and waves of people from Anatolia came to settle in the area, which was why most of the remaining Jews moved out of Kuledibi to other districts of Istanbul.

Apart from Neve Salom – Istanbul's largest synagogue – another smaller but more attractive synagogue and a small butcher's shop selling kosher meat, there was no longer any trace of the Kuledibi Jews who once lived there. There were, of course, the "ownerless" houses and shops that I had learnt about three days before.

Impoverished Anatolian families with lots of children now lived in Kuledibi, not forgetting, of course, the daytime population of chandelier wholesalers and electricians. Actually, if you looked carefully, a gradual change had started in recent years. The area was slowly taking on a new identity as people bought up the houses and started restoring them. My bookstore had been the first shop to sell anything other than chandeliers, and now there were several bars, cafés and even a few expensive hotels in the neighbourhood. A Spanish woman had opened up a bar serving tapas daily and paella one day a month, and there was even a jazz club that drew in the intellectuals.

Towards noon, I called Candan in the hope that she might have found out the necessary information. Pelin had still not arrived at work and I was trying hard not to call her. One of the difficulties of working with young people is having to put up with the vagaries of their lives.

Candan, that wonderful woman, came up with a name and telephone number. Kasım Bey: 0 538 318 44 54. She told me to say that Varol from the Charities Commission sent his regards.

My heart was pounding as I dialled the number.

My conversation with Kasım Bey was short and to the point. Apparently it was not the done thing to discuss such matters over the phone. We agreed to meet at the Duvardibi Tea Garden in Sultanahmet after work. I put the phone down, realizing too late that we had not discussed how we would recognize each other. I wondered if I would be able to pick out a bribe-taking state employee by his appearance. It would be a good test for me, as one who claimed to have such in-depth knowledge of Turks.

Believe it or not, after the briefest hesitation, I made my way between the twenty or so tables in the tea garden directly to where Kasım Bey was sitting. This exercise undoubtedly showed I was a good observer of Turks. However, I cannot deny that there were certain external factors that helped me.

Several tables were taken by young couples who liked to spend romantic early evenings at this tea garden where the music, termed *arabesque* by Turks, sounded like the meowing of cats.

Other tables were occupied by Turkish families out for an evening stroll – two adults and at least four children.

Northern European tourists were sitting at the tables without any shade, exposing their arms and calves to the shimmering heat of the sun and gazing with endless interest at the dregs in the bottom of their coffee cups. I could have bet a hundred to one that eventually one of them, a German, would ask the waiter for a spoon and start eating the coffee grounds. Germans are the only people who never forget, even as grownups, the tale fed to them as children that anything edible we leave on a plate will cry.

Then there were four tables, each with a single man sitting at them. One was a handsome young man who was reading intently and could not possibly be Kasım Bey. That would have been too good to be true.

The man at the second table looked well past the age of retirement, for a civil servant.

The man at the third table could have been Kasım Bey.

So could the one at the fourth table.

Thinking of the question "Which part of a man do you look at first?" that frequently appears in women's magazines, I found myself looking at the men sitting at the third and fourth tables. Ah, but you're wrong – I was looking at their legs!

Kasım Bey was the one wearing brown sandals with white socks.

His shirt was dark blue and crisply ironed.

It was only when I stood next to him that I noticed he stank of sweat.

He got up and we shook hands.

That evening, I went out with Selim and a few of his lawyer friends and their wives with their streaked or dyed blonde hair. We went to an Italian restaurant in Zincirlikuyu, or maybe it was Esentepe. These wealthy, characterless districts of Istanbul were very alike and had never really interested me. I'm sorry to say I could hardly tell where Zincirlikuyu started and Esentepe ended.

There were more waiters, head waiters and commis in the restaurant than there were customers. I counted, and there were exactly twenty people there. I caused a bit of unease around our table when I started talking about hidden unemployment figures and the social upheaval caused by unemployment. As I spoke, they gave each other sidelong glances, thinking I wouldn't notice; and then the bald, strangely sexy man sitting opposite interrupted to compliment me on my Turkish. It was nothing other than a crude attempt to change the subject and I found it maddening.

In revenge, I said, "Oh yes? You, too, speak very good Turkish."

I have to confess it wasn't original – I pinched it from a novel.

I hate to think women are more stupid than men, but it's only men who laugh at my plagiarized jokes.

However, the splendid bald creature didn't succumb. Instead, he asked, "Where did you learn Turkish?"

"In Turkey," I replied, deciding that my revenge was now sufficient, as I caught Selim narrowing his eyes in exasperation at me.

"I was born in Turkey," I added.

My mother was a German Catholic and my father was a German Jew. They escaped from German fascism and settled in Turkey, where they stayed long after the war ended. I was born in Istanbul and spent the first seven years of my life here.

For the rest of the evening, they avoided unpleasant topics such as social upheaval, employment, tax rises or the forthcoming elections, preferring to laugh about things like the ridiculous cost of a horrid bottle of Chianti.

I wouldn't say I was anti-capitalist, but, apart from my friends and my lover, I really disliked rich people. Any reader thinking that such people probably disliked me too should note that the splendid bald creature hung on my every word throughout the evening, right in front of both his wife and Selim.

As soon as we got into the car, Selim picked a fight as if it had been my fault. Or rather, I should say he was silent and tight-lipped. He wasn't the sort of person to row and he would certainly never start one. But his silence would drive me mad and make me say all sorts of things so it always ended up with me starting our arguments.

They'd go something like this:

"Aren't people strange? You know, what they talk about and so on."

Selim remains silent.

"Any serious topic seems to be taboo."

Selim remains silent.

"Is Chianti at that price ever drinkable?"

Selim remains silent.

I feel I want to scratch his face.

To put my fist through the windscreen.

To kick him in the eye with the heel of my shoe.

To force the dog ends in the ashtray into his mouth.

To smash his brains.

To throw the remains of his brain to the alley cats.

Argghh! Most of all, I hated myself!

"Stop the car. I'm getting out."

He stopped immediately! See what I mean? As if we were playing out a lovers'-tiff scene for some lousy movie where a girl gets out of the car and bangs the door, hitches a lift and gets raped. Or something else awful happens to her.

A long list of swear words was building up inside me. In two languages. German and Turkish.

Of course I wouldn't actually swear at Selim, not out loud.

The fifty-dollar sea bass was still being digested in my stomach. Goodness knows which seabed it came from, but it had a very grandiose name on the menu and was paid for by my lover, probably the highest tax-paying commercial lawyer in the city that year. I pulled out a wad of notes – with Turkish lira you always have to pay in wads – and left them on the seat as I climbed out. I wasn't going to slam the door. Everything was dramatic enough. Tragic. Disastrous. Pathetic even.

Before I closed the door, he reached over the seat and held my arm.

"Don't pull that ugly face," he murmured.

His words were like a slap in the face. Pow! Right in the middle.

If only he had said something different. Something like, "Don't be ridiculous" or "Are you crazy?"

I closed the door behind me.

Everything else like house-hunting, the rubbish-collection tax I'd forgotten to pay for years and the stupid high-fashion heels suddenly lost all significance.

"Will you please get back in?" he said. He had now got out of the car and was standing next to me, holding open the door I had just closed and waiting. Waiting for me to get in. The money was still lying on the seat. If I got back in, I'd have to pick it up and put it back in my bag.

For that reason alone, I hailed a passing taxi. Just to avoid taking back that money.

I had an appointment with my accountant at 10 o'clock the next morning. Before leaving home, I checked to see if Pelin had arrived at the shop. She hadn't turned up at all the previous day. However, she was there. We don't communicate much by phone. Neither of us really wants to.

I applied some face cream that claimed to reduce puffiness under the eyes, but there was really no point wasting time in front of the mirror covering myself all over with such things so, deciding to ignore the cellulite, I put on my Jackie O sunglasses and went to have a sugarless Turkish coffee at the Firuzağa Café near where I lived.

From there, I took a taxi to the accountant's. I quarrelled with the driver for going too fast. Turks are crazy drivers. They're always speeding off to some important business, without a second to lose. As if rushing will close the gap they've opened between themselves and the civilized world. Traffic lights have even been fitted with digital chronometers to show the number of seconds remaining before they change. They count backwards: 20, 19, 18... 9, 8, 7... We're living in a country where every second is of vital importance! The instant those pedestrian zeppelins – mostly housewives and bearded old men – see there are, say, seven seconds to go before the lights turn red, they start running like there's no tomorrow, just to avoid waiting for the green light to come round again. What on earth do they expect to do with the fifty-one seconds they save?

My driver was worse than the pedestrians. Taxi drivers are maniacs anyway. Even if they don't start that way, they become first-rate maniacs within a year of driving in Istanbul.

It was a good thing I hadn't brought the car and took a taxi that morning. My argument with the driver calmed me down. Even his snidest comments wafted over me like a shiatsu massage. Or aromatherapy. A jacuzzi with a bouquet of oils added. Fifteen minutes in the warm waters of a jacuzzi, followed by scented oils kneaded into the muscles, creating fragrant smells and settling the nerves.

I tipped the driver, something I would never normally do.

By about two o'clock, thanks to the cream I'd applied around my eyes, I looked like a new woman. I was sitting with Pelin, silently chain-smoking. It was a sluggish day. We had only sold three cheap paperbacks. I decided that unless some miracle occurred in the next half-hour, I'd phone Lale. The right side of my head was numb with pain and I'd just taken a couple of aspirin. Having eaten nothing since the sea bass the previous evening, I realized my stomach was starting to rumble. And the aspirin had done nothing for my migraine.

I desperately wanted to be the sort of woman who gets in a fluster over finding a place for her five-year-old daughter at the nursery of a well-established school like the German High School. I wanted to be making phone calls all over the place seeking out influential contacts. That was the kind of problem I wanted in my life: problems suitable for my age.

I wanted to be one of the women with highlighted hair who complain about their snoring husbands, wear lamé ballet pumps, vote for social democratic parties and live in an apartment block with a swimming pool.

I wanted to be aiming to lose a kilo in weight, just one kilo, to smoke those long, thin women's cigarettes with flowers in the filters, to read Danielle Steele, to complain to my female friends that sex with my husband was over, and to cry as I listened to Mariah Carey.

My mobile phone rang. Just once, then it stopped.

With feverish, almost shameful excitement, as if hunting for treasure, I went into the mobile's menu to see my unanswered calls. There was one number. Not Selim's, because he kept his undisclosed and it never showed up on the screen. This was an actual number.

Quivering and trembling, I called it.

My caller turned to be Kasım Bey. The bribe-taking civil servant from the National Real Estate Bureau.

Love it or hate it, the telephone connects people to life. After speaking to Kasım, I felt better. We were to meet that evening at the same time and place as before. Just having an appointment with someone, anyone, made me feel better. I ate two toasted cheese sandwiches, drank some tea and went to the chemist for migraine pills. I didn't call Lale. She was depressed enough anyway, so I refrained from loading her with my problems. Now, once again, I could love my friends, enjoy luxury make-up products, revel in the fact that I wasn't the mother of a five-year-old girl, and not feel obliged to smother myself all over with cream. I also loved the fact that I wasn't married and had no problems in my sex life.

I walked from Kuledibi to meet Kasım Bey in Sultanahmet, along streets cooled by downpours of rain a few days before. I adored Sultanahmet and Yerebatan Sarnıcı, the ancient underground reservoir. I often used to go there if I was feeling very depressed, even worse than on that day. The water dripping from the ceiling would comfort me. Yet, isn't that a form of torture? Is it in fact possible to use absolutely anything to torture people? Can torture consist of something that would normally give pleasure?

I stroked the external reservoir walls that jutted out onto the pavement, as if they housed a sacred place or a sepulchre. The officials looked at me strangely as they tried to close the doors at the top of the steps that twisted and turned as if going down a bottomless well.

Kasım Bey and I were drinking tea and talking about the forthcoming elections. I was trying to work out which party he'd be voting for, but I didn't ask him. However, Turks have no qualms about asking each other such questions, not even about how much money they earn. Kasım Bey kept complaining about the difficulties of managing on his low public-sector wages. It was clearly a preamble leading up to a request for a bribe. Finally, he named a sum, saying that it wouldn't be just for himself, but that he had to distribute it to others who would see the job got done. They would share it. Meanwhile, I was converting the sum he had named into euros. It wasn't unreasonable. He wanted three hundred euros, twice the amount of the increase demanded by my landlady. So little. So cheap. I was going to pay it anyway, whatever the figure, because it would give me the chance to buy a property and escape the tyrannies of landladies for good. If it didn't work out, it would merely be a gamble that didn't pay off.

I went to draw some money out of the bank, and Kasım Bey waited for me at the tea garden. He had with him a list of four addresses in the Kuledibi area that were about to be turned over to the Treasury.

"The court case is still ongoing," he said. "When it's over, they'll be put up for sale. Have a look at them, miss, and we'll go for whichever one you like best."

Before returning home, I called in at the Cactus Café, where I collapsed onto a bar-stool by the door like some lonely old tramp and ate a Mediterranean salad. It was my favourite salad, almost an antidepressant in itself – soothing for the nerves.

But, like all small pleasures, the pleasure of a Mediterranean salad didn't last for long.

I'd been better off when I was single, without Selim, before he had even entered my life. I had hope then. I had that secret hope of starting a relationship that would last for ever. I also had a few dates. I certainly wasn't like this, torn to pieces and suffering like a wounded animal.

I pressed my hand against my ribcage as if I were in physical pain. Was it possible for a wounded heart to have physical manifestations? Had I forgotten all about the scars of my long singleton days? Had I forgotten how a single word could reverberate in one's head? Over and over, like a stuck record. I opened my mouth wide and let out a silent scream. As I did when I was a child. Like the screams I used to make in my room under the bedclothes.

Why did that quarrel seem so important? It wasn't even a proper row.

26

I shan't drone on about how I passed that night. I was brought up to believe that people should work through their crises on their own and never show defeat. It was a stupid petit bourgeois mentality, but it had been drummed into me. Or maybe being petit bourgeois was genetic and had nothing to do with nurture.

I felt quite good in the morning, which was a surprise. Life is full of surprises! Isn't it surprising that people can't even predict their waking mood? I felt as if I'd just spent years with shaven-headed priests in a Buddhist monastery where spiders were spinning webs over the monastery doors. I felt as if I was flying, as if I weighed no more than seventeen kilos. However, I pulled myself together, or at least most of myself.

I dressed colourfully in a green blouse that revealed a bit of cleavage, a sand-coloured skirt with a slit at the back and red slingbacks with ridiculous heels. I looked like a girl on the make again, but this time with orange hair. I felt the orange hair gave me more chance of finding a man to grow old with.

As soon as I left the house, I realized I wasn't quite together enough. It was obvious, because I could hardly keep myself upright.

I felt blood oozing down my legs as I walked towards my car. Warm and sticky. Alarmed, I felt my legs with my hand. It was just sweat. Sweat! A physical reaction to mental or emotional suffering. Whenever I was in that sort of state, I would feel as if some part of me was starting to bleed, but of course it never did.

I got into the car and put my foot down on the accelerator. There were four addresses to find. I needed to keep focused on apartments. I could do it. One of the addresses Kasım Bey had given me the previous day might turn out to be my future home. If I didn't like any of them, my money wouldn't be wasted of course, because he would keep finding others for me until I found one I liked.

"We're not conmen, miss," he had said with sincerity. Should one believe the assurances of a civil servant who accepts bribes? The truth is I didn't know. Paying bribes wasn't a daily occurrence in my life. I had no occasion to do it. Why would the owner of a little bookstore need to bribe anyone?

Contrary to expectation, my stomach had not heaved as I handed over the bribe money. I hadn't felt any self-disgust when I gave the wad of money to Kasım Bey. Many of my acquaintances paid bribes – maybe that was the reason.

Selim!

With superhuman effort, I stopped myself from letting my thoughts get locked around that name. I needed to find an apartment to keep my mind focused. An apartment that would mean using up all my savings, selling my car, getting loans from my mother and brother. Yes, an apartment.

Look at me. Had I even thought of buying an apartment until a few days ago? Hadn't I been looking for a place to rent? How quickly I'd warmed to the idea of buying property, stacking up debts all over the place and putting down roots in this city.

I was in no mood to get stressed about finding a free parking place, so I decided to pay up and leave my car in a little car park close to my favourite tea garden in Kuledibi. From there, I went on foot to find the addresses. The first two buildings looked very disappointing from the outside. But the first was better than the second. It was a detached, narrow-fronted house, probably with a garden at the back. I'm talking about a proper house, not an apartment block. A family with countless children was living in it, which would mean having to force them out if I were to buy it.

The third address was just behind the second, in Papağan Street, one of the streets that opened onto Kuledibi Square. I'd passed it countless times, not just the street but this very building, and each time I'd gazed longingly at it. How come I hadn't realized that one of the addresses on Kasım Bey's list belonged to this building?

I thought I was going to break down in tears at the front door.

That was another surprise.

Such is life.

I didn't manage to see my very own future apartment, because I couldn't get anyone to open the door, but I did see an apartment on the floor below when I went back to the building ten minutes later. I blurted out some silly words in convincing tones to the man who opened the door, saying that I'd heard there was an apartment for sale around there and did he know of one in that building.

He had Mongolian-type features, probably a Tatar, and he was clearly less amused by my patter than I was.

"You're too late, madam. This one was sold a month ago," he replied with a serious expression on his face.

"You're joking," I said.

"Why should I joke about it, madam? It was for sale and a buyer turned up with thirty-two thousand dollars. The new owners have given us three months to get out. I don't know what they intend to do with it. Live in it, I think. This area has become much sought after recently. But you know that, of course, because you want to buy something here too."

"OK," I said, "but could I have a quick look inside? Just to get an idea of prices."

The man opened the door wide, but before I was even inside he remarked that he thought he knew me from somewhere.

"Yes, we're more or less neighbours. I have the bookstore on Lokum Street," I said.

"Which is Lokum Street?" asked the man. Turks are like that – they don't even know the name of a street two feet away. That's why streets get defined by some building on the corner – say a mosque, pharmacy, supermarket, school or hospital.

"It's the street that goes down to the Austrian High School," I said.

"Oh," he said. "Is there a bookstore there? I've never noticed. That's strange because I like reading. But I don't really have the time, what with work and so on. You know how it is."

The building spread along the street like a top-quality limousine gliding round a sharp corner. All the windows at the back looked out over the Bosphorus, which, you will appreciate, was a very rare feature. The views from the first floor were magnificent. The Bosphorus was even visible from the toilet window. On the hill behind, you could see Topkapı Palace on Sarayburnu. If you leant your head to the right, you could see the golden building of Sirkeci station where the Orient Express once terminated, the minarets that had turned the Byzantine Hagia Sophia into a mosque, a car ferry waiting by the shore, a passenger ferry trying to get alongside the jetty at Karaköy, a sombre-looking tanker, and tiny fishing boats that looked like mere specks on the water. In the distance to the left was the Bosphorus Bridge with its constant stream of cars. Oh, the wonders of Istanbul!

The views from the apartment still to be sold would be even more magnificent. After all, it was higher up, on the second floor. The apartments were 220 square metres. I hadn't written that down incorrectly. Exactly 220 square metres, with six rooms plus a living room. No bathroom of course. The building was at least 150 years old. With high ceilings! Yes, it was in a state of decay, but that was the least of my worries just then.

# 3

I called Kasım Bey the moment I got back to the shop. He said he'd heard nothing about the apartment being sold, but he'd go and see the charity's lawyer to find out more and would call me back as soon as possible.

"I couldn't get anyone to open the door, so I didn't see inside the apartment you meant. Can you do something about that?" I asked.

"Be patient, miss. Don't be in such a rush. All things come to those who wait," he said.

But I am not the waiting type. Never have been. I wanted to see my new home that day, or the next day at the very latest. I just couldn't wait to see inside the apartment and plan how I would arrange my furniture, what colour I'd paint the walls, which room I'd convert into a bathroom...

Over the previous two years, I'd had plenty of time to realize that it wasn't much good just sitting around, praying for Turks to dig into their pockets and invest their last cents in a book.

I rushed out of the shop.

If only I hadn't. If only I hadn't had that horrible row with Selim and become so embroiled in house-buying as a means of getting over it. If only I'd been calm and patient and waited for Kasım Bey to call.

But that wasn't what happened.

Not at all.

There was no warning of impending disaster.

It came completely out of the blue.

First, I walked all around the building. God, how majestic it was! It had a beauty that made you quiver inside. Then, taking care not to arouse suspicion, I paced in front of it trying to work out its measurements. It had to be over thirty-nine metres. Unbelievable.

I went inside and up the marble staircase to view my future home. The front door was still closed. Of course, there was no reason why it should be wide open if nobody lived there. However, as someone who had lived in various squats during her days as a student in Berlin, I felt I had a certain amount of experience in these matters, and you didn't need to be an astrologer to work out that there were squatters in there. Probably a family with seven or eight children. I knocked on the door again, this time more decisively.

I put my ear to the door, expecting to hear the shuffling steps of an exhausted mother of seven or eight children. After a pause, I knocked again, at the same time looking around for a bell. If only I'd asked the man downstairs to tell me who was living in this apartment. I tried again, this time hammering with both fists.

"Hold on!" shouted someone inside. "Keep your hair on."

The door suddenly flew open.

I found myself face to face with a man. I didn't know what to say. Should I say why I'd knocked on the door? The man had no idea what to say either. First of all, he looked me up and down from top to toe. Then he leant forward, trying to see down the neckline of my green shirt. He had a bulbous nose and skin so dark it was almost aubergine colour. There was actually something rather charming about him. Either that or I was still seething from my recent quarrel with Selim.

"Hello," I said. "I've been told there's an apartment for sale here. Is it this one?"

"No. It's not," he said, moving to shut the door.

"Is this apartment yours?"

"Yes, it is." But he was clearly lying.

I leant on the door with my hand to stop him from closing it.

"May I see inside?"

He waved his hand in the air as if to indicate that I was mad.

"I just told you – it's not for sale. So what's the point of looking at it?"

If I were the sort to be scared off by bullies, I'd have been sitting at home doing embroidery, or making lace edgings to put on hand towels.

A man's voice called out from inside, "Osman! I can't wait any longer."

"I'm coming," replied Osman in a polite tone of voice. Or as polite as a thug's voice can be. He pushed the door towards my face.

I don't do bodybuilding and I'd never claim to be capable of cracking a dozen slabs of marble with one hand. In other words, there was no way I could prevent him from closing the door. My only option was to put one foot inside and squeeze my body into the space between the door and the door frame, which is what I did.

"What are you doing?" he said, without a trace of the politeness I'd just heard in his voice. "What do you want?"

He was getting annoyed. I was too. In any case, I'd been looking for someone, anyone, I could have a fight with that would put them behind bars.

"Hold on, don't I know you?"

I said nothing. I was busy thinking about what to do next. I was, of course, well aware that I was behaving like a lunatic.

"I want to see this apartment," I said, my voice as edgy as my nerves.

"Why are you being such a bloody nuisance, woman?"

He got hold of my arm and tried to push me out of the way.

The man inside had still not even bothered to look out to see what was going on.

"I just want to see inside this apartment," I repeated.

"And I told you it's not for sale," he said, tapping his ear with his forefinger. "Are you deaf?"

"No, I'm not," I said. "How would an idiot like you know if it's for sale or not?"

"What did you say?"

"I said idiot! Bloody idiot."

The idiot went for my throat and started squeezing it. It wasn't really that bad. I mean, he wasn't squeezing hard enough to kill me. Still, the moment he let go, I started to yell. I was still in the gap between the door and the door frame and I was screaming blue murder.

"Police! Police! Help!!"

We must have looked quite ridiculous. The man now had his hands over his ears and was shouting, "Shut up! For God's sake, shut up!"

Despite all the noise and hullabaloo, the man inside had still not looked out which, even as I was screaming my head off, I found strange.

It seemed even stranger when I thought about it afterwards.

The Tatar from the floor below came to my help. Some Romanian labourers working on the top floor also came rushing down, but it was the Tatar who saved me. He invited me in and sent out for some tea.

I was halfway through a cigarette by the time he asked, "What happened, madam?"

"I wanted to see inside the apartment. But the man turned nasty for no reason."

"Why? You looked at this one a short while ago. The others have exactly the same layout. So why? Why did you..."

"The apartment upstairs is about to come on the market. Apparently there's no owner. It used to belong to one of the Jewish families who lived in Kuledibi. Property that has no owner is turned over to the Treasury and gets sold off after a certain period of time."

"Oh, my dear lady," he said, laughing. "Do you think those men are going to let you have it? Do you have any idea who they are? They're not like us. Trust you to pick that one!"

"What do you mean by 'they're not like us'?"

He took hold of his trouser legs and pulled them up carefully before sitting down on the chair opposite me.

"Everyone knows that. You know the car park next to the grocer's, don't you? How many years have you been in Kuledibi?"

"A little over four years."

"Ah well, in that case, you wouldn't know about the building that was demolished on that plot. Must be six years ago. Would you like more tea? I'll send out for it right away. You've just been through an ordeal and it'll do you good. Excuse me a moment, I'll order the tea and be right back."

So, it seemed that I'd encountered a true Istanbul Tatar gentleman in this odd place.

When he returned, he again carefully pulled up his trouser legs to maintain their crease before sitting down.

"Well now, what was I saying?"

"The car park," I said.

"Ah yes." He pursed his lips and shook his head slightly.

"Until six years ago, there was a historic building where that car park is now. I don't know if it had an owner, but, even if it did, it would have made no difference. Those men weren't the sort to worry about a mere landlord. You should be grateful that you got off so lightly. You must have heard what happened in Ortaköy? They burned down a huge school. It wasn't the same lot of course, but these men are in the same business. They burn down buildings to make car parks. You must have heard how they burned down a school because the headmaster wouldn't let them use the playground for a car park."

"I didn't know," I said. "I don't read the newspapers."

He nodded knowingly and made no further comment. He ran his forefinger over the table next to him and looked long and hard at it, checking to see if there was any dust, then rubbed his finger and thumb together.

"Excuse me, but may I ask you a question?" he asked, looking a little embarrassed, with his head on one side.

Oh no, I thought, what is he going to ask that makes him feel so uncomfortable?

"Of course."

"You have a slight accent and it aroused my curiosity. Are you an immigrant?"

I relaxed.

"Yes."

"From the Balkans, perhaps? I hope you don't mind my asking."

"From Germany."

"Oh, are you a daughter of one of those worker families? If you are, you don't count as an immigrant." Was he disappointed?

"My parents are German, not Turkish."

"But my dear lady, what are you saying?" He opened up his hands effusively. For a moment, I thought he was going to embrace me, but he didn't venture that far. "You mean your mother tongue is German? And yet you speak such excellent Turkish. You even speak it better than some Turks. And when you... Of course, there's something a bit foreign about your looks. But, as you know, there are so many different types of Turk."

Very appropriate for this man in particular to be making this comment, I thought.

"You're right," I said, just wanting to put a stop to all this. "I must get back to my shop. Do drop in if you ever have the time."

"You can't go yet. I've just ordered tea. It'll be here any moment. Sit down, I can't let you go like this. You're still in shock from what you've been through."

I don't like to think how many teas I might have been forced to drink if Pelin hadn't called me on my mobile.

Even before I woke up, I knew it was going to be a bad day. In that semi-conscious state between sleeping and waking, I found the idea of having no man in my life again unbearable. I started to cry in my sleep. But it wasn't a dream. It was real.

Not that I would tell anyone. Oh no.

I set off for the shop looking very glum and not even smartly dressed. Pelin was nowhere to be seen again, which I wasn't really sorry about. By noon, a couple of customers had been in. One made some pretty good purchases. He was about to go on holiday and said he always read crime fiction when he was away "to clear his head". Actually, he didn't give the impression of being someone whose head was ever very full, but naturally I kept my thoughts to myself. I'm not one to bicker with everyone who exchanges a few words with me, especially if they're customers.

The telephone rang three times, but none of them were those silent calls that, as I knew from experience, Turks make when a relationship ends. They call their former lovers and then hang up without saying anything, just to make sure they're not forgotten. Obviously, Selim thought he had no need to remind me of him. And he wasn't wrong.

I was passing the time sitting in my rocking chair and putting on make-up when the shop door opened noisily. My mascara brush almost poked my eye out.

37

It was the man from yesterday. The car-park man who had seized me by the throat.

"What do you want?" I yelled, springing to my feet. It was only afterwards I realized that in my haste I'd dropped my mascara brush and stepped on it.

"Who the hell do you think you are?" The guy was spitting the words out through his teeth.

"You're not on your own turf here, you brute! So watch what you say," I shouted. My manic courage in such situations surprises even me. In fact, of course, it wasn't a situation that required real courage, because half the district, led by Recai the local tea-boy, had gathered outside the window to see what was going on and I knew they'd intervene if things got out of hand.

I considered shouting "Police!" again, just to get the man worried. However, this time there was a real possibility that the police would actually turn up and I disliked the police just as much as any car-park owner or property developer.

The man lunged towards me with one hand raised as if intending to seize me by the neck again. However, one thing was different this time. Allowing him to replay that suffocation scene in front of all those people would severely damage my standing as a local trader. I had to do something and – as you will appreciate – I had very little time to think. I made a rash decision.

And – well, there's no point prolonging this – I picked up a ceramic ashtray and hurled it at his head.

There was a nasty cracking noise. Like the sound of two stones hitting each other.

It was strange. Very strange.

The ashtray hit him just above his left ear and it started to bleed.

When I say bleeding, his ear, or rather his head, was bleeding really heavily, making a large, bright-red stain round the neck of his yellow T-shirt. Recai and his mates were inside instantly, looking in horror at me and the man, who looked as startled as if he'd just seen a UFO, and at the blood dripping from the hand he'd raised to his head. I stood there without saying a word. What could I say – "Get well soon"?

Was it because of the blood-and-guts movies I'd seen? Had films like *Fight Club*, *The Matrix* and an overdose of James Bond had a bad effect on me? Or crime fiction? Had Ruth Rendell and Patricia Highsmith led me to this? Perhaps it wouldn't have happened if, like normal women, I watched *Tea and Sympathy* and *Gone with the Wind*, read *A Farewell to Arms*, and had a penchant for cats, birds, insects and children. Why couldn't I have had a shop selling romantic fiction?

The man pulled himself together and walked out, hurling threats in all directions. Veysel Bey, the carpenter, ran to the kitchen to fetch me a glass of water. They sat me down, gave me a cigarette and lit it. The way they were patting me on the back suggested that my prestige had at least doubled.

Naturally, Recai was the first to let his curiosity get the better of him.

"What happened, Miss Kati?"

"Well, you saw what happened."

"Did he want something from you?"

"Why don't you ask him, Recai?"

"We need to get back to work now, miss," said Veysel Bey.

"Of course," I said. "Thank you all so much."

One by one they left.

Shortly afterwards, Gaffar Bey, from the snack bar, came back.

"Miss Kati, don't get me wrong, but I feel it's my duty to say this. After all, we've been neighbours for so many years and we do business with each other..."

Actually it was a one-way business. I paid him for the toasted sandwiches I bought from him but, in all those years, he had never once bought a book from me.

"Of course, Gaffar Bey," I said.

"Those men are bullies. You know that too. Just make sure you don't leave the shop empty from now on. After all, it's your bread and butter. People say better they take your money than your life, but they also say money is the key to life. It's my duty to say this because I think of you as a daughter."

"Thanks, Gaffar Bey," I said. "Thank you so much."

I'm not stupid and of course I'd been considering what I should do. After all, I was a mere mortal who went home at night. The streets would be deserted, the shop empty...

The shop would be empty, but there was all that insurance! Hee hee! Insurance against terrorist attacks, violent action, flooding, electricity outages, earthquakes, fire and a whole host of other things, whether I was in the shop or not. My insurance policy, which I renewed every year, no expense spared, was just there waiting.

On the way home, I planned a whole evening eating strawberry ice cream and dreaming about how I would use the insurance money. I was fed up with house-hunting, Turkish men and trying to sell a non-essential product that was neither the meat nor potatoes of life in a country suffocated by an economic crisis. Of course, I could always live in Berlin. But nothing could be worse than that!

Or could it?

Would my life really be worse in Berlin, where winters lasted eight months, snow fell in October, the streets were deserted and people looked glum, mean and discontented?

I was still contemplating this nonsense when someone pressed a finger unrelentingly on the doorbell.

It was Pelin. She looked a mess. Before entering my apartment, she asked if she could stay with me. From the look of her two large bags, she wasn't meaning for one night only. Naturally, I would never have turned her away, even if she'd asked to stay for a hundred nights. There was still some humanity left in the world.

She didn't appear desperate to talk, so I told her what had happened to me, making sure she understood that things might have worked out differently if only she'd deigned to come in to work that day.

"So now I don't have a boyfriend or a job," grumbled Pelin. How could she say that? My business, which I had set up and laboured over, was falling to bits, yet that was all she could say. Not a word of sympathy.

"If it makes you feel any better, I've just split up with Selim," I said.

"You'll make it up."

I pounced on her words. Did she really think Selim loved me that much?

"Why do you think that?"

"You broke up just recently, didn't you? It didn't last a week."

"It's different this time," I said, lowering my eyes.

"You said it was different last time. People don't split up unless a third party comes into the equation. If people just quarrel, they always make up."

How wearisome it is when girls of that age philosophize about relationships. So irritating.

"Has Deniz got someone else in his life then?"

"The soloist who sings with his band. A girl called Nurten. He denies it of course. It's the usual male tactic – deny everything, even if you're found in bed together."

"Maybe he denies it because there really is nothing between him and the girl."

"I phoned her."

"Oh my God! You did what?"

"I phoned her."

"And?"

41

"It was gross."

"How do you mean? What did you say to her?"

"I asked if she knew whether Deniz had a lover."

"Awesome! And? What did she say?"

"She said that it's nothing serious, just sex!"

I put my hand on my chest. These modern ways were just too much, even for me.

"Yes, that was gross indeed," I said.

"I told you."

"What's going to happen now? What will you do?"

"I won't do anything. It's all over. It would help if I could stay with you, just while I look for somewhere to live. I have to get my belongings from Deniz's place and make a new life for myself," she said, gathering her hair up on top of her head. "Now it seems I've got to look for a job too."

"Would you like some strawberry ice cream?" I said.

# 4

The shop was still there. Safe and sound. I'd become so quickly caught up with the idea of getting insurance money, I didn't know whether to laugh or cry. Mentally, I was preparing to pack a suitcase that very afternoon for the Bahamas, the Dominican Republic or at least Antalya. Now, since I couldn't leave Istanbul, those plans were laid to rest and I had to start searching for a home and a lover again. I also needed to tell Kasım Bey that I'd given up on the apartment in Papağan Street and he should find some others for me. And maybe I'd find a way of making up with Selim. I also had to go and pay my back-dated refuse-collection tax. My poor delicate shoulders were sagging under life's load.

As I went into the kitchen to make some tea, I heard the door open. I thought Pelin must have finally woken up and come into work, because it was highly unlikely to be a customer. What Turk would actually weather a stock-market crisis by reading a book?

I peered out of the kitchen.

Impossible. It couldn't be.

It was Batuhan.

I couldn't conceal my astonishment.

"Hey!" was all that came out of my mouth.

"Why the surprise? Wasn't it obvious that I'd be knocking on your door first? Or didn't it occur to you that they'd give this job to me?"

I looked at him blankly. What on earth was he talking about?

I had no idea. Or was he talking about yesterday's incident? Had the murder squad started taking on personal assault cases? What was he on about?

"What job? Which door?" I asked sharply. I'd been looking for a reason to get cross anyway.

"You do realize you're the chief suspect in the Osman Karakaş murder case, don't you?"

"What? Is this some sort of candid-camera stunt? Anyway, who is Osman Karakaş?"

He laughed ruefully and said, "I only wish it were a stunt. Unfortunately not. You have to come down to the police station with me."

"Don't be ridiculous, Batuhan," I said.

"I'm serious. Osman Karakaş was killed yesterday evening. A number of people saw you fighting with him and his brothers say he had no enemies apart from you."

"Don't be ridiculous," I repeated, as it dawned on me that Osman Karakaş must have been the car-park man.

"If you say 'Don't be ridiculous' one more time, I'll have to charge you with insulting a police officer in the course of his duty. Hopefully, you know me well enough to realize that whatever happened between us previously will not prevent me from doing my duty."

"Cuuuut! Cut! Cut!" I wanted to scream. Did this idiot really believe that anything had happened between us? The way he was talking, he deserved a much more derogatory term than "idiot" – but I won't be crude.

"Do you seriously think that I killed somebody? This is a joke, isn't it?"

"No, it's certainly no joke. Osman Karakaş was found dead this morning in his office at 3/6 Papağan Street. With a single bullet in his leg," he said. "You, of course, know all this better than I do," he added, with another rueful laugh.

I refrained from saying "Don't be ridiculous" yet again.

"Please sit down."

"We have to go to the station for you to make a statement."

"Very well. But sit down for a moment and then we'll go."

He sat down.

Just then, the shop door opened. It was a customer.

"We're closed," I said.

"What do you mean 'we're closed'? You're most definitely open. I'm standing inside your shop this very moment." It was a woman. If things continued like this, I felt in serious danger of becoming a misogynist as well as a misandrist, which I'd been for some time.

"We're not open for business because we're stocktaking. I do apologize and would be delighted if you could come back this afternoon." How did I manage to utter so many words without losing my cool?

The woman left, slamming the door behind her.

I collapsed into my rocking chair and put my head in my hands.

"Let's start from the beginning. The man I quarrelled with yesterday has been killed. Correct? The man from the car-park mafia. Correct?"

He nodded in agreement.

"His brothers say I was his only enemy. Have I misunderstood anything so far?"

"No, you've understood correctly."

I clenched my fists to stop myself throwing an ashtray at Batuhan's head.

"For God's sake, does it sound reasonable to you that a female bookseller would be the sole enemy of a car-park gang member?"

He stood up, took a packet of cigarettes out of his pocket and offered me one.

"I don't know. It's still too early to say. I have no evidence to support any such claim. I'm just stating what we've been told."

After a few minutes, I called home. Pelin was out, so I called her on her mobile to tell her not to dawdle and to come straight to the shop. I asked Batuhan to wait until Pelin arrived.

At the station, they ordered tea for me. An officer typed up my statement, read it aloud and asked me to sign it. The text was full of spelling errors, but I signed it.

Osman's brothers were also brought in to give statements. One of them made a lunge as if he was about to strike me. Another, who looked no more than fifteen or sixteen, seemed to be the only one with a tongue in his head.

"That woman attacked my brother. She made his ear bleed. My brother Osman said, 'Let her go, we never lay a finger on women,' then in the evening, this happens. He didn't come home last night. We knew something was wrong straight away. That woman's sick," he snarled.

The brother who had just lunged at me sidled up and, out of police earshot, whispered in my ear, "Who's going to take care of you then, cunt?"

I felt sick.

"My father is the German Minister of the Interior. He'll take care of me, dickhead," I whispered back. The man's eyes almost popped out of his head.

Two hours later, they said I could go, but I was barely able to move. I felt as if my blood had completely drained away.

Batuhan was waiting by the door. He took my arm affectionately and drew back a strand of hair that had fallen over my face. The man was clearly a bit unhinged. Only that morning he'd been questioning me about a murder!

"You're OK, aren't you?"

"Ugh," I said. "What a load of nonsense that was."

"Let me buy you a meal for old times' sake. I know a good kebab house in Laleli."

Batuhan's behaviour might give the impression that we had indeed once been in a relationship, but I swear that would be very far from the truth. I first met him when he was working on a murder case that involved a friend of mine. That had been over a year before. Something had happened between us that ended disappointingly for him. But you couldn't even call it a fling. Anyway, what could come of a fling between a policeman and a woman who hates the police as much as I do? Still, it was disappointing.

Taking full advantage of Turkish police privileges – which they exploit with primeval relish – we drove, without stopping, down several "no entry" streets before coming to an abrupt halt in front of the door to the kebab house. I had no inclination to eat a kebab and wasn't even sure if I could manage any soup.

"So the man was killed in his office," I said. Until that moment, both of us had remained tight-lipped.

Batuhan gave me a teasing look. I'm not kidding when I say I felt violent. I had difficulty restraining an urge to fly across the table and land a punch on his smug face. After this, I would definitely never touch anything other than *Wuthering Heights*.

"Look," I said, "if you really think I'm a killer, then there's no point in us eating kebabs together. Collect whatever evidence there is, have me arrested and get it over with. You know my shop and you know where I live." I took my bag and got up from the table.

He grabbed my arm and his face broke into a grin. Where were the man's principles? Having adopted a position, he could at least stick to it! But no, men's brains don't work like that.

"Sit down, sit down. Don't get cross so quickly. Why are you being so touchy?"

I didn't like him calling me touchy. Asking me why I was touchy, especially on a day when I was being accused of killing some thug, was likely to make me lose my temper. Somewhere inside me, a ball of anger exploded. It took only a second to reach my throat. I tried to swallow it and keep it trapped in my throat so that it wouldn't burst out of my mouth. I kept on swallowing. Experts advise taking deep breaths when you're upset. I inhaled the smell of kebabs with four deep breaths.

It was no good. Completely useless. I got up and went to the cloakroom.

I wanted to make that man regret the day he was born and never set eyes on him again. He wouldn't have been the first person I'd cut out of my life. I studied my face in the mirror. What was happening to me? Why was I so irritable? If this went on much longer, I'd have no one left in my life. Already, my mobile phone had stopped ringing. Should I start taking antidepressants? I had to find a way of getting through this with the least amount of damage, with or without Prozac. I'd ask Özlem for the name of a psychiatrist next time I spoke to her.

By the time I returned to the table, I'd pulled myself together. Batuhan had finished his Adana kebab and was putting away a portion of baklava. What an appetite! He tried to squeeze a sliver of baklava into my mouth but I refused, saying I was on a diet. Men have a certain way of treating women who are dieting. He didn't miss the opportunity.

"Hah. Now I know why you're so touchy. Dieting has affected your nerves."

I tried to pretend I hadn't heard the word touchy. He carried on jabbering.

"You don't need to diet. You're already thin. It wouldn't look good if you got any thinner. Anyway, Turkish men like plump women. You know that."

I refrained from blurting out, "Who said I wanted Turkish men to like me?"

Instead, I smiled.

*

The best thing about being perceived as a murder suspect by a person of reasonable intelligence was that it created a great excuse for calling Selim. So it was true – every cloud, in its way, does indeed have a silver lining.

Before going to the shop, I went home to make my phone call. However, as soon as I stepped inside, I changed my mind. I didn't want to be chasing after him or anyone else. If necessary, I'd fork out and hire myself a lawyer. That way, if Selim and I ever got back together, it would mean I hadn't sacrificed the pleasure of being able to needle him by saying, "You abandoned me in my hour of need."

I tried to make a plan. I wasn't prepared to sit at home, meekly waiting for the Turkish police to finish their investigation. I'd proved I was a genius at solving murder cases once before, and I was quite prepared to take on and solve the murder of Osman Karakaş like a professional detective.

After taking a shower, I put on some proper clothes to rev myself up a bit. By the time I left the house, I was almost high on adrenalin.

As I was knocking on the door of the late Osman Karakaş's Tatar neighbour, it occurred to me that I really should start re-ferring to this dear man by name. After all, he had come into my life as such a force for good. How would I like it if people always referred to me as "the German"?

When Yücel Bey saw me, he put his hand against the wall to steady himself and stop himself from falling. He was clearly very surprised.

"Ah, my dear lady, did they let you go? I heard the police had taken you in. What were they thinking of? A lady like you. Come in, please. I'm sorry, my office is a bit untidy. I've found a new place, you see. We haven't signed the contract yet, but I thought I'd make a start on sorting out the paperwork. Would you like some tea? Or something cold?"

I hadn't been able to get a word in edgeways until then, so I didn't miss my opportunity.

"I won't drink anything, thank you. But if you have time, I'd like to talk to you."

"Even if I didn't have the time, I would make time for a lady like you. Come in. I'll sort out my files tomorrow. So, what was it you wanted to talk about?"

"Did you see the murder scene? Do you know how they found the body?"

"Oh yes, I did, unfortunately. It certainly wasn't something anyone would actually want to see. But I went upstairs because I heard shouting, and also partly because of that terrible incident that happened to you. Otherwise, I'm not an inquisitive person. Never get mixed up in other people's business. You don't often hear fighting going on around here. But now we've had two incidents in two days. I'm baffled by it all. Actually, I was worried it might have something to do with you."

"What did you see, Yücel Bey? Please tell me."

"He was lying there on the floor. Stone dead. His name was Osman, as you know. He was the eldest brother. There are lots of siblings. I know five of them and there must be more. They're from the east, but I don't know which province. Really, I suppose, you'd have to call them *İstanbullu* now. I'm told they've been here for over fifteen years. In Kuledibi, I mean. They were probably somewhere else in Istanbul before that. But I wish you'd have something to drink. It doesn't feel right. Shall I send out for some tea? Do let's have some tea."

I nodded my assent to keep him happy. He ordered tea over the two-way phone by the front door, and came back to sit down in the chair opposite me. As always, he lifted his trouser legs carefully before sitting. He was a tall, robust-looking man in his sixties, with thinning hair. I wondered where he lived. Where would such a man live in Istanbul?

"Do you live around here, Yücel Bey?"

"No, madam. Is this any place to live?" he replied. Then he glanced at me and said, "What I mean is, this is no place for people like us. I live on Vatan Road. We used to have a single-storey house with a garden, but we sold it to property developers. I don't know what got into us. Having a garden was such a great blessing. It's only with age that people understand the value of certain things. We still have a house and garden out at Silivri. It's a paradise there. We grow a few vegetables in the garden. Eat home-grown tomatoes. My eldest son is an agricultural engineer, so he's interested in..."

He went to open the door and came back with the tea-boy, a mere child, who bowed his head in greeting. Obviously, our Recai didn't cover this area.

"Sorry 'bout what 'appened, miss."

"What?"

"Sorry 'bout what 'appened. We 'eard they took you in."

"Thanks," I said.

The boy bowed his head again and left.

"Wow," I said. "My fame has spread."

Yücel Bey seemed uncomfortable that the tea-boy had not only recognized me, but had seen me in his workshop. Taking an enormous handkerchief out of his pocket, he mopped his brow.

"I'll go if you like," I said.

He was stroking a brown mole by his nose, thoughtfully, and appeared not to hear me.

"I'll go if you like," I repeated.

Blinking, he looked at me.

"What did you say?"

"If talking to me is a problem for you, I can go."

"No, no. Don't be absurd. Why should it be a problem?" He stopped for a moment, still deep in thought, then added firmly, "Of course not. Why should you go?"

"Well, in that case, I won't take up much of your time," I said, pointing to the pile of files lying on the floor.

"Let me explain to you what I know. If that's all right with you." I lit a cigarette.

"I'm here by half-past eight every morning. Business has been bad recently because of the economic crisis. There are no orders and, as you see, I have nobody working here. When there was work, this place provided a living for ten people, but now I'm thinking of winding the business down and retiring."

"What do you do here?"

"We produce made-to-order packaging. I'll show you if you like. This, for instance, is a shirt wrapping," he said, getting up and taking a bundle of polythene wrappings out of a cupboard.

"This sort of thing," he said, handing me some wrapping with "Kenzo Shirts means Quality Shirts" written on it. I managed not to smile.

"We also do gift packaging. Tie packages like these, for instance."

Yücel Bey pulled out a long, thin transparent plastic box and put it in my hands. It had "cT – cafer Ties" written on it.

"I'm going to sell some of the equipment. A smaller place will do for me now. I only need the occasional order to see me through. I have a small pension and the children help out a bit. But we don't want to be a burden to them. We own the apartment we live in and people need less money as they get older, my dear. My wife and I will manage."

"I'm sure you're right. Do you mind if I take notes while you tell me what happened today? I can't keep everything in my head," I said, hoping to steer us back to the main topic of conversation.

"Of course. Of course. Oh dear, am I boring you with my chatter? I'm sorry. Once I get going I don't know when to stop. Especially when my audience is a beautiful young lady like yourself."

Smiling, I thanked him. Anyone seeing that smile would never have believed I was the same woman who had hurled an ashtray at Osman's head the day before.

"As I said, come what may, I'm here by half-past eight every morning. This morning was just the same as usual. After I arrived, I took all the files out of the cupboards and started sorting out papers. If I'm not mistaken, it was just after nine when I heard footsteps upstairs, then someone started shouting down the telephone. I knew the voice. It was Musa, the next oldest brother after Osman. The windows were open of course, but I couldn't understand what he was saying. However, I could tell he was agitated. A bit later, I saw two more brothers rush upstairs," he said, adding somewhat sheepishly: "I sensed something odd had happened, so I opened the door slightly as they went up."

I made a head movement indicating that I believed he had definitely acted as any law-abiding Turkish neighbour would.

"Then I heard a loud yell, so I went up too."

"And?" I said, getting excited.

"Osman was lying on the floor, right by the front door. He must have crawled there. There was blood all over the place. Pools of it. Dark red, dried blood." He covered his mouth with his hand and shook his head from side to side, his eyes filling with tears. "He was like a son to me. We'd been friends for years."

I looked away so that he could compose himself and get back to the story.

"Our offices have the same floor plan and he'd obviously crawled from the back room to the front door. He'd been wounded by a bullet. You know how it is in films when they write the killer's name in blood? Well, I followed a trail of blood that led directly to the back room to have a look. There was certainly enough blood around for it. The brothers were in shock of course. Özcan, the youngest, was on the floor crying and embracing his brother. Musa was crouched down smoking a cigarette. I thought no one had seen me going into the back room, but Nevruz did because he came after me. That's why I couldn't stay in there long. My guess is that there was a really big fight in that room. Everything was turned upside down. The chairs were on their sides and there were papers everywhere. It was complete chaos."

"I suppose you weren't able see if the killer's name was written in blood?" I said, with a tinge of irony. Still, it wasn't impossible.

"Out of the question! The police arrived within ten minutes and they wouldn't let anyone inside. A crowd of locals had got into the building but the police sent them all packing. It wasn't a film set, after all. There are so many idlers in this country. All the local tradesmen were here. You'd think they'd have better things to do, wouldn't you?"

"Did any of the police speak to you?"

"Yes, a young one. I told him what I knew. But I don't know a great deal, as you see."

"You've known the family for a long time though."

"Yes, fifteen years is quite a long time. You could almost say I brought Osman up. He used to serve tea at the café I went to in Tophane. He was just a child then. I knew his father too. He was a porter. I used to give him work when I could. The poor man died young, and the children were left without a father. They lived around here in those days, but later moved to the Bağcılar area where they had friends and relatives. Or that's what Osman said. Oh yes, there's another thing. When the father died, their mother married an uncle, the father's brother. I thought at the time, 'What sort of tradition is that?' I say uncle, but he was only a boy, barely older than Osman. Not a day over fifteen. Within a year, Osman was also married, to a cousin on his father's side. They never marry their daughters off to strangers. We were invited to the wedding, but didn't go. My wife doesn't like crowds, especially if they're people she doesn't know. To be honest, I didn't feel like going either. I don't know why. Basically, they're good boys. Deep down, they're all right. Very polite and respectful. People from the east are like that. Always respect their elders. They were the ones who found this workshop for me. I used to have a place in Tophane until about ten years ago. Osman was a hard-working lad. He worked his socks off as a waiter at that café. Old Abdül Efendi, the café owner, took a real shine to him. Dear, dear, he's passed away too," said Yücel Bey with a deep sigh.

"The old man had a son who became a heroin addict and died," he continued. "One day, I found the son in my workshop basement. He'd bound a rag around his arm and was injecting himself. I said to him, 'Do you have any idea what you're doing to your father, my boy? This addiction will kill you.' But his eyes were all glazed. Dear God, I feel terrible just remembering that scene. He died not long after. Tall and slender, like a willow branch, he was. There was no colour left in his poor face because of that poison. People said he used to beat his father to get money out of him. But I never saw that. Poor Abdül Efendi, what could he do? After his own son was dead and buried, he treated Osman as a son and gave him the café. Osman worked very hard and paid back every penny. 'My debt's all paid off, Uncle Yücel,' he said to me. He used to call me Uncle Yücel. For a while, things went well for him after he took over the café, but somehow or other he got involved in some shady deals. They say a water bottle breaks on the way to the spring, don't they, dear lady? I said to him, 'Don't misunderstand me, son; we've known each other for years and I feel like a father towards you, but the things you're getting involved in never end well.' Osman said, 'What can I do, Uncle Yücel? I've got fifteen mouths to feed.' That uncle turned out to be a layabout and Osman was having difficulty keeping everything going. So the poor boy was forced to get involved in these shady deals."

"Do you mean the car-park business?"

"He started with little things, before the car parks. He bought the car park six years ago. Or rather, they burned down that building. We arrived one morning and that huge thing had vanished into thin air. I didn't understand any of it, of course. What would I know about burning down a building to make a car park? Istanbul never used to be full of bandits like this. I come from Salihli, near Izmir. We came to Istanbul when I was a boy. That was sixty-odd years ago, so I know all about the old times. It was lovely in those days. You never went down Beyoğlu without wearing a suit and tie. Istanbul just isn't the same any more."

"So, did Osman change after he took over the café?"

"He got himself a car within two or three years, so he was already hungry for something more. He'd say, 'I'm working on a deal', but I never knew what kind of deal. He was barely scraping by. A smart boy but..." he said, stopping suddenly.

"Dear me," he said, clapping his hand against his forehead, "he's passed away, poor lad. I still can't take it in. I feel as though I'm talking behind his back like this. But I don't mean any harm, I'm just telling you how it was, aren't I, my dear?"

"Of course," I said. "Moreover, what you've said will be very useful. Have you told the police all this?"

"No, my dear. They didn't ask. Do you think what I've said might be useful?"

"Definitely."

"Tell me, how did the quarrel happen? Did Osman come to your shop?"

I nodded and said, "I think he was going to threaten me."

"Well, he's paid the price. He wasn't a bad person, Osman, but he could never accept defeat. That was just his nature."

I nodded again.

"What sort of business was Osman caught up in?"

"To be honest, I don't really know, so whatever I say might be a lie. They used to say all sorts of things at one time. Some people said he was... I don't like to say it, but... into pimping, others said he was selling drugs at the café. They also said he ran gambling sessions in the basement there. Later, I heard he had a car park in the backstreets of Beyoğlu, towards Tarlabaşı. I don't know how much of that's true, of course. Oh, and they even said he was taking protection money from shop owners to send to some terrorist organisation. But don't believe everything I say, because I saw none of this with my own eyes. Whatever he did, he made money somehow. These days, nobody asks how you make your money. The only important thing is whether you have it or not. He had 'rich peasant' written all over him."

"Who? Osman?"

"Of course. He had a BMW. It was too big to go down this narrow street so he'd get out at the corner. When I asked my youngest son how much it would have cost, he just said, 'Megabucks, Dad,' which is the message that BMW pushed out. Who would think it? How things have changed."

"How did you hear that Osman had been to my shop?"

He waved his hand. "Oh, my dear, everyone knew that he came back with his ear covered in blood. News spreads fast around here. I'm sure you attracted the attention of all the locals by refusing to give in to him. We heard about it immediately. Good for you, is what I say. You have to put people in their place in situations like that. It's a jungle out there, isn't it, my dear?"

"Is it?" I said. "Is it a jungle?"

"Your shop is opposite Veysel, the carpenter, isn't it? Veysel Bey is old Kuledibi stock, from the good old days. What times we had together! You wouldn't believe it now, but lots of money passed through these hands. 'Easy come, easy go' is what we used to say about all the money we got through at the poker table. Some nights, I'd go home having paid out enough money at that table to build ten or fifteen apartment blocks. But I swear I haven't so much as touched a playing card for over ten years now. You know what? We wasted the best days of our life. The very time when we should have been making money. Thank God, both my children completed their education. I have two sons. One's an agricultural engineer. The other's an accountant. I have to be grateful for that. When I look at some people's children... At least ours are straight as a die."

I didn't want to be rude, but I had to interrupt him, otherwise he would have carried on talking about his children.

"Is there anyone else who knew Osman well?"

Yücel Bey fixed his eyes on the window and thought, stroking the large mole on his face.

"My dear lady, ask any of the old Kuledibi folk. They all knew him. But I doubt if they could tell you more than I can. Just a minute, let me think," he said, still stroking the mole.

"Osman had a lady friend he was infatuated with at one time. I've no idea how you'd find her, but she used to visit Osman's a lot. We'd bump into each other downstairs in the lobby almost every day. I'm talking about five years ago. Maybe more."

"Don't you know her name?"

"I used to know it. I knew it because she brought out a CD later on. I even saw her on television one evening. Very indecently dressed she was too, I must say," he said, pointing to his chest. "If you ask me, it all stemmed from that time. After all, my dear, what was she doing visiting a family man?"

"Her name?"

"I'm trying to remember," he said, tapping his fingers on his calves, as if playing a trumpet. "Was it Rüya? Or Hülya? Something like that. People like that use stage names, don't they? It certainly won't be her real name. Yes, I remember she used to sing wearing a mermaid outfit with a sort of tail on it. She even dyed her hair blonde. When she came round here, she was never blonde. But I recognized her instantly and I still remember her song. She wore the mermaid outfit because it went with that song."

He started singing in a low voice:

> Across oceans, from the depths, I came to you
> Embrace me, give me warmth, let me be with you
> Hold me tight, I'm so cold, and yearning for you

When he'd finished singing, he looked at me shyly.

"Sorry about my voice, but it went something like that. It might be worthwhile finding that woman. It's three or four years since I saw her on television and I've no idea what she's doing now, of course. How would I? Osman always had lady friends, but this one lasted a long time. Youngsters nowadays would probably say they were an item."

He stopped suddenly, and then added, "You can't help knowing what's going on when you're neighbours and living on top of each other."

"You're right," I said. I'd made a note of the lyrics in the hope of finding somebody who remembered them.

# 5

I returned home without calling in at the shop, hoping that over the weekend the local tradesmen would forget about what had happened. I called Lale, the only one of my friends likely to remember a song from four years ago.

"You'll be joining the Prozac club soon. It makes everything seem much better, I can assure you," she interrupted. Yet I hadn't told her half of what had happened in the four or five days since we had last spoken. Prozac was what kept Lale and half the Turkish women in her circle going. The other half were on herbal antidepressants.

"Can you find me someone who knows about Turkish music?" I asked, after we'd been on the phone for over an hour. I was holding the handset in my left hand, my right arm having gone completely numb.

"I'll find you just the person. Someone who can even tell you the name of the company that issued the album. Why don't you come over this evening? We'll go and eat farmed sea bream at caviar prices in Çengelköy. I want to see your face one more time before you go to jail."

I was in no mood to laugh at this joke, even if it meant hurting my friend's feelings.

Lale gave me the mobile number of Erdinç Sarıak, the greatest record producer of all time. I called him immediately.

"Yes?" said the man who picked up the phone.

"Hello, I'm a friend of Lale Çağtan—" I said.

The man interrupted me before I could say any more.

"Oh, how is my Lale? It's absolutely ages since we spoke. We go way back. She's splendid. Absolutely splendid. I don't think I know you. Are you wanting to make a recording? I'd have to listen to your voice first. I'd do anything for Lale, but I have to be professional about these things. You do too, no doubt. Of course, we no longer have the backing of Lale's media outlets..." he said, breaking off with a shrill laugh. Lale had been editor of *Günebakan*, Turkey's largest-selling newspaper, until she was sacked a year ago, since when she'd been unemployed.

"Well, actually, I didn't want to make a recording—"

"What do you mean? You didn't actually want to, but would if I insisted?" He laughed chirpily again. To himself of course, because I had no intention of joining in with anyone's laughter.

"No. I wouldn't, not even if you insisted."

"Then what's your problem, darling?"

"I was going to ask you if you remembered a singer who was on the scene three or four years ago."

"Well, that sounds like an excellent question."

I read out the lyrics and added, "She sang this song wearing a mermaid outfit. They said her name was something like Rüya or Hülya."

He burst out laughing.

"No, sweetie. It wasn't Rüya or Hülya. See how wrong people can be? Never mind, they can't help it. The poor girl's name was Eftalya. Don't you remember her? Eftalya the Mermaid?"

I thought I'd heard the name.

"Eftalya the Mermaid was a stage name. Such a shame the song was so awful. The idea wasn't bad. But what a waste! Bad production, embarrassing song. That was clear from the start. Her real name is... Oh, it's on the tip of my tongue. I even know where she is at the moment. She runs a guest house at Mount

61

Ida. Way out in the country, not far from Troy. Called Goose Mountain nowadays. What on earth is her name? Wait a minute. Rauf will remember."

I think he put his hand over the handset, because I could hear him talking to someone, but not what they were saying.

"Her name was Habibe Büyüktuna. Isn't Rauf splendid? He remembers everything. Never forgets. Like an elephant. Splendid. Absolutely splendid."

"Yes, he sounds really splendid. Are you certain about the guest house at Mount Ida?"

"Of course I'm certain. She's not bad, Habibe. That is, compared to others in this business."

"What's the name of the guest house?"

"You're a demanding girl, aren't you, darling? Let's see if Rauf knows that too. I have a terrible memory for names. By the way, what was your name? I didn't ask, did I?"

"Kati."

"Kati?" I waited for his response. Or at least a question.

He didn't ask. This time he spoke to Rauf without covering the handset. When he finished, he came back to me.

"Did you get that, sweetie?"

"Yes, I did. Many thanks. You've been really helpful."

"Oh, absolutely my pleasure." The last thing I heard was that frightful laugh.

I called up directory enquiries and spoke to a weary-sounding woman. There was no telephone number registered for the Zeus Guest House.

"Can you try another number for me, registered in the name of Habibe Büyüktuna?" I said.

"Is it a Burhaniye number too?"

I said I thought it was.

"Ah yes. I've found it. Have you got a pen?"

An automatic voice slowly dictated the number.

I called it immediately.

If only someone would pick up...

But no one did. Typical! I'd had more than my share of disappointments over the last few days, don't you think?

I went back to directory enquiries. This time, I asked a different switchboard operator if there was an Istanbul number registered in Habibe's name.

There was. It was on the other side. You don't really need to know this, but the city of Istanbul is split into two parts, on the Asian and European sides of the Bosphorus. I'm a European and live on the European side, which is why I refer to the Asian side as the "other side".

I called the new number straight away. I would have been amazed if anyone had answered.

Never mind, life isn't always amazing.

There are few times when you can wear jeans and still present the image of a woman who follows fashion. Well, that year they were definitely in. I tied back my hair, which had begun to spiral out of control through neglect, put on a pair of jeans with a denim jacket, and went out. I hesitated for a moment, twiddling my keys in front of the car, wondering whether I should drive. I was so much on edge that I was afraid I might actually run over any pedestrians who annoyed me. Yet if I took a taxi, there was a very good chance of ending up at the police station with the driver. People who take taxis in Istanbul have to be prepared to brave that risk. However, in my current situation, I thought that might be a risk too far.

I was no longer free to roam the city at will! I seriously considered walking to Beşiktaş and taking a motorboat from there to the other side. I suppose it wasn't impossible, walking through all those exhaust fumes to Beşiktaş.

Then I stopped messing around and jumped in the car. After all, I was a civilized individual, wasn't I? Yes?

And how civilized. I went down Akyol slope, through Fındık to Beşiktaş, and onto the bridge that took me to the Asian side where I turned off towards Üsküdar. All this without a single wrangle with anyone. I parked the car in front of Lale's place in Kuzguncuk, again without a harsh word to anyone. My self-confidence was back. Thank goodness for friends! Without them, I would never set foot outside Cihangir and mingle with normal people.

Lale was all dressed up, waiting for me.

I think we must have been missing each other. We hugged tightly.

"I've made a reservation. They promised me a table by the water. But families come out in force on Fridays, so we mustn't be late."

"Fine, then let's go. But just a moment, I need to make a phone call. I tried before I left home and no one answered. She may be back by now. It's that singer whose name I got from your friend Erdinç."

I dialled the Istanbul number of Habibe Büyüktuna. Someone picked up as soon as it started to ring.

"Good evening. May I speak to Habibe Büyüktuna, please?"

"Who is calling?"

"My name is Kati Hirschel. She wouldn't know me, but..." I stopped, not knowing what to say.

"Why are you calling Habibe Büyüktuna?"

"I'd prefer to explain that to her myself," I said, thinking I might increase my chances of speaking to her if I made myself sound a bit mysterious.

"This is Habibe," said the woman.

"Good evening, Miss Büyüktuna," I said, as if I was just starting our conversation. "My name is Kati. I have a bookshop in

Kuledibi. I met an old acquaintance of yours the other day – Osman Bey."

The woman let out a wail on hearing Osman's name. If not a wail, a very strange sound.

"My Osman's dead," she said.

I was astonished. Bad news certainly travels fast.

"I'm so sorry about your loss," I mumbled. "That's why I'm ringing you. It seems that the family are holding me responsible for his death." For a moment, we were both silent. "That's not exactly correct, but in a way it is."

The woman was still absolutely silent, but I knew she hadn't put the phone down because I heard her sniff.

"Oh, grow up. How could you have killed Osman?" she said with no hint in her voice that she had been crying.

"To be honest, that's exactly what I'm wondering. But the police need to be told this. So do the brothers."

"Where are you?"

"I'm at a friend's house in Kuzguncuk," I said, thinking Lale would kill me if I didn't go out with her for dinner that evening.

"Good. I'm in Koşuyolu. Write down this address."

I had no option but to do as she said. There was something irresistible about her voice.

Promising Lale I would return within half an hour or an hour at most, I left and jumped into a taxi at the Kuzguncuk rank. Taxis from ranks are a cut above those that roam the streets of Istanbul. At least their interiors don't stink, and the drivers don't insist on filling your head with their ideas on politics and the EU. They also don't drive at such crazy speeds. In other words, you can get into them without having to fear for your life.

"This is it, miss," said the driver. We'd stopped in front of a group of horrendous-looking apartment blocks. About twenty of them lined up side by side. The balconies served as storerooms for the people who lived there. Discarded washing machines, mangles, barrels, wooden chests, dilapidated pushchairs, Scandinavian-type chairs without their cushions, a twelve-place Formica dining table – all waiting hopefully in the copper rays of the evening sunshine for the day when they would be taken inside again.

Habibe Hanım lived in E Block, number twenty-four. She had told me the bell had the name Büyüktuna by it. In Turkey, it's not customary to have only a surname by the doorbell. If a woman puts just her surname next to the bell, it indicates that she lives alone but doesn't want her neighbours to know that. Unlike Cihangir, not every district is welcoming to people who live alone.

I took the lift to the sixth floor.

There were four doors on that floor. I pressed the bell of the one that was slightly ajar and, putting my mouth close to the gap, called, "Habibe Hanım?"

"Come in. Come in. I'm in the kitchen," she said. It was the voice of the woman I'd spoken to on the telephone.

I closed the door and stood indecisively in the entrance hall.

"Don't bother to take your shoes off. Come in as you are. I've been out of Istanbul for two months and the place is filthy," she called from the kitchen, which was to the left of the front door.

I waited quietly by the kitchen door, listening to Habibe unpacking food and cramming it into the refrigerator. I always feel shy when I'm a visitor in a Turkish home. I feel like a spy intruding on people's privacy. It has something to do with the importance Turks attach to their homes, the very personal way they fill them with scores of knick-knacks, and the little secret details that give away the identities of the occupants. I think I'm a bit afraid of Turkish homes. They make me feel both voyeuristic and stifled by the dread of seeing something I shouldn't, something I will have to try to erase from my memory. I never go right inside unless a member of the household tells me to do so.

That was why I stood like a lemon by the kitchen door, waiting to be rescued by an invitation to sit down.

"Would you like a coffee?" asked Habibe Hanım.

"It's too late for me to drink coffee. I wouldn't sleep."

"Something cold? Iced tea?" This had become fashionable in Turkey. But having read the ingredients on the carton, I think it's a most disgusting drink. However, it's rude to refuse everything offered by a Turkish host, especially if you've only just met and are trying to establish a relationship.

"That would be lovely," I said.

Habibe Hanım put two cartons of iced tea and two glasses on a tray and turned towards the sitting room. It wasn't far. The kitchen and sitting room adjoined each other.

The sitting room was crammed with furniture: a huge dining table, a glass case of neatly arranged tableware, a television, a few marble-topped tables of different sizes and a three-piece suite that looked most uncomfortable. I sat down on one of the chairs and she sat on the sofa. As soon as she sat down, she lit a cigarette.

"So, do you want to tell me what happened?"

"Well, actually..."

"How on earth did you find me? Tell me that first."

"Well, Osman Bey..." It sounded odd to me. Should I have said "the late Osman Bey"? Or would that have been too hurtful? I stopped indecisively.

"Yes?" Her small but pretty-coloured eyes were sizing me up, waiting impatiently for me to continue. I decided that she didn't really care how I referred to Osman. It was a bit odd really. Was this really the same woman who had wailed at the mention of Osman's name on the telephone?

"And?"

"On the floor below Osman's office, there's a packaging workshop. The owner is someone called Yücel Bey. You may know him. A tall, elderly man."

She shook her head. Clearly my description wasn't very good.

"Yes?" she said again, this time almost ordering me to continue. Had I been capable of steering the conversation, I would have asked questions about the rent of her apartment, her fuel costs and whether people at the Mount Ida guest house got on with each other. However, never mind steering the conversation, I couldn't even control my arms and legs. When I tried to take hold of the glass of iced peach-flavoured tea, it slithered between my fingers like a fish onto the ugly factory-made carpet.

I jumped up.

"Show me where you keep your floor cloth and I'll wipe it up," I said.

The woman didn't bat an eyelid.

"Oh for God's sake, sit down. The cleaner's coming tomorrow," she said, pointing to the chair where I'd been sitting. "Did it spill over you?"

I felt my trousers. Fortunately they were bone dry; otherwise it would have been an expensive evening, because they were part of a trouser suit.

"No," I said, "but what about the carpet?"

"Never mind the carpet. I'll fetch you another tea." She went back into the kitchen. You'd think that at least I should have been spared having to drink that synthetic iced tea with its chemical peach aroma, wouldn't you? But no.

She waltzed back into the room with a carton in her hand and plonked it on the table.

"So, what did the man downstairs say?"

"He mentioned you. He didn't know much about you, but he remembered your Mermaid Eftalya act on TV."

She leant back in her chair and laughed at this. A lovely, seductive laugh. I have to say it was the last thing I expected to hear in that apartment, sitting by a factory-made carpet with a former mistress of that thug Osman.

"Darling, you mean there are still people who remember?" She continued as if talking to herself, "It gives one faith. Such a long time ago."

The woman must have been about ten years younger than me, so for her four or five years seemed like a long time, whereas, for me, four or five years was beginning to feel like just yesterday. How awful.

"You're not an easy woman to forget," I said. I wasn't just saying that in the hope that a compliment would soften her up.

"That's an interesting comment for a woman to make."

"Actually, it's important for women to make comments like that." When I get going, I can be very good at bullshit. My problem is that I soon get bored and can't keep it up. However, it clearly had some effect because Habibe Hanım slammed her glass down, spilling cold tea that gradually spread over the table and would leave a sticky mark.

"Why on earth do we drink this stuff? It's nothing but sugared water, for God's sake," she exclaimed, as she went to open a cupboard underneath the television. "What would you like instead?"

I leant sideways to see the bottles inside the cupboard. I chose a whisky, with ice and soda of course.

We'd covered a lot of ground by the time we got back to talking about Yücel Bey. My dinner with Lale had gone completely by the board. What could I do? It was a matter of life and death for me.

Lale was still up when I returned to Kuzguncuk in the middle of the night. Ever since she'd been unemployed, she'd given up going to bed early. I found her sitting in the garden, smoking a cigarette.

"What was she like?" she asked.

"Very unappealing to begin with. I almost turned round and came straight back. Then—"

"Then you set fire to your chair with a cigarette and somehow struck up a friendship."

I don't like people knowing me and my little quirks so well. I don't like it at all.

"The glass slipped out of my hand onto the floor."

"Hey, well at least it was something different," said Lale, and she stormed off to bed with an accusing expression on her face as if I'd stood her up.

I hadn't learnt much from Habibe. However, the evening hadn't been completely wasted because she'd had the grace to share with me the name and telephone number of Osman's current girlfriend. Habibe knew her. When speaking of her, she'd turned bright red and started fanning herself with an old newspaper.

I phoned the new girlfriend the next day around noon.

"May I speak to İnci Hanım, please?"

"I'm her assistant. İnci Hanım is sleeping. You can leave your name with me."

"She won't know me. My name is Kati. I'll call again later. What time will she wake up?"

"In three or four hours," said the assistant, and put the phone down.

I called back after three hours. I had nothing better to do, so I wasn't going to forget. The assistant's response had obviously been designed for people with full diaries and agendas. But there are still a few people like me who rely on their memory.

This time, a different woman answered. I thought it must be İnci Hanım herself.

"İnci Hanım?" I asked.

"Yes, that's me."

"My name is Kati Hirschel. This morning—"

"Oh yes, you called while I was asleep. Hafize told me. If you're trying to sell me something, I can tell you straight away that I'm not interested. And I don't want to take part in any telephone survey."

"No, no. I'm not selling anything," I said, thinking it was the first time I'd heard of surveys being conducted over the phone. "I just want to talk to you about a matter concerning Osman Bey."

"Osman? Did he owe you money? Look, I've never got involved in Osman's business. Go and ask his brothers. If you don't know where they are, I'll give you a phone number."

At least she hadn't started to sob on hearing Osman's name.

"It's not to do with a loan. It's quite... How can I put it? It's complicated. Shortly before Osman was killed, I had a quarrel with him. I have a shop in Kuledibi." Was I making any sense to someone who didn't know what had been going on?

"So? Hurry up with whatever it is you have to say."

"Because Osman Bey was killed after that quarrel with me, they think I killed him."

"Who does?"

"The police," I said, "and his brothers."

"I don't know about the police, but it's a bit strange for the brothers to believe that."

There was a short silence, then she added, "Is this some sort of practical joke?" This woman's brain seemed to work pretty well.

"It's hardly a joking matter, is it?" I said.

There was another silence. I was biting my lips, a habit that I hate.

"How did you find me? And what do you want?" asked the woman finally.

"I thought you might be able to help me find the real killer. I got your phone number from Habibe Hanım." I couldn't recall Habibe's surname.

"Habibe?" she said. Another silence. Meanwhile, Habibe's surname came back to me.

"Büyüktuna," I said.

71

"Yes, I know who she is," she said. "How do you two know each other?"

"I met her because of all this," I replied. A long silence.

"İnci Hanım..." I started, but was unable to finish my sentence.

"I'd like to find the killer even more than you would. But I don't think I know anything that's of any use to you. More's the pity," she said with a deep sigh. "You said you had a shop in Kuledibi. What do you sell? Chandeliers?"

"Crime fiction," I said, thinking she would dismiss this as stupid.

"You're not serious? I adore crime fiction. I love Lawrence Block's burglar. Who is your favourite?" Her voice was rising with excitement and I now recognized it as a voice that could only belong to a crime-fiction fan. Was this conversation all a dream? Or was I really talking to a gangster's moll who loved detective stories?

"Mine? At the moment, my favourite is Minette Walters, but it's always changing."

"Minette Walters? I haven't read any of hers," she remarked, her voice rising in pitch to that of a spoiled little girl. "Well, in that case, bring a Minette Walters with you when you come, and let's see if I like it."

Before putting the phone down, she said something else. Actually, it was a prophecy.

"You know, I sense you're going to solve this crime. My senses are very powerful. When we meet, I'll do a tarot reading for you."

She had said she wanted to meet somewhere where we could sit outside, so that we weren't exposed to cigarette smoke, and I had asked her whereabouts she lived. The only open-air place I could think of in her area was the Bebek Café. Selim and I had been going there for breakfast recently, so perhaps it wasn't the best choice for me. However, it was a good place for İnci and me to meet, even if it risked reviving memories of happier days.

Bebek is one of the districts along the European shore of the Bosphorus, in my view the loveliest. If I were richer, or if rents were lower, I would definitely live there. Selim lived in a beautifully renovated old house on one of the hills just behind Bebek. I didn't like using the past tense for him, but I had to face up to reality. He was now relegated to my past. I was feeling pretty adamant about that.

I couldn't face opening up the shutters and struggling with the locks again in order to pick up a Minette Walters from the shop, but I didn't want to take her a used book from home. She might not have appreciated that. I, on the other hand, love books that have already been read by others. You sometimes find things between the pages. I don't mean anything romantic like a pressed flower, but maybe a tea stain or a cake crumb. It amuses me, especially if someone I know has read the book.

I went to Candan's shop. She was also an avid reader of crime fiction and kept a good collection. She was bound to have some Minette Walters in her shop. Sure enough, I found them as easily as if I had put them on the shelves myself.

I set off for my rendezvous a little early and drove fast to allow time for tea and a cigarette before İnci Hanım came. It's quite reasonable for people to have cigarette intolerance. For someone whose mother has died of lung cancer, even smoking at the next table can be intolerable. I've certainly come across people like that.

By the time she arrived, I'd smoked not one but two cigarettes in succession. That wasn't because she was late, but because I was an expert at getting through cigarettes. However, I suspect that isn't something I should boast about, either to my friends or my readers. Oh, what the hell!

I'd described myself to İnci Hanım, but she hadn't said a word about her own appearance. If she had, "I'm pregnant" would have been enough. Obviously that was the reason for her cigarette avoidance, rather than a mother who died of lung cancer. Despite her condition, or perhaps because of it, she was very beautiful. She resembled the woman in *The Big Sleep* – Lauren Bacall, if I'm not mistaken.

She looked at the cigarette packet on the table.

"I used to smoke a lot. It was difficult to give up and I'm amazed I haven't started again with all that's happened," she said, toying with the collar of her shirt. She was wearing a frilly shirt, covered in large red flowers with green stems, and black trousers. In my book, it was a perfect maternity outfit.

"When I was thinking about having a child, the hardest part was the thought of giving up cigarettes," I mused. "Not to mention finding a man who would make a good father, of course."

"You're right there," she said, with a smile that revealed all her teeth. "I was just making the best of what I had." She shrugged her shoulders and added, "Now he's gone, there's nobody left."

She didn't really look sad at all, but was merely stating a fact objectively.

"Is it Osman Bey's?" I asked, indicating her belly with my chin. She nodded.

"I had an appointment with my solicitor today. That's where I was before I came here. See what I've been doing, with Osman's body barely even cold?" she said. Raising her eyebrows, she added, "Don't think it's easy. But I have to protect my child's rights. I'm not giving up on the inheritance."

"Were you married to Osman Bey?"

"It's because we weren't married that I went rushing off to the solicitor. I'm trying to make sure my child gets his share of the inheritance."

"But he had a wife, didn't he?"

She opened her palms upwards.

"God knows. He married a relative, of course, but he told me it was never made official. He married very young and said they never got around to having it officially registered. I don't know, maybe he just said that to lead me on."

"You mean they were married by an imam?"

She shrugged.

"Lots of people do it. Istanbul's migrant districts are full of couples married by imams." She looked me up and down and added, "But how would you know what goes on out there?"

Actually, every district in Istanbul, including Cihangir, was brimming with couples married by imams.

"Does a religious wedding mean the wife and children by that marriage can't inherit?"

"Well, that's the crux of the matter. According to the solicitor, any children considered to be Osman's, that is if he is registered as their father on the birth records, can be beneficiaries of the will. But the wife can't inherit unless she has an official marriage certificate. And that's the position I'm in," she said, passing her hand through her blow-dried hair. "I couldn't care less what happens to the others. All I want is for my child to have his inheritance."

My face probably showed how strange I found the way she said that.

"Don't get me wrong. I loved Osman as much as this child I'm giving birth to – and that's a lot. But I've had enough of big promises. I try not to raise my expectations so that I don't end up being disappointed. That's all."

"How long had you known Osman?"

"Didn't Habibe tell you?"

"She didn't really tell me much. Anyway, it doesn't concern me. I'm just trying to save my own skin," I replied.

"You're right. Why should it concern you? When I think about what she did, I can't help getting worked up. I don't know what she told you, but that tale about me stealing her lover is..."

75

"Tale?"

"Just as I thought. Oh, that woman. I wish I understood her problem. She says the same to everyone. Did she really tell you that?"

"She said that she was once Osman's lover and that she introduced you to Osman," I said, wondering if it had been a lie. "Anyway, it's not important," I added.

"Now he's gone, it's not worth fighting. Is that what you mean?"

"Something like that."

"But what she says is all lies. Habibe didn't introduce us. Osman picked me out himself because he liked me. I was at high school and I was a good student. We used to live near Osman's family, in the same neighbourhood. He used to see me going to and from school. I wasn't the sort of girl to be dazzled by people with luxury cars and stacks of money. Don't get me wrong, we were very poor, but that's another matter. As soon as I was out of school, I'd do piecework, sewing sequins on sweaters. The money I made was my contribution to the household expenses. I thought Osman might provide me with a way out of that life. That's all. I'd long since given up on fancy ideas like 'only you can save yourself'. Youth is supposed to be innocent, but mine was like falling down a deep, deep well, where after a certain point every ray of hope disappears, yet still you continue to fall."

"What sort of person was Osman?"

"He wasn't a bad man. Otherwise I couldn't have put up with him for so long. Culturally, we were very different, of course. That bothered him more than it did me. For instance, he couldn't bear it if I read a book. There were no books at home. I would read them secretly and then throw them in the rubbish bin. For a book-lover, that was akin to murder. The first thing I did after hearing Osman had been killed was to chuck out the rubbish bin. Would you believe it? I couldn't bear looking at that rubbish bin. It was like a bin of guilt." There was silence.

"Can I have a cigarette?" she said.

I'm not one to lecture people.

"If you like," I said.

She didn't say a word until she was halfway through the cigarette.

"After you phoned, I called Özcan, Osman's youngest brother. He's a sensible kid."

"I had the honour of meeting him. But he didn't seem very sensible to me."

"Excuse me, but can I ask you something? Are you really German?"

"I prefer to say that I'm an *İstanbullu*, but yes, I am German by origin." She smiled.

"Don't get me wrong. You speak Turkish very well, which is why I asked. You even use the old-fashioned terms properly and only have a very slight accent. You can tell sometimes, in certain words. I'm very fussy about language. I always used to get top marks for Turkish at school."

"How did you know I was German?" I asked, wondering if it was because of my new orange hair.

"Özcan told me on the phone. He said your father's the Minister of the Interior in Germany."

"What?" I said.

"Your father..."

"My father's dead. He died years ago. Where did that come from?"

She raised her shoulders, making her look as if she had no neck. Then I remembered. I'd said it after the police took my statement when one of Osman's brothers made threats at me. He must have actually believed me. So what if my father had been a minister? What strange things grab people's attention!

"Did you give up school on account of Osman?" I asked.

İnci Hanım seemed to like talking about her schooldays.

77

"No, I wouldn't have done that. I was in my last year when we met. I graduated from high school. It was a commercial high school, one of the vocational schools where they send children from poor families so that they can start earning quickly – you may have heard of them. They teach bookkeeping, typing and so on. For a vocational-school graduate, getting into university is no more than a distant dream. I wanted to study, to go to university and absorb all that culture. Now, perhaps I can do it. If I get any money, that is. Maybe one of the private universities, because they're easier to get into than the state ones."

"If you really want it, nothing is impossible," I said.

She twisted her lower lip.

"Doesn't it seem strange? One person dies, a second is born, and a third one feels free for the first time in her life..."

"While another is accused of murder," I said.

She smiled, showing her thirty-two teeth once again.

"Don't. Nobody's accusing you of murder."

"Did Özcan say that? Only yesterday, he was practically foaming at the mouth when he accused me in front of the homicide police."

"The main suspect is the uncle. It was Musa's idea to accuse you to divert suspicion away from him."

"Who is Musa?"

"Musa is the next brother after Osman. He runs the car park in Kuledibi. Or rather the car park runs him. He's a real idiot. What can you expect from someone that dumb? According to Özcan, the police never took those accusations about you seriously, so I don't understand why you are."

"It's not something to be taken lightly. They took my statement and made me sign it."

She shrugged.

"Round here they come and take statements just for a traffic accident."

"But that's normal. At least it's because you've witnessed an accident, not for no reason at all."

"Have you spoken to a lawyer?"

"I don't want to hear the word lawyer," I said.

"Why? Have you been cheated by one?"

"What made you say that?"

"I don't know. They say lawyers are swindlers, don't they? That's probably why."

I lit a cigarette, signalled to the waiter and ordered two more teas.

"My lover's a lawyer, but we've just split up. Less than a week ago," I said.

# 6

Osman died from a bullet wound to the leg. Or rather from loss of blood. The wound itself wasn't fatal, more a "watch your step" message. "They probably just got into a fight," İnci had said. Osman's office was a wreck. Chairs, tables all over the place. Whoever was there had pulled out a gun. A shot to the leg. A warning. Neither the gunman nor Osman thought it would end in death.

But Osman had a gun too, didn't he? Couldn't he have fired back?

According to İnci, he never went around empty-handed.

When I asked what she had meant by that, İnci replied that my Turkish was so good she'd forgotten it wasn't my mother tongue, and that it meant he never went out unarmed. However, it was possible that he wasn't carrying a gun in the office, just as he didn't carry one at home.

This meant Osman would have been armed when he came to my shop. I tried to recapture his entry. I hadn't noticed what he was wearing. Or if there was a bulge around his waist. One thing I knew for certain was that I needed to pay more attention the next time I hurled an ashtray at anyone. You never knew who they might be. As Yücel Bey said, it was a jungle out there.

İnci had invited me to her apartment for dinner, but so much social activity within a few days was too much for me. Besides, I was of the view that people shouldn't be too familiar when they've only just met. If I had gone, she'd have given me a tarot reading.

The next day was Sunday. When I woke up and realized this, I wanted to bang my head against the wall with exasperation because it meant the previous day had been Saturday and I'd forgotten all about my Saturday morning rendezvous with Yılmaz at the tea garden in Firuzağa. It was my fault for refusing to carry a diary – just because I didn't want to behave like a typical German.

I got up and rushed straight to the phone. When I'd arrived home the previous evening, there hadn't been a single voicemail, which was not impossible since Pelin was now around to answer the phone. Pelin hadn't been in when I arrived home and she hadn't left me a note. So Yılmaz hadn't rung. It infuriated me that, never mind my mobile, he hadn't even rung me at home. After so many years of friendship, I felt I could expect that much from him. Thinking up a few choice words to say to him, I dialled his number and woke him up.

"Don't you have a clock? Today's Sunday," he said. If it were possible to kill someone down a phone line, I can assure you I wouldn't be sitting here writing this now.

"I wanted to apologize for yesterday," I said.

"Let's talk later," he said.

Scratching my head, I went into the kitchen. I needed a really good cup of coffee. Even something milky, like a cappuccino. There had to be some of that stuff you can mix with water to make a concoction that resembles cappuccino. I opened a cupboard and took out a large tin containing single-portion bags of powdered cappuccino. It was still three months before their sell-by date. That was good news. The bad news was that I also noticed the ingredients, one of which was something called Stabilizer E339. There was no way I was going to drink anything containing that stuff even if, on that lovely September morning, the whole world claimed it was harmless to human health. I went back to the sitting room to order a packet of Turkish coffee from the window. In Istanbul, you can call down to the local shop like that. Ordering by telephone is also an option. But why do that, when you can call out of the window? I shouted down to young Hamdi, asking him to bring me up a packet of Turkish coffee.

Five minutes later, Hamdi was at my door with the coffee. Another reason to love Istanbul and the Turks. In Berlin, I would probably have to scour half the city to find a shop selling coffee on a Sunday morning.

I finally managed to wake Pelin by slurping my Turkish coffee loudly on the balcony outside her bedroom.

"Why did you get up so early?" she said, having managed to stagger as far as the balcony door without opening her eyes.

"It's not early at all. It's nine o'clock," I remarked.

I heard the flush go in the bathroom. Then a door shut with a bang. She'd gone back to bed. I continued to sit there like some sort of vagrant until, finally, the telephone rang.

It was İnci. My new friend.

"Good morning. Did I wake you up?"

"No, darling. I got up at least two hours ago."

"I woke up early this morning, too. Never do usually. I've just been talking to Özcan. He's Osman's youngest brother, as you know. He's like a friend to me. He still doesn't get why you're interested in this business. Poor kid, he's not a crime-fiction reader like us," she said, with one of her wonderful laughs. I could just visualize all those pearly teeth.

"I started on one of the books you gave me last night. It's very gory, isn't it? I think I'd better read it after the birth, because I'm not going to be able to put it down."

"Mmm, don't read it at night, otherwise you'll never get any sleep."

"Have you seen the papers today?"

"No."

"After two days, it's made page-three headline news in three of them. I don't know how, but they got hold of Osman's passport photo and they also found out he'd had a fight with his uncle over money. That was all."

"You said you spoke to Özcan."

"Hah. That's why I called you, actually. Özcan is coming to see me this afternoon. You said you wanted to ask him a few questions, didn't you?"

"What time shall I come?"

"Come early. Come now, if you like. We could look at the tarot cards. Have you had breakfast? We can have it together."

"Fine," I said.

İnci's home was immaculate. Like that of every good Turkish housewife. In fact, like Istanbul in general: spotless interiors and windows, with balconies and streets too filthy to set foot in. That's why I complied so willingly when asked to remove my shoes at the door. She gave me some high-heeled house slippers with feathers on: size thirty-six. They didn't fit my feet of course, so I put on some men's slippers that were there. Slippers of a dead man. As I put them on, a cold hand seemed to pass rapidly up my body, from my feet to my head. I felt as if I too might become a corpse because of those slippers. As if death was a contagious disease, like leprosy. I took them off and put them back on the hall stand before entering the sitting room.

While I guiltily drank my second coffee of the day, İnci told my fortune with the tarot cards. The chariot card appeared. It signified that I would be taking a big step forward. There would be a great change in my life. Apparently, it's the only tarot card to forecast any change for the good.

"You'll find a new lover and be happier than ever," she said.

Actually, I'd have preferred the change in my life to be a new home, rather than a new lover. Was that so strange?

İnci proudly showed me the baby's room where everything was all ready for her son. He was to be called Osman Emir and was due in three months. I felt obliged to feign interest by making a close examination of the piles of tiny outfits.

We talked about Habibe for a while. İnci commented that the mermaid costume was the reason why her album hadn't caught on.

"Mermaids have no sexuality because they have no sexual organs. What man do you think is going to fancy a woman with no legs and no whatsit between them? Women didn't like her either, because she showed too much cleavage. Nobody's going to find a sexless mermaid they've seen on TV so memorable that they have to go out and buy her album, are they? Of course not. So it didn't sell. In that business, you're marketing sexuality, not a song."

I commented that one of Hans Christian Andersen's most beautiful and charismatic fairy-tale heroines was a mermaid.

"See, that just backs up what I said. In this world, a character without sexuality can only be a heroine in a fairy tale, not a singer trying to get her CD sold out there to real men and women," she exclaimed.

Maybe she was right. What do you do with a sexless singer?

Özcan rushed for my hand as he walked in. It was awful. Turks kiss the hand of anyone older then themselves and raise it to their forehead, out of respect. We ended up almost wrestling in the middle of the room while he tried to kiss my hand and I resisted. In the end, with İnci's help, I won.

Özcan said he was very upset about what had happened to me. I studied his face intently to see if he was being sarcastic. But no, he was serious. Yet if he was upset, why had he previously tried to convince the police that I committed the murder?

He seemed to read my mind. "It was Musa who said you must have done it. I just went along with him, miss. But it had nothing to do with you, did it? You don't go and murder everyone you have a quarrel with."

I nodded. He was just a kid of fifteen or sixteen. He was bound to go along with what his elders said.

"Your uncle—"

"He ran off with my brother's money on Tuesday night. Osman had a payment to make early the next morning so he'd taken the money home for safe keeping. My uncle found it somehow and ran off with it. We always keep an eye on him because we know he's no good. He must have taken it while everyone was asleep. We let our folk know it had gone in the hope of getting some back before he'd spent it all. But they haven't come up with anything yet. Nor have the police. Drink, gambling, women – that man's into everything. He probably regretted taking it and went back to see Osman. Then I expect they got into a fight and he ended up shooting him."

"Did he always carry a gun?"

"No way, miss. My uncle's pathetic. We keep an eye on him. But he's no good. Osman's given him jobs at several places, but he always picks a fight with someone within a couple of days. He makes any street thug seem like a gentleman. We only put up with him for my poor dead father's sake."

"But if he didn't have a gun, what did he shoot with?"

Özcan looked at me as if I were some species of extinct panda.

"Miss, where do you think you're living? This is Turkey," he said. "Getting hold of a gun is no problem if you have the bucks. Show me the cash and I'll have it for you in half an hour. Only the best, what's more."

"What business are you in?" I asked.

"We don't deal in guns. I said I could get you one, not sell you one of ours."

"That's not why I asked. What other business are you in, apart from car parks?"

"All kinds of things."

"How many car parks do you have?"

"Let me see," he replied, and started counting aloud using his fingers. "Two streets in Beyoğlu are completely ours. And Tarlabaşı. You already know the one in Kuledibi. And we have a large one in Cihangir."

"When streets get closed to traffic, they're turned into car parks. Is that how you got yours in Beyoğlu?"

"Yeah, that's right. We have the whole of İmam Adnan Street and Büyükparmakkapı Street."

"Where do you get permission to turn streets into car parks?" I asked out of curiosity.

"From the council. We pay our taxes, down to the last penny. We're doing people a service. What would they do if we didn't operate car parks there? Where would they leave their cars? Do you have a car, miss?"

"I do," I said.

"Well, if you went for a night out in Beyoğlu, where would you park? You wouldn't want to leave your car just anywhere. There are tramps, thieves and glue-sniffers all over the place. They get high on those thinners, take hold of a nail as long as your arm and scratch along the sides of cars, one end to the other. Who's going to keep an eye on that scum? The police can't be chasing after them twenty-four hours a day. Tell me miss, would you leave a brand new car parked in the road these days while you go out drinking?"

I couldn't understand why Turks always seemed to think I was an idiot. Because I was German? Because of my orange hair? Anyone living in Istanbul knew about the scam of scratching cars and breaking off side mirrors to force people into using car parks.

"What do you do apart from running car parks?"

"All kinds of things," he repeated, clearly not wanting to elaborate further.

"Did Osman have a café?" I asked.

He looked at the floor and replied, "It was after the café that he went into the car park business. The first car park he bought was in Tarlabaşı and things gradually grew from there."

"And what's your job?"

"I go round the car parks. It's hard work getting people to do their job. You have to watch them twenty-four hours a day, otherwise things get out of hand. Musa looks after the one in Kuledibi, and I take care of the others. I'm on the go day and night."

"Who was the first person to find Osman?"

"Miss, you sound like the police with all your questions," he said, taking some black worry beads out of his jacket pocket and fiddling with them nervously.

"I'll go and make some coffee," said İnci.

"Don't bother," Özcan said, rising from his chair when İnci got up. "We're just talking, there's no need for coffee." He sat down again as İnci went into the kitchen.

"See, she's left carrying my brother's child in her belly," he said, and he put out his tongue to make a noise, as if spitting into the middle of the room. "Bastard! Excuse me miss, but it makes me mad just thinking about it. I can't help it. I grew up without a father. Osman was like a father for me. Now, God willing, I'll be the same for his child. My brother's woman won't want for anything."

I stroked the end of my nose with a finger, thinking that Özcan's fantasies might not fit in with İnci's plans.

"Where does your family come from, Özcan?"

"We're *Vanlı*, miss."

"Lake Van," I murmured to myself. The only thing I knew about Van was that Turkey's largest lake was there. "Are you Kurdish?"

"Yes, miss, we're Kurds."

"Do you speak Kurdish?"

"No, miss. I was born and brought up in Istanbul. I understand when I hear it, but I can't speak it properly. My brother Osman could. My mother picked up Turkish from watching TV and I swear her Turkish is as good as mine. She's a clever woman. I always say if she'd been educated, she could have been Prime Minister. She'd have done a better job than the present lot."

"You know they're allowing Kurdish courses to start up now, don't you?" I said. That summer, parliament had passed a reform package to comply with EU Legal Harmonization, which meant it was now legal to run Kurdish language courses.

"Yes, I heard that. But I want to learn English, miss. Knowing English would really open up the world for me."

"What would you do if the world opened up?" Was that an odd question, I wondered?

"Everyone needs English, miss. If you go on the Internet, it's all in English. These days, you're only half a man if you don't know English. Kurdish is our mother tongue and I'm all for it... But it's like Turkish. Useless, the moment you leave Turkey."

"Do you want to live abroad?"

"No, miss. I'm happy here. What would I do abroad? Of course, it would be different if I was going off travelling. We have lots of folk in Germany – two of my uncles are there. They keep telling me to go out, but I won't go to Germany. Why go somewhere full of Kurds and Turks? We have them here in Istanbul, don't we, miss? Germans too," he said, pointing at me. "Why should I go to Germany?"

"I agree with you. So where would you like to go?"

"I want to go to America. To see what it's like. They rule the world, don't they? They must know a thing or two."

"Have you started learning English?"

"I would've signed up for a course this month if all this hadn't happened. But that's unlikely now because I'll be taking over the business. My brothers aren't bothered about the family."

"How old are you?"

"Seventeen. But I look older, don't I, miss?"

"Yes," I said. What else could I say?

"People grow up fast when they have responsibilities."

"How many brothers and sisters do you have?"

"Five brothers and seven sisters. I'm the youngest. The others are all married. That's village mentality for you – my mother married them off early. She wanted the same for me, but I refused. It's not like the old days. There's no way I'd get married without meeting the bride first. All my brothers are married to cousins. I've never once seen them take their wives to the cinema. They just sit at home saying nothing, except maybe, 'Dinner's ready. Are you hungry?' I want to marry a girl who goes out to work and meets her friends instead of spending all day at home watching TV."

İnci brought in the coffee. Özcan jumped to his feet again at seeing İnci. This was presumably out of respect. İnci held out the tray to me first. It was my third coffee of the day, but, yet again, I couldn't refuse.

"You were just saying that your brothers aren't bothered about the family. Why is that, do you think?" I asked, hoping that İnci's presence wouldn't inhibit our conversation.

"Everybody's gone their own way, miss," replied Özcan, blushing slightly at being caught revealing family matters in front of İnci.

"Kati is a very good friend of mine, Özcan," said İnci, winking at me. "You can talk freely to her. Anything you say here stays within these walls."

"Did you know each other before?" said Özcan, looking in astonishment from İnci to me.

89

"Of course. I knew Kati before I met Osman," İnci said, and, turning to me, asked, "How many years is it?"

"Must be seven years now," I said. "You were still at high school."

Özcan was no more likely to buy that than I was to believe he was seventeen.

"Why didn't you say so?" he said, slapping his knee.

He jumped up and was about to lunge at me and attempt to kiss my hand again, but checked himself this time.

"I'm sorry, miss, but how was I to know?" he said, sitting down again. "Did my brother know?"

"No, he didn't," said İnci. "As you know, he didn't want me to see anyone. I lost contact with all my friends."

That much was true. İnci didn't have a single friend other than her daily help, Hafize Hanım, which was why she was clinging to me as if I were a lifebelt.

"You're German, aren't you, miss?"

"Yes I am."

"Why are you in Turkey?"

"In Istanbul," I corrected him, because I felt myself to be an *İstanbullu.* "I like it here."

"But miss, what do you like about it? The noise? The crowds?"

I didn't answer. How could I explain to this young lad that I loved the underground cistern, Sülemaniye mosque, the Galata Tower, Tahtakale, and the talkative, friendly Turks and Kurds?

"You said Musa was the first person to find Osman, didn't you?" asked İnci.

"Yes, Musa found him. Osman hadn't come home the night before. We all live in the same place. Osman built it for us. There's a floor for each brother. My mother and uncle are living on my floor until I get married."

"That's normal for them," said İnci. "When a woman's husband dies young, they marry her off to a brother of the husband. That's how mothers come to be married to uncles. But the uncle he's talking about is roughly the same age as Osman. About thirty, isn't he, Özcan? Young enough to be her son."

"It wouldn't happen nowadays. Our folk had only just arrived in Istanbul then. They brought their village traditions with them."

"Don't you also have a tradition out there that you have to find your brother's murderer and kill him?" I asked. I wasn't being serious, but realized I'd said the wrong thing when I saw Özcan's face turn bright red.

"Don't go into that, miss. You're talking about blood feuds and there's no end to that business. But this isn't the Wild West. This country has police, gendarmes and courts. It's up to them who gets punished and how," he said, still playing nervously with his worry beads.

"Of course. Nothing like that will happen here," said İnci.

Just then, my mobile rang. It was Pelin.

"Where are you?" she asked.

"I'm at a friend's place. What's the matter?"

"Batuhan's been calling you since yesterday. Batuhan is that policeman, isn't he? I forgot to leave you a note when I went out yesterday, so I thought I'd better let you know he'd been calling, in case it's something important. I don't think he has your mobile number and I didn't want to give it out without asking you. If he calls again, shall I give it to him?"

"No, don't," I said. "Take his number and I'll call him back. I used to have it, but it might have changed, so write it down. Has anyone else phoned?"

"Yılmaz and Lale phoned, but they said it was nothing important. They just rang on the off-chance."

Selim was still holding out then. So was I.

As I put my mobile in my bag, Özcan looked at his watch.

"I have to go, miss. I came round because İnci asked me to, but I left the business without anyone in charge."

"Wait," I said. "Tell me, how did you find Osman?"

91

"It was Musa who found him. We suspected something when Osman didn't come home that night. He wasn't answering his mobile, so we called İnci," he said, lowering his eyes for a moment and blushing slightly. "He wasn't with her. Then when Musa went to the office in the morning, he found Osman lying on the floor by the door. He told my brother Nevruz and me to get round there. Then the police came a bit later. They took photos and roped the area off. They were going to do a post-mortem to see if he really died from a bullet wound, but they haven't told us anything yet."

"Did you tell the police that I did it?"

"No, miss. When the police asked if he had any enemies, we said he'd had a quarrel the day before with a local woman shopkeeper and maybe she had some sort of grudge against him. There was nothing wrong with that, miss. We just said what happened. In any case, his ear was all covered in blood. It was still like that when he was buried. We couldn't just say nothing about it, could we?"

"Did you say your uncle stole the money?"

"He admitted it yesterday, when the police started getting heavy with him. Then they asked me and Nevruz if it was true, and we said it was. There's nothing for you to be worried about, miss. You're in the clear."

I phoned Batuhan as soon as I got home. I'd used up an awful lot of time and energy before managing to escape İnci's clutches.

"I've been calling you since yesterday," he said.

"A friend's staying with me and she's only just thought of letting me know you'd rung," I said.

"I rang to say you're off the hook. We have a very strong suspect. You're more or less in the clear."

"Did you really think I could have killed someone?"

"You've no idea the things we see. People aren't like melons, you can't tell what they're like inside just by smelling them."

"Have you found the uncle?"

"Which uncle?" he said. I clapped my hand to my forehead. How did I know about the uncle?

"How do you know about the uncle?" he said.

This time, I said, "Which uncle?" It was a futile attempt.

He pretended not to hear my question. "How do you know about the uncle?" he repeated.

I couldn't think of a single plausible lie.

"I've spoken to Osman's brother. The one called Özcan."

"Hah! Our amateur detective is on the case again. Didn't you get enough kicks out of the last one? Look, babe, it's better if you don't get mixed up in this, because even I can't protect you."

Never mind the rest of that last sentence, I was furious that he addressed me as "babe".

"I don't think I asked you to protect me," I said. Actually, I shouldn't have said that. Not because women who are abandoned by their lovers are expected to behave impeccably towards every good-looking man they come across. No, not that at all. The reason I shouldn't have said it was that lots of information about the murder was just waiting to spill out of Batuhan's mouth.

"Fine then. Suit yourself," he said icily.

"Wait. I didn't mean to say that."

"Then what did you mean to say?"

"What I meant was that you can't protect me, because we're not together every minute of the day."

"Well, that's up to you, isn't it?" he remarked.

Argh!

It was Fatma Hanım's cleaning day. She hadn't been the previous week because of a family wedding. In the meantime, the apartment had become as dirty as the Istanbul streets outside. Fatma Hanım and I had breakfast together.

"You know about these things, so tell me, is Europe going to let us in?" she asked, looking extremely serious as she spread cholesterol-free margarine and jam on her bread.

"How should I know, Fatma Hanım?"

"You're European, aren't you? You must know," she said. Getting no response from me, she continued, "I don't think they'll have us. Look who's in charge. A bunch of conmen. Did you see the news yesterday?"

"No, I didn't," I said. Fatma then proceeded to tell me in great detail about the Environment Minister who had been giving jobs at the ministry to his mates. Fatma couldn't read or write, but she never missed the news on television.

"Europe is stringing us along. You can tell them Fatma Hanım says so. They'll never let us in."

My mobile rang once and fell silent. I could find out who it was by going into "missed calls", so there was no point fretting about it. A blessing of technology. I called the number. It turned out to be Kasım Bey.

"Why do you always ring and hang up, Kasım Bey? Why don't you say anything?" I asked. Was I really so naive? Maybe Turks have good reason to treat me like an idiot.

"Your business is going to be sorted out, miss. I wasn't calling for nothing," he said. Only then did I realize he was letting the phone ring once before hanging up so that I would pay for the call.

"Has there been any development?"

"I got someone to look at the file and I've spoken to a solicitor. He says the case will be finalized within a month, two at most. No relatives eligible to inherit have been found and the owner isn't around. All done and dusted. Just so you know."

"Was that apartment being rented out?"

"No. It's empty. It's being put straight onto the market. If you like, I could keep it aside for you to rent, but there's no need."

"Are you sure it's not being rented, Kasım Bey?"

"Miss, listen to what I say. I have the computer right here in front of me. Is a computer going to lie? We haven't rented it out."

"But there are people in it. It's not empty."

"Ah, well, that's nothing to do with me. Once you buy the apartment, you'll have to reach an agreement with them, stuff a few million lira in their hands and chuck them out. You could also get them out by going to court, but why make a solicitor rich? The best thing is to negotiate. I can help with that if you like. It's not really a woman's job. When the time comes, I'll see what can be done. In the meantime, don't you worry your pretty little head about a thing."

"In that case, the ball's in your court," I said.

"You're quite right, miss. That's very true."

I went out. The apartment was no place to hang around anyway. Fatma Hanım was cleaning the sitting-room windows and singing at the top of her voice. I don't understand why Turks insist on cleaning their windows even in the rainy season. I suppose there must be a reason.

The time had come for me to inform my landlady whether I would be moving out in two months' time or staying for another year. Staying would mean paying an extra 150 euros on top of the monthly rent of 1,800 euros. I might just be able to persuade her that in the current climate nobody could afford to pay the sort of money I was paying, and get her to accept a more reasonable figure. After all, buying the apartment in Kuledibi would mean using up all my savings and taking out a loan as well. On top of that, I'd have to pay for repairs. Financially, I was clearly way out of my depth, not to mention my emotional doubts about living in an apartment where a person I knew had been killed.

Instead of taking my usual route through Çukurcuma and Galatasaray, I decided to go to the shop via Tophane. Both sides of the road were lined with cafés full of men playing backgammon or card games. I went up to an elderly man standing in the street smoking a cigarette and asked him which café belonged to Osman, not because I thought I might one day need to know, but out of curiosity.

I went over to the café the old man had pointed out with his calloused finger, sat down on one of the chairs lined up outside and ordered a tea. I don't know what it's like in the outlying districts of Istanbul, but in the central areas people no longer bat an eyelid if a woman sits down in one of these men's cafés. Not long ago, say fifteen years, when I decided to settle in Istanbul, no respectable woman would have dared do such a thing. If she had, she wouldn't have been left in peace. All the men in the cafés would have left their card games and backgammon boards to go and stare at her. Some things change so quickly.

The way people dress in Istanbul is another thing that has changed rapidly. Fifteen years ago, only tourists wore low-cut tops and shorts, and the natives would turn round to stare at the arms and legs of foreign girls. Nowadays, all middle-class Turkish women wear shorts, miniskirts and tops with cleavage bursting out, even from high necklines. It wasn't only women's clothing that had changed. Men's had too. Turkish men, who always used to wear trousers and moccasins in the summer heat, never exposing so much as a big toe, were now walking around in sandals and shorts. Lale put this change in dress customs down to a succession of subtropical summers in Istanbul. I'm not a sociologist like Lale, but in my view, it's Turkish mentality that has changed, not the climate.

One of the steep roads going from Tophane to Kuledibi passed right in front of *my* apartment. As I was drinking my tea, I began to think I should stop dreaming about buying anything, forget about the money I'd given to Kasım Bey and find somewhere else to rent. But before reaching a final decision, I needed to walk past the apartment to take a last look at what I would be giving up.

I called out to the waiter and paid my bill. He was a good-looking lad with a shaven head and enormous eyes. Osman would have been that age when he first came to Istanbul. Eleven or twelve, thirteen at the most. Nothing could convince me that families who migrated from their villages to the city in the hope of a "better life" actually found it. At least, not for several generations.

Housing wasn't the only thing I thought about as I was drinking my tea. I also decided that, from then on, I wouldn't stick my nose into things that didn't concern me. Especially when my own life was in such turmoil. After all, I had no connection, close or tenuous, with Osman's murder, which was how I wanted things to remain. Interrogating people and listening to their dreadful life stories was of no use to me whatsoever. I was never going to make a career as a detective. I already had a job that I loved. Being the proprietor of Istanbul's only crime-fiction bookshop was quite an achievement, wasn't it?

But life does not always turn out according to plan. Surprises leap out at us. Nightmarish surprises.

I sensed there was something wrong even before I got there. To say "sensed" is a bit of an exaggeration. Two of my five senses were assailed by a noisy crowd of people shouting and crying outside on the pavement.

At first I thought it must be Osman's funeral cortège. People often need something tangible like a coffin to be able to comprehend death. Then, I decided that was a stupid idea. Why would they bring Osman, or rather his coffin, down the street where his office was?

However, it couldn't have been just a local fight that had brought so many people out. Maybe it was a traffic accident. Maybe.

I went up to the crowd and picked out a girl with a red kerchief edged with little gold trinkets and asked her what had happened. She didn't answer my question, but just sized me up and said, "Have you got a cigarette?"

I pulled a packet out of my bag. She took two and, loosening her headscarf, stuck one behind her ear, then stood waiting for me to give her a light. Which is what I did – what else could I do?

"So, aren't you going to tell me what's going on here?"

"I thought you were a tourist," she said.

I abandoned the idea that those two cigarettes might get me anywhere and approached a young man.

"What happened?" I asked.

"We've no idea. These women and children keep shouting. I don't know if someone's died or what. The police will be here any minute."

There are two sayings in Turkish for what followed: "speak of the devil" when someone's arrival is unwelcome, and "good people appear at the mention of their name" when it is welcome. I was undecided as to which of these sayings was appropriate when, just after the young man spoke, someone else took hold of my arm. I turned around quickly and saw it was Batuhan.

"Another murder?" I asked as soon as I saw him.

"Good morning, Kati Hanım. What a nice surprise," he said. Had my Turkish been twenty times better, I would have realized he was being facetious.

"You know I work around here," I said. Was any more explanation necessary?

"It's an old woman," he said, nodding towards a nearby building. "She lived in the basement with her son and daughter-in-law. They both go out to work in the mornings, so she was alone at home. Her grandchildren were in the country."

"And? A murder?"

"Robbery. We reckon it was for the bracelets she was wearing. We think they panicked and knifed her when she cried out."

Following the economic crisis, there had been a significant rise in the number of robberies and thefts in Istanbul. Actually, I think the Turks put up with it all pretty well. It's no secret that poverty was the reason why the crime rate had soared. Penury poisons the character of a society. However, wealth alone cannot repair the character of some societies. Take Germany, for instance. Try waiting at a Berlin bus stop when the bus is five minutes late, if you have the stamina, and see how those monsters, each with enough money in their pockets for a taxi, elbow, push and trample over each other to get onto that bus. You would be instantly convinced that, for the sake of universal peace, Germans should on no account ever be denied their social benefits.

"Have you got more work to do here? Can I get you a tea?" I asked.

"I'm waiting for someone from the prosecutor's office, but it won't take long. I'll come round to your shop," said Batuhan.

"No," I said. "Come to the tea garden, not in the square but the one further down. Ask for the mukhtar's office and it's next door to that – called Café Geneviz."

As I set off walking, my mobile rang. A most inconvenient time as far as I was concerned. It was İnci saying that she'd forgotten to ask which perfume I used, which wasn't normal for her, but yesterday her mind was all over the place.

"Scorpio," I said.

"I knew it!" she cried. "We're in the same zodiac group. I'm Cancer."

I didn't tell her that I'd given up all that at the age of twenty-one, after a bitter experience with a Pisces boyfriend I'd fallen for in the belief that water signs were compatible. I find less and less to believe in as I get older, but I wouldn't want anyone to age before their time.

I waited for Batuhan, smoking a cigarette and drinking tea at Café Geneviz, confident that the shop was in Pelin's safe hands. My phone rang again. Sometimes that happens. After days of not ringing at all, it suddenly doesn't know when to stop. But it didn't even occur to me that it would be him. I'd given up all hope of hearing from Selim. You stop assuming you're everyone's top priority as you get older.

"How are you?" he said, in a voice that sounded as if he was walking on broken glass. Can a single utterance give that impression? Definitely.

I would have given anything to be able to say, "I feel like shit. Absolute shit!" But I couldn't. It wasn't in keeping for someone of my age to stage a tragedy out of a separation. I'd experienced enough melodrama by the time I was thirty to see me through any subsequent failed love affairs.

However, I wanted to say something meaningful in response to his question. Something appropriate for a lover who hadn't phoned for days and, when he did, merely asked how I was.

"I'm managing," I said.

"What does that mean?"

"It means just that."

"Are you still upset?"

"Did you call to ask me that?"

"We'll talk another time if you like. See you later."

He hung up without even waiting for me to say goodbye. Actually, I had no intention of saying goodbye; if only he had waited. I called back.

"You hung up on me."

"Kati, let's talk later, when we're both feeling a bit more positive." It was pretty obvious he meant "let's talk when *you're* feeling a bit more positive", wasn't it?

"I was feeling very positive until a moment ago. Has it never occurred to you that it might be *you* who makes me negative?"

"In that case, there's no point in us talking any more."

"Yes, I agree. Goodbye." This time, it was me who hung up.

I bit on my thumb to fight back the tears and counted silently up to ten. If I'd counted to a thousand, it would have made no difference. Anyway, chanting numbers is all very boring. Count sheep for insomnia, count numbers for nerves, count, count, count...

I went to the café cloakroom and washed my face. Gazing at the mirror, I asked my reflection why I'd hung up, as if my mouth was a decision-making entity completely separate from the rest of me. I got no answer, of course.

I suddenly felt a heaviness come over me, as if I'd gained thirty kilos. My weight changes constantly, depending on my psychological state. I felt like a sprinter trying to run with tightly bound ankles. I wasn't even a sporty type, so I could barely move my feet. But I needed to pull myself together because Batuhan was about to arrive at any moment. Also, there was no alternative. I couldn't go home and crawl under a blanket because Fatma Hanım was trilling out her songs behind the curtains there. And I couldn't go to Lale. You can't go crying over silly love problems to a woman who relies on antidepressants to keep herself going.

When Batuhan arrived, no one would have guessed that I'd had to work so hard to pull myself together. Getting older isn't always such a bad thing. Any woman with a shred of experience about surviving the pain of separation knows that the next time it happens she will ultimately survive again. That knowledge lies deep in the subconscious. But why couldn't the unspecified time indicated by "ultimately" have been "right now"? It's not that simple, of course. Unfortunately not. One man told me he lived his life as a series of compartments and simply closed the door behind him when he moved from one compartment to another. He had explained this with great pride. If I had such a theory, I'm not sure I'd have boasted about it to all and sundry. In fact, what managed to pull me together when Batuhan arrived was neither the "right now" nor the compartment theory. I'd had a moment of enlightenment. I'd realized that the most important thing was that Selim hadn't given up before I had. That was hugely significant, don't you think?

I might have grown out of many things, but I wasn't too old for these little relationship games.

Batuhan arrived looking serious and in no mood for light-hearted banter. Thank God! I wasn't either.

"Do you know how much blood there is inside a human body?" he asked.

I hadn't the slightest idea.

"How much?"

"Four to four and a half litres."

"So?" I said.

"I was just thinking. I wonder how much blood the old lady lost. It looked to me as if her body was completely drained. There was so much of it."

Was there really enough blood to shock a burly murder-squad officer?

Batuhan continued to explain, but seemed to be talking to himself.

"He threw the murder weapon down next to the corpse. Maybe that will provide a trail that leads us to the killer. But I doubt it. Nowadays, even kids know all about fingerprints. Why would he leave the stiletto behind? Probably didn't want to take it with him because it was covered in blood. Yet he would have been covered with blood himself, especially his hands. The front door was open. He must have realized there was no one else at home. At any rate, nobody came when the woman cried out. If anyone had been at home, then... But it's not just a question of fingerprints, several other things have to be investigated. If we were to find fingerprints on the stiletto right away, then I'd say the perpetrator was mentally deficient. But if we don't find fingerprints, then it's very odd. It couldn't be premeditated murder. An old woman like that..." he muttered to himself, as people do when they're trying to put their thoughts in order.

"Perhaps he wiped the stiletto before throwing it away," I said.

"What did you say?" said Batuhan, turning to me with a startled look.

"I said maybe he wiped the prints off the stiletto before throwing it down."

"It didn't look as if it had been wiped. The stiletto handle still had blood on it. If it had been wiped, the blood traces would have disappeared with the fingerprints. Did you know that just a single eyelash can lead us to a murderer these days? The man in the street may not know that much about advances in forensic science, but fingerprints... Who knows? Maybe there are still people out there who don't know about them. We've no idea what sort of person we're dealing with here. Kuledibi is hardly Manhattan."

So even the police looked down on Kuledibi residents. I needed to look into this before deciding to move there.

"Couldn't the killer have worn gloves?"

"Of course he could. I didn't say he couldn't, did I? But in that case, our original theory doesn't hold. Why would a robber go around wearing gloves in order to take two bracelets from the arm of an old lady? That is, of course, if his original intention had been to steal the bracelets. There was no sign of force on the woman's arm. No sign that he tried and failed to remove the bracelets. Superficially, at least. Anyway, the bracelets were loose enough to come off easily. The woman had cancer. She'd lost a lot of weight recently. Or so the daughter-in-law has just been telling us. The killer could have removed the bracelets without even touching the woman if he'd wanted to. There's something odd about this."

"So, what conclusion should we draw from all this?"

"We think the son and daughter-in-law probably did it. Or one of them acting alone."

That's how the police mind works. If someone is killed, they go straight for the nearest and dearest. If the victim is a woman they accuse the husband, and if it's a man they accuse the wife. They probably even have statistics to back this up. However, as a good crime-fiction devotee, I always suspect the involvement of a secret lover or someone from a murky past. I'm rarely wrong.

I certainly didn't subscribe to the police theory that if an old woman is murdered, the killer is most likely to be her son or daughter-in-law. My suspicions were leading me in a completely different direction.

Actually, I never got tired of talking to Batuhan, especially about murder. I certainly didn't want him to stop talking about the Osman murder. Yes, I know, I'd only just decided to stop sticking my nose into things that didn't concern me, but listening to a murder-squad officer fishing around in the dark for ideas didn't really constitute being nosy, did it?

"There's something I don't understand," I said, changing the subject. "How can a person die from a bullet wound in the leg? In films, people get shot in the leg as a threat. Then they appear in the next scene hobbling around with a wounded leg, not in a graveyard surrounded by a crowd of weeping mourners."

He took hold of my leg to demonstrate. At least I hoped that was the reason.

"An artery runs from here to here. This artery was lacerated by the bullet. If he'd been shot in the knee, or anywhere else in the leg, there would have been no danger, as you said."

"Was the shot deliberately aimed at that point?"

"You mean the thigh?"

"Did the killer deliberately shoot at the thigh?"

"There's no way of knowing. I think it was an unfortunate accident. The infamous uncle is unlikely to know that much about anatomy. Anyway, now it's your turn. Why did you talk to Özcan?"

"Well, I was a suspect in this murder case, wasn't I? So I had to collect evidence to clear my name."

"If I'd known you were going to take it so seriously, I wouldn't have played that joke on you. You made a statement at the station, didn't you?"

"I did. And that's why I was sure you weren't playing a joke on me."

"What did you sign yourself as on the statement? Because you seem to have become an amateur detective."

"Nobody told me who or what I was supposed to be while I was there."

"What do you mean? It would have been at the top of the statement that you read and signed. It must have said 'suspect'."

"So I was a suspect, was I?"

He repeated what I said, apparently amused by it. I guess he thought I was flirting.

"Why do you always put down policemen and lawyers?" he said. "Do you think you're the only person in this country with any brains? If a poor car-park owner gets killed, especially by a gun, do you really think we're going to arrest an unassuming proprietress of a bookshop two streets away?"

"Don't you dare try to tell me how brilliant the police are," I said, my voice possibly sounding sterner than intended. I've never wanted to be described as unassuming. "I have serious doubts about the brilliance of the police, especially the Turkish police," I continued. "Only last year, you arrested a scrawny shoe-shine boy for the murder of a burly businessman, didn't you? So, why not repeat this success by arresting 'the proprietress of a book-shop two streets away'."

His face reddened. He'd never been the pale and pretty type, but now he looked darker than usual. I hardly ever read the newspapers, yet even I could list at least ten cases of scandalous police behaviour. But it was no use attacking an individual police officer. You had to go after the institution. As far as I was concerned, Batuhan was not a true representative of the institution to which he belonged.

There was a silence. I found myself fervently wishing for one of our phones to ring, just to break the silence. At times like that, my mother would say, "An angel has just passed over us." If there were such an angel of silence, I'm certain it would never come within a hundred miles of Istanbul. No angel would be able to tolerate the noise of this city. Anyway, it wasn't that kind of silence.

I lit a cigarette.

"Was the gun used to shoot Osman licensed?"

"Our work isn't usually that easy," he said, mockingly. "We have to use our heads occasionally."

"But you must know the sort of gun it was from the bullet."

"We do."

"What was it?"

"What do you intend to do if I tell you?"

I shrugged my shoulders. Indeed, what did I intend to do?

"We found a 9mm bullet lodged in the wall. It had been fired from a revolver. So, having learnt that, what are you going to do now? Did you understand what I just said anyway?"

"No, I didn't," I said. But the fact that I hadn't understood didn't mean I wouldn't find a way of understanding. My brain might have failed to register any information about guns since childhood, but I was still an avid crime-fiction devotee.

Yet again, Batuhan had become annoyed and stormed off. Our relationship seemed to get more nauseating by the day. I had no idea why he was still hanging around. In fact, until our encounter the previous Friday, I had thought I'd got shot of him because he hadn't called me for over a year. Yet when we met up again, we had carried on exactly where we left off. Was there anything left of the eternal love, sexual attraction, passion or whatever his feelings had been for me?

I was forty-four years old and still couldn't claim to understand men. Why they do what they do, or not, as the case may be, made no sense to me whatsoever. In fact, I'd more or less given up trying to understand. I often wondered if women became lesbians because they'd wearied of men, or asexual if they'd had enough of both men and women. But then, how would people become necrophiles?

No, that was too much, even for me.

I have to say that if you have a mobile phone, you do expect friends to keep in touch with you on it. Istanbul's streets were brimming with people whose phones rang constantly. So people certainly used these devices. I seemed to be the only person whose friends still behaved as if I didn't own a mobile and insisted on calling me on my landline, either at home or at work. When I arrived at the shop, Pelin handed me a long list of people who had phoned. The first person I called was Lale, to ask why she refused to contact me on my mobile.

"You can't talk easily on a mobile," she said.

"I think you're just being stingy. Go on, admit it."

"Darling, you're the German, not me. I'm told that in your language you say 'suitably priced' instead of 'cheap'. Nothing is ever cheap according to Germans. Isn't that right?"

"Of course, darling, you're right," I said, in a voice that made it clear I was humouring her.

Normally, I never missed an opportunity to squabble with Lale, but I had too much on my mind for that. Apparently, Lale also had plenty on her mind, because she didn't elaborate further.

"Shall we go out for a meal this evening? We need to make up for Friday evening," she said.

"Are you inviting me?" I asked.

"Oh no. We'll do it German style. Each pays for what they eat."

I spent the rest of the day mooching around at the shop and phoning the list of book distributors Pelin had given me. I decided I wouldn't bother to go home to change and collect my car, but just hop in a taxi to go across the Bosphorus. After all, I was hardly likely to meet the man of my dreams at a fish restaurant in Çengelköy. And if I did, I was hardly going to complain that the reason I'd missed out on the love opportunity of a lifetime was that I wasn't wearing a backless black-silk dress and teal-coloured stilettos.

That's what I thought. But nobody ever knows beforehand how they will react to such a situation if it occurs. Therefore, to be on the safe side, it's always worth wearing high-heeled sandals, even to go out to the corner shop. Or fishnet tights, if it isn't sandal season.

"I think you must be starting the menopause," Lale said.

I thought only heterosexual men made idiotic sexist remarks like that. And misogynist homosexuals. However, Fofo would never say such a thing, not because he isn't a misogynist but because he's a PC homosexual. Selim might think that way too, but, like Fofo, would never actually say as much. I believe in interrupting anyone who makes stupid comments like that. They should keep their ideas to themselves, whoever they are and whatever the reason.

The only way of dealing with people who refuse to stop spouting such rubbish is to pretend not to hear and to cling to the notion that the spoken word is ephemeral while the written word endures.

That's what I did. I simply ignored what Lale had said.

"Can you imagine? Selim actually hung up on me," I said.

"Have your periods become irregular?" she asked.

As you know, I'm inclined to violence and a voice deep inside me was yelling out instructions to smash the water jug on the table and rip out this woman's guts.

"You realize I'm only forty-four years old," I remarked.

"What does age have to do with it, darling? Anyway, forty-four isn't too young. In fact, I think it's exactly the right age."

"You can be so cruel. To young people as well as old," I said, with just enough malice to make my point. I just couldn't help it. I mean, Lale wasn't exactly young. She was only five years younger than me.

"Especially young people with no professional future," I added. That was really below the belt. My dear friend had spent the last year hanging around at home waiting for job offers.

"Hey, I wanted to talk to you about that," she said.

Amazing! Was her treatment for depression actually working then?

"About what?" I said.

"I've had an offer. Not in the media, which is why I can't make up my mind. But I think it's going to be very difficult to get a newspaper editorship now. And since nobody is going to offer me a job as a correspondent..."

"What's the offer?"

"It's in advertising. From a company that's newly formed and very ambitious."

According to Yılmaz, my friend in advertising, that line of business was very precarious in Turkey just then. I felt sure it was the same in other countries, but the only people I knew in the international advertising world who might have kept me informed had moved on to writing autobiographical novels.

"Why don't you talk to Yılmaz? It might not be quite the right job for you," I said.

"My savings have all but gone, and I can't bear living hand to mouth. This crisis is never going to end. So what else can I do?" she said, looking tense and thoughtful. Then she suddenly smiled.

"If the Germans hadn't come here and scooped up our business opportunities, I might have opened a bookshop selling crime fiction," she said, laughing.

As I tried to get to sleep on the uncomfortable sofa bed that Lale had made up for me, I felt glad I hadn't wasted time going home to change. What small things give us pleasure when life is hard!

# 7

It's always acceptable to visit someone who has been recently bereaved in order to offer condolences, even if you don't know them well. Turks are like that. They regard it as good manners and are pleased to have you there, especially if you're a neighbour.

For that reason, I didn't think twice about entering the building where the old woman had died the previous day.

The door of the basement was wide open. There was a pile of shabby shoes outside. It was a mess. Like the inside of my head. Like the streets of Istanbul. Like the political, economic and social situation in Turkey. That pile of shoes outside the door assumed an authentic representative value when I added my fashionable and expensive red slingbacks. Among those twenty or so pairs of shabby, down-at-heel shoes, mine stood out as extremely smart footwear that had probably cost more than the other nineteen pairs put together. It was an approximate reflection of income distribution in Turkey, where each lucky person in the top five per cent earned as much as the remaining ninety-five per cent put together.

I entered a room full of women who had their heads covered and were dressed in flowery skirts and blouses. Muslims don't have traditional mourning clothes. It's normal to wear everyday clothes on such occasions. Everyone was whispering in hushed tones. When they realized I was there, they stopped to look at me. An elderly woman sitting on the carpet patted the floor next to her and said, "Come and sit here, my dear."

I knelt down on the floor. It wasn't pleasant being the object of such curiosity. A woman rose to her feet and shook my hand.

"Welcome," she said.

I needed to say something, to explain who I was.

"We're neighbours. I have a shop near here," I said. "May I offer my condolences? I was passing by here yesterday and..."

"May she rest in peace," they said in unison.

"The shop that sells books, is that one yours?" asked a young woman wearing a headscarf.

Actually, there's no point mentioning that she wore a headscarf, because all the women had their heads covered. Not a single woman in that room had her hair showing.

"Yes. In Lokum Street."

"I went there to get my daughter's school books, but the young lady said they didn't keep that sort of book," said another woman.

"Are there different sorts of book?" asked someone.

"We don't sell school books. We sell novels," I said.

"Of course," said a young girl. "There are novel books and poetry books, aren't there, miss? They're never sold in the same place."

"That's right," I said, thinking what a strange conversation this was. "Was it your mother-in-law who died?" I asked, addressing the woman who had said "welcome" to me.

"I'm her daughter. My sister-in-law has gone to ask her boss for some time off. It's all so sudden," she said, starting to cry. A few of the women sprang to their feet and started whispering words of consolation to her, their lips moving as if saying prayers.

The woman sitting next to me took hold of my arm and pulled me towards her.

"She was my older sister. Very ill, she was. God bless her. But she's been spared any more pain now. The way she suffered...

112

God knows best of course, but it was sad she had to go that way."

A woman picked up a bottle of cologne that was next to the television and sprinkled it onto the hands of the other women in the room. "Her daughter-in-law was out in the streets half the night," she said. "There's never peace and harmony in a home if the woman isn't back by evening prayers. Is it women's business to get involved in party politics these days?" The atmosphere in the room suddenly turned icy. Nobody seemed to know what to say. The silence was eventually broken by the young girl who had talked about "novel books".

"It was cancer, miss."

"So you must be a granddaughter," I said. "Do you think I could have a glass of water?"

The girl got to her feet and I followed her, feeling relieved to escape from that room.

"Do you live in this apartment?"

"Yes. We came back yesterday evening. Me and my brother go to our village for the summer vacation. We help out there. My mum and dad can't go because they both have jobs."

"How did it happen?"

The girl's eyes filled with tears. I should be ashamed of myself, I thought. The girl covered her mouth with her hand and began to sob. When she leant her head on my shoulder and started crying, I felt obliged to stroke her hair, or rather her headscarf.

"She was very ill. So really, she's been spared," I said. "She would have suffered a lot of pain. God took pity on her and spared her."

"Don't say that, miss. The whole place was covered in blood. She was stabbed all over her belly." She moved her hand in a way she thought a belly-stabbing action would be.

"Why was that, do you think?"

The girl was no longer crying. "I don't know. For her bracelets, maybe? But if you saw those bracelets, you'd know they wouldn't fetch anything. They were like strips of tin. She used to say she'd give them to me if I got to be a teacher."

Someone called from the sitting room, "Figen, your sister Nurten's leaving."

Obviously, I was never going to get proper answers to my questions in that crowd.

"I should go too," I said.

"Miss, can I ask you something?" she said.

"Of course," I said eagerly, knowing that it meant I would be able to ask something of her in return.

"Wait a minute then, don't go yet."

"All right."

"Just wait here, please," she said as she went to see her sister off.

Finding myself alone in the kitchen, I started to examine my surroundings, as any good detective would do. A row of sacks, presumably containing winter food supplies from the village, was lined up on the floor in front of the worktop. There were several dishes of food laid out on a wooden table. On the wall was a large poster for the United Endeavour Party. It showed a young girl in a green dress and white headscarf looking at a book with her hands open as if in prayer and tears streaming from her blue eyes. Just above her head was the party logo: a white crescent moon rising in an azure sky at the centre of an emerald outline of Turkey. You didn't have to read the newspapers every day to know that the crescent moon emblem belonged to Islamic parties. Nor that the UEP was currently the fastest-rising Islamic party in Turkey.

Next to the refrigerator was another poster for the same party: Say NO to the plunderers of Turkey! Say YES to United Endeavour! UEP for better tomorrows! On this poster, the familiar green outline of Turkey stood out from a picture of dry, cracked earth.

By the time Figen returned, I was sitting on a stool and even smoking a cigarette. There's no need to ask for permission to smoke in Turkish homes, except of course in those of my friends or Cihangir residents. Some of the Bach devotees who live in Cihangir think it's very modern to ban smoking at home. Even in the open air, they wave their hands about as if chasing a fly away if you smoke near them.

"Miss," she said, bending towards me as if to whisper something very important in my ear. "I really need to get out of here."

"Why's that?" I asked. Given that I was being used to assist her in her escape, I thought this question was justified.

"I have to see a friend. I've been away in the village for two months so we haven't been able to meet."

"Is it a boyfriend?" I asked. Just my curious nature, I'm afraid.

"He's a sort of fiancé. We made promises between ourselves. I won't be long and I'll come straight back, but I don't know how to get out. If you said you had a book for me at your shop, I could leave with you. I'd be back within two hours, I promise."

Should I have told her there was no need to make such promises when talking to me?

"Yes, but would they believe the book story?"

"They would if you said it."

"You mean they wouldn't believe it if it came from you, but they would from me?" I asked.

"Yes," she said. A bit illogical, wasn't it?

"Who should I speak to?"

"I'll get my aunt to come into the kitchen and you can tell her. Say, 'The girl's in a bad way, she's really distraught about the old lady.' I'll keep crying while you're talking. Then say, 'I have a book for her that will comfort her.'"

This sounded stupid to me. I pursed my lips.

"If you say the word 'book', they'll think it's something important. I swear I won't stay out long. I'll be back in two hours, miss."

Her flow of assurances and those strange party posters were all too much for me. "OK then. Go and call your aunt," I said, unable to believe I was being drawn into this. But what was there to lose?

The aunt entered, wiping her eyes with the corner of her headscarf.

"You didn't even sit down. I'm sorry. I didn't look after you properly. There are so many relatives here, bless them. But I've hardly had time to catch my breath."

"I just popped in, anyway," I said, thinking I should probably have said a bit more, but that was the best I could do in Turkish. "Figen is very upset about her grandmother and I want to give her a book to read. Let her come to the shop with me. It'll do her good." I felt as if I was taking part in some surreal film.

Meanwhile, Figen was displaying her acting talents, with much heaving of shoulders and loud sobbing. The tears flowed by the bucketful.

"Well, I don't know. What would her parents say?" said the aunt.

Figen started crying and sniffing again, more noisily than ever.

"Auntie, I feel really terrible. My eyes are streaming. I think I have a fever. Oh Nana, Nana."

Figen was beating her ribcage with one hand, her knees with the other, and crying out, "Nana, Nana."

I repeated the tale about going to my shop to get a book. It was dreadful.

"Well, go along then. What's the book called? What shall I say if your mother comes?"

"Say I've gone to get a book. I need it for school. Our teacher gave us some homework. They didn't have the book in the village. School starts again next week, doesn't it? You can tell my mum I went to get a book for school. Say that miss has it and doesn't want any money for it. She doesn't need it any more. What would a grown woman do with a book anyway? She's going to give it to me. I might as well have it if it's free, otherwise I'd have to pay for it. There's no end to expenses. You just have to

116

set foot outside the door and you've spent five million Turkish lira. Isn't that right, miss?" If she'd gone on much longer, I think I'd have passed out.

"Indeed. What would I do with the book? I'm a grown woman," I said, holding out my glass for more water to help me swallow. How had I ended up here? Why was I staring at UEP propaganda? Why the sudden need for me to get so involved with these people?

Figen disappeared into another room. When she returned, she didn't look any smarter than before, but she definitely had more material covering her. How could people carry so much material on them? No part of her was visible except for her hands, half her forehead, her nose and lips. Involuntarily, I tugged at the sleeves of my T-shirt. But it made no difference what I tugged at. Next to her, I looked stark naked.

We left together. I took a deep breath as we stepped out into the street.

"Miss, let's go this way. My mum will come the other way. If she sees me in the street, she'll make me go back," Figen said, tugging at my arm.

"Fine, you go down there. We'll go our separate ways from here," I said, feeling so deflated I was even prepared to forego any information I thought I might get from the girl.

"No miss, you can't do that. I have to telephone Mahmut to tell him to come to your shop so we can meet there. If my mum sees me out in the street, she'll break my legs."

I was going out of my mind. Seriously. The girl was looking at me as if she was about to burst into tears. And I needed no convincing that she could repeat her ability to dissolve into floods of tears at will.

I took my mobile out of my bag.

"Call Mahmut now and arrange to meet him somewhere. But not at my shop, you wouldn't be able to talk comfortably there," I said.

"Oh, please, miss. Don't let her see me out in the street," she said.

The first signs of a migraine had appeared.

"Fine. Let's go to the shop," I said.

At the shop, Pelin was burbling away, helping some customers who were gazing indecisively at the shelves and picking up the odd book then putting it back. It felt good to be back in my own civilized world. I took Figen through to the telephone. While she was whispering on the phone, I lit a cigarette and waited for the customers to leave.

As soon as the door closed behind the last customer, I said, "Is he coming, your fiancé?"

"He's going to try and get permission. I said I'd call again in ten minutes. You don't mind, do you miss? He can't make calls at work."

"Do you belong to the United Endeavour Party?" I asked, in a leaden voice.

Her face lit up on hearing the name of the party.

"Of course, miss. We all belong to UEP," she said, pronouncing it *yoo-ep*. "You can't be a Muslim if you don't belong to UEP, can you?" she said.

I refrained from pulling at her headscarf and tearing her hair out. After all, I'd decided I wouldn't stick my nose into matters that didn't concern me.

"Do you work for the party?"

"My mum does, more than the rest of us. She goes round to people's homes to organize women's meetings."

"Doesn't your mother have a job?"

"Yes, she cleans at the Haliç Sports Club. When she finishes there, she does Allah's work. It's her salvation. Who are you going to vote for?"

Elections were to be held within a few months.

"I don't know yet," I said.

Figen nodded her head. "Vote for UEP. The others are all corrupt. They've ruined Turkey. The Muslim people have been walked all over. Their wives and daughters have fallen into prostitution."

"Does your mother work late hours for the party?"

"Sometimes she comes home in the middle of the night, miss. She's given so much of herself to the party. My dad doesn't say a word. She's doing Allah's work, not going out and enjoying herself. If she gets just one vote for the party, she's achieved one good deed."

"What does your father do?"

"He serves tea at the Council."

"Beyoğlu Council?"

"Yes."

The chairman of Beyoğlu Council was a member of UEP.

"Did your grandmother belong to UEP as well?"

"Of course, miss. We're all working for Allah."

"Do you think your grandmother was killed for her bracelets?"

Figen didn't reply. She was busy looking at her watch.

"Miss, can I phone again? Sorry miss."

Pelin was watching me and the girl with wide eyes. I signalled with my eyebrows for her to join me in the area we used as a kitchen, because I owed her an explanation.

When I returned, Figen was standing there looking glum.

"He can't come. Couldn't get permission because there are too many customers today. I came all this way for nothing. I'd better go back straight away, miss," she said.

"No, wait a minute," I said. "I want to ask you a few questions."

"Miss, my mum will be waiting for me at home," she said.

"That's not very Muslim of you. Didn't we have an agreement? I help you and you help me?" I think Pelin was convinced I'd gone completely mad.

119

"Quick then, miss. There are lots of people at home and I have to help my mum."

"Was your grandmother very sick?"

"She didn't have any pain, but we could tell the end was near. She couldn't go out at all. She needed to have check-ups, but there's no doctor in the village. Even if there was, the doctors out there aren't like the ones in Istanbul. It's different in the cities."

"Has she always lived with you?"

"No miss. She came to us after she got ill. She didn't want to give up her allotment and animals. After Nana came here, we started going out there to help Grandpa."

"Do you think she was killed because of a robbery?"

"You don't get robberies around here, miss. My brother says it's because all the robbers are neighbours and a robber doesn't steal on his own patch. Anyway, what have we got to steal? Nana had a couple of bracelets, but they weren't even taken. If you're saying there's another reason... But what would anyone want from us, miss? Who'd have anything against us?"

"Perhaps it was because of all this party business," I said.

"No, miss. Why would that be? Anyway, what would Nana have to do with anyone in another party?"

"Well, why then? What does your brother say?"

"He doesn't say anything."

"What did your grandmother do at home all day?"

"Just lay in bed. She wasn't in pain, but she was very weak. She used to be such an active woman, a real go-getter in her time. But this illness took it all out of her."

"Didn't she get bored spending all day at home?"

"Bored? Any woman who's used to working would get bored. And village work isn't like the work here. Out there, people work from dawn till dusk. Nobody stands around doing nothing in the village. That's the life she was used to. Of course she got bored doing nothing. She used to help Mum with the housework and cooking here. And she did that knitting with five needles, making socks for my brother to sell at the market. Those socks used to sell really well in winter. My Nana was a beautiful knitter, God bless her soul. I'll bring you a pair," she said, getting up.

"When she wasn't doing housework, did she use to look out of the window?"

"Of course. Everybody does that, don't they miss? Why do you ask?"

"I was just wondering if she used to sit in front of the window, because when I came to your place, there was an empty place on the divan."

"Yes, that corner was where my Nana sat, miss. She always watched the street from there to see who was coming and going. She didn't watch TV. 'Never got used to it,' she'd say. My aunt doesn't let anyone sit in Nana's place. She says it has to stay empty."

"Did she read newspapers?"

This time Figen laughed.

"What newspapers, miss? Do you think she could read and write?"

"Maybe she looked at the pictures."

"No, miss. Newspapers in the village? Nothing like that has ever entered our house. Who'd pay out good money for that kind of thing every day?"

It had occurred to me that maybe the old woman was killed because she'd seen Osman's killer. The woman would have to have been a very reliable witness for the killer to commit a second murder. Enough to frighten him into taking a serious risk. In which case, he must have thought the woman would be able to identify him. In other words, he was well known. Either that or he was someone who was always around there. Say, for instance, the uncle.

The uncle was still on my list of suspects.

Or, it might have been a well-known person from Osman's circle, who was also known to the old woman. If there was anyone like that, of course. If Osman knew anyone well known.

The only way to find out was to call İnci.

That's what I did. She said she was making dolma and asked me to go round for dinner.

After closing the shop, Pelin and I walked home together. She asked me if she was the reason I kept going out in the evenings.

"I can go to another friend's place if I'm bothering you," she said.

Pelin is Turkish. I forget this sometimes. And she at times forgets that I'm German, though she doesn't really know what Germans are like.

"Look, I'm not Turkish. I'm an in-your-face German and I'd tell you to go if I was bothered about you staying," I said.

"Would you really say that to me?"

"Definitely."

"I'd rather die than say that to anyone."

"I know. You're a polite, hospitable Turk. And I still have just a little bit of German left in me," I said, demonstrating with the tips of my thumb and forefinger. Some things just never change in people.

Osman had lived well. I knew nothing about his wife, but the feast his lover prepared for me that evening was splendid.

"I can't stay long," I said, but not until we'd finished eating, of course. "I was out yesterday evening, too, so I'm a bit tired. But I wanted to ask you something."

I told İnci about the old woman's death and my suspicions. She listened attentively. A bit too attentively, really. I was beginning to see myself as someone of importance.

"The police came today," she said earnestly. "They've finally found out about my existence. See, you're faster than the police."

This was a compliment beyond my wildest dreams. I smiled, sinking my neck down between my shoulders. I was faster than the police, yeah!

"What did they want?" I asked, my voice coming out like that of a spoiled little girl.

"They asked all sorts of things. Like where was I between seven-thirty and nine-thirty on the Thursday evening. I said I was at home, watching TV on my own."

"Did they ask what you were watching?"

She looked hard at me.

"No, they didn't," she said. "They just asked whether or not I was alone."

I suddenly remembered the bit under my chin where it was starting to sag, and how massaging it with a few rhythmical movements helped me to think.

I learnt from İnci that there had been two people in Osman's life who could be described as "well known". One of them was a former footballer. He had played in premier-league teams and was crowned "goal king" in 1989. But Turkish football wasn't as high profile in the Eighties as it is today. Even if it had been, I doubt if an old woman would be able to recognize any of the players.

The other well-known person was an actor who had been a centre-right MP for one term. He was a favourite in the old-school Turkish cinema, memorable for his roles in romantic films. An idol of young girls. A dark, handsome, moustachioed Anatolian guy, who graced the posters on their walls. He came from the same village as Osman. His name was İsmet Akkan. A king among men.

İnci said that İsmet was a gambler. His friendship with Osman had indeed started because they came from the same village, but it had developed because of their shared passion for gambling. After casinos were banned in Turkey, they went off on gambling sprees together for six years or so. At first they went to Bulgaria, but more recently they'd been going to Northern Cyprus. Was this murder because of a gambling debt? Or something like that? Just then, I could think of no other reason.

İsmet Akkan was famous enough for an old woman to recognize him. The average Turk would have memorized every scene of at least three of his films. You didn't have to be a TV addict to recognize İsmet Akkan. Even I knew a couple of his films backwards from catching their weekly screenings on daytime television.

I didn't manage to leave İnci as early as I'd intended. As a result, I arrived home too late to call Lale. I needed her to get İsmet Akkan to contact me.

While I made some green tea, I prepared myself to listen sympathetically to the latest developments in Pelin's life. Every so often, whether we like it or not, it's necessary to take an interest in those around us. After all, we humans are social beings.

When I awoke in the morning, I felt as if the wrinkles around my eyes had decreased. Occasionally, a good night's sleep can have that effect. Standing in front of the mirror, I massaged cream into my face with tiny circular motions and took more care over my make-up than I had for days. If I called in at the hairdresser's, there would be nothing to stop me looking as gorgeous as ever.

I called Lale before leaving home. She said she'd find someone who knew İsmet Akkan. Her interview with the advertising company wasn't until the following afternoon, so she could spend time phoning around that day.

I had a blow-dry, manicure and pedicure at my local hairdresser's. Even after all these years, whenever I go to a salon or encounter one of those immaculate women in the street, I feel grateful to be living in Istanbul where prices are so reasonable.

*

The shop was heaving with customers. People were saying the economy was moving, thanks to pre-election spending by the political parties and last-ditch efforts by MPs. So even I had good reason to put up with the plastic flags sporting party logos that were fluttering in the streets. I spent the whole day dealing with customers and recommending books.

Because of the volume of business, it was evening by the time I had an opportunity to go to the building where Osman was killed. I found that when I stood on the marble steps leading from the main door to the street I could see the corner where the old lady used to sit. Therefore, as I'd guessed, it was extremely likely that she had seen the killer. I sat down and stared at the basement window, trying to recreate in my head what had happened. I didn't know what time the murder was thought to have taken place. İnci had said the police asked her where she was between seven-thirty and nine-thirty on Thursday evening. Did that mean they thought the murder was committed between those times?

There was nothing for it but to phone Batuhan. He said he was driving and couldn't speak for long. Still, he could have at least given me that much information. He didn't. Apparently, it was forbidden to discuss cases that were still ongoing. I'd become used to his inconsistencies long ago, so I didn't even get riled.

Pelin invited me to go along with her and her friends to a rock bar that sold cheap beer. Out of courtesy, I think. She must have known better than I did that, in my current state, I could never go and sit in a rock bar. Anyway, I had other plans for the evening that didn't entail putting on a jacket and tying my hair back.

I prepared myself some muesli with yoghurt. Not because I thought it was the best thing to eat on evenings I spent at home alone, but it does no one any harm to live healthily occasionally. I sat with my dish of muesli in front of the computer and went to the Turkcell Superonline homepage. I'm not ashamed to tell you what I was about to do. They always say, "If it makes you feel ashamed, don't do it," don't they? Well, I wasn't ashamed or embarrassed. What was there to be ashamed of?

I was going to try and find the password for Selim's email account. To find out what was happening with regard to me. Naturally.

The password was the problem. Not being an ace hacker, I would have to do it by trial and error. I decided to try numbers first, then words. I had a few possibilities in mind.

First, Selim's year of birth: 1950.

Second, his university graduation year: 1976.

Third, his favourite and most studied historical event: 1789.

It was none of those.

I looked up the dates of the Magna Carta and the Bill of Rights in an encyclopaedia, thinking they might appeal to a lawyer who liked history. It was neither of those. Midnight passed and desperation was setting in when I entered Tarkovsky, the name of his favourite film director. Then, barely able to keep my eyes open, I tried both *diabolo* and *diabolos*, followed by *veritas*, *vino* and *justitia*. I went on to the names of his beloved Kant, his favourite author Stephen King, his mother, father and siblings. By this stage I'd decided I would abandon him for ever if his password turned out to be the name of a more distant relative. I tried the brand names of the cigarettes, cigars and cologne he used. I had thought that anyone who worked as hard as Selim was bound to choose an easily remembered password, but it seemed I was wrong about this. As about so many things. I tried to think once more of all the things Selim would find easy to remember. He would never remember the date we first met. If we were married, maybe he'd remember the date of our wedding. I would have tried my own birth date, except that he'd forgotten it the previous year.

As I sipped some foul-smelling herb tea, it occurred to me that I hadn't tried my own name. At least he had so far not forgotten my name. So why not? Kati. I typed it in.

Trrrt. Selim's incoming emails opened up in front of me.

His password was my name. The four letters of my name.

Oh, my darling. Bless you. My one and only darling.

I can't tell you how emotional I felt. How many men use their girlfriend's name for their password? I felt I should hang my head in shame for the rest of my life, atoning for all the past and present wrongs I had inflicted on that dear man. My romantic Turkish man. My King of Hearts.

Teardrops were running down my cheeks and dripping onto the computer keyboard. While I'd been thinking how *diabolo* might be a suitable password for him, it turned out that he'd chosen the name of his angel, which was me. Did I deserve such a man? An intrinsically wicked woman like me?

I was squirming with embarrassment. I wanted to call him straight away and have my wounded spirit tended in his arms. To rest my head on his little paunch and have the badness in my head wiped away. To be loyal to him for the rest of my life and never again hurt his sensitive feelings. To marry him, learn how to make dolma, even his favourite meatballs. To nourish him with meals cooked by my own fair hands. To wake him with kisses and whisper in his ear that breakfast was ready. To iron his underpants. I would never make a fuss about the amount of alimony he gave his ex-wife. I would dye my hair blonde, have highlights if necessary. I would drink tea with his friends' wives. I would greet him chirpily at the front door when he arrived home. I would massage his tense shoulders. I would love him more than any other human in the world, more than all the cats, birds, flowers, insects and children. My darling. Did I really deserve to be loved so much? I was trembling inside. His name was burning my lips. My lips were scalding. My heart was fluttering.

I went into the sitting room, poured a whisky and wandered around the apartment letting the ice clink in the glass. I downed it in one and poured another. You can't become an alcoholic in one night, after all. I finished the second one quickly, too. At some point I would have to be realistic. I had to accept that I was never going to learn how to make dolma, that ironing underpants was not really my thing, and that I had no intention of waiting by the door to greet anybody. I poured a third whisky.

If I changed my password to "Selim", I would consider my debt repaid. Even in international relations, that would be a sufficient gesture of reciprocity. No more was required.

I woke up to the chirruping of the telephone. Or rather it woke me up. I ran to the study where the landline was. It's amazing how one can run so far at the moment of waking, despite bumping into walls. It was Batuhan. He had been driving when I called the previous day, which meant that he'd been unable to talk and so on and so on. He seemed to be having a crisis of regrets. It suddenly occurred to me that he might be married. That when I phoned him the previous day, he might have had his wife with him. The things I think of when I've just woken up! Would a woman who stuffed tomatoes or ironed underpants come up with such a thought? No way. Impossible.

Batuhan was still prattling on. If only he'd stop for just a moment. My head was bursting. So early in the morning. He said he was coming to my neighbourhood that day. To Kuledibi. We could have lunch together. His police salary seemed to be limitless when it came to feeding me kebabs. How could he afford it? Was he trying to compete with my beloved top-tax-bracket lawyer? Aren't the wages of state employees supposed to be low in Turkey? And aren't policemen state employees?

"I'll only come out to eat with you if it's on me," I said, thinking it was time I made a contribution to the nation's police force. After all, I lived there and was the bearer of a noble Turkish passport. It was the least I could do for the Turkish police.

I was thinking my usual early morning rubbish. Selim knew that side of me so well.

"Don't be late," I said. "The place I'm taking you to closes early."

Outside it was dark and overcast. Likely to rain. The rains that had brought floods two weeks before were obviously going to start again. Pelin hadn't come home the previous night. I called the shop to check if she was there. She told me a German newspaper wanted to interview me for an article. Would Turkey manage to enter the EU? Everyone expected me, as a German living in Turkey, to have an answer to this huge question. The reporter would call again around noon. He definitely had to see me.

Before leaving home, I called Lale again about İsmet Akkan.

"My friend hasn't managed to get hold of him yet. His mobile's been turned off. But she's found his brother. If not today, they'll definitely set something up for tomorrow, don't worry," she said.

I wished Lale all the best for her job interview.


I bumped into Recai the tea-boy in front of the shop. He was carrying a tray of teas and staring at the sky with a worried look on his face.

"Not long before the rains come. It's the Americans' fault, miss. They've ruined the world, pulled the stopper out. There are floods everywhere. Did you see the news last night? Houses floating on water. They say it's because of the weapons they use to fight wars with. What happened to those things that can see inside caves so that there's no need to use guns? Did they ever manage to get Bin Laden? All lies, miss, all lies," he said.

I was trying to get myself inside the shop.

"Your teas are getting cold, Recai," I said.

"There's no point having tea if we can't enjoy it, miss. People do nothing but complain." Waving his hand, he went down the narrow street towards the square.

There's no way of avoiding politics. Everyone has at least thirty ideas that they're ready to spout about. Talkative Turkey.

Pelin thrust the telephone receiver into my hand as soon as I entered the shop. It was Günther Schmidt, the correspondent from the *Wochenzeit* newspaper.

"I'm extremely busy at the moment," I said, thinking that it was time I gave up having boring meetings with German reporters who knew less about the world than Recai.

"I'm in Istanbul for a week. We can meet whenever it's convenient for you."

"In that case, call me again before you leave," I said.

The rain had started. Nobody was likely to come in to buy a book in that weather. I can't say I felt sad. And I wasn't sad to cancel my lunch appointment with Batuhan. I spent the whole day slouching around with Pelin, even reading a newspaper at one point. The things people will do when they feel out of sorts!

Pelin cooked dinner that evening: okra and lamb casserole. I still hadn't grown used to the existence of this vegetable. It didn't taste bad, actually. With a lot of lemon and tomatoes. But if I spent forty years without okra, I doubt if I would ever give it a thought. Pelin was amazed that most Germans didn't know what it tasted like. So what? It's possible for a nation to live without eating okra, to grate courgettes into their salads like cucumbers and to think their version of pizza is man's greatest invention ever. Anyway, who can compete with the beautiful variety of Turkish cuisine? Though I can't help thinking that Turks go too far occasionally. I still find it a bit weird to eat animals' intestines and brains.

We were just getting ready to go to bed early when Lale rang. Her interview had gone well and she'd got the job. She'd also made contact with İsmet Akkan, who would be waiting for me at his office the following day at five o'clock. She gave me the address and telephone number. Before going to sleep, I made my plans for the next day, which the weathergirl said would be dry.

I woke up to find rays of sunshine trying to filter into my room, the beautiful sunshine that follows a day of continuous rain. It's awful how people's morale is so subject to the weather. One day without a glimpse of the sun and we sink into depression and feel we've aged overnight. There then seems little point in forcing down the muesli, foregoing coffee to reduce cellulite, applying rejuvenating creams, face masks, or even trying to give up cigarettes. I decided to have a morning coffee to celebrate the sunshine. To compensate, I would apply cellulite cream after my shower. It said on the packet that for best results it had to be used regularly, but if it was good for my psyche it was bound to do something for the cellulite.

I shook Pelin to wake her up and told her to go and open the shop. She proclaimed that ever since she had been staying with me she had opened up the shop on her own every single morning. I replied that I was on the verge of old age and already greatly distressed by cellulite and the wrinkles on my face, that there had been no word from my lover in case she hadn't noticed, that I didn't have friends to help drown my sorrows by taking me to rock bars serving cheap beer in the evenings, that life was cruel to women of my age, and that our situations were totally different. She appeared convinced and left, dragging her heels. I went off to the hairdresser's to have my hair coloured. Not the local one this time. Once a month, I ventured out to a salon in Nişantaşı for colouring. Actually, Nişantaşı wasn't far from Cihangir. But going to that district was such a tiresome manoeuvre that I always felt as if I was travelling miles. I couldn't bear how the women there dashed about with their expensive highlights and designer-label carrier bags. They unnerved me. Lale said the reason I found them

131

intolerable was that subconsciously I was afraid of becoming like that myself, or rather that I recognized the potential.

Oh well.

After leaving the hairdresser's, I went to Karaköy before going to the shop. This area had lots of street stalls selling all sorts of strange things, from Vitamin E tablets to condoms. Behind the stalls were shops that were almost completely hidden from view, and one of these was a retailer of guns and hunting gear. Or it had been when I was last there two or three months previously.

It was still there. I sighed with relief to see its shop window display of guns and cartridges. Inside were three people serving and four customers. I stood outside looking at guns in the shop window until two of the customers had left.

"I'd like to look at a revolver," I said to the young lad at the counter, as if I'd come to buy a crew-necked sweater. He stared at me blankly.

"Were you looking for something in particular?"

Obviously, I needed to know a bit more about guns to maintain my pose as a proper customer.

"Well actually, I wanted some information. I wanted to find out about the special features of a revolver," I said, with a smile engaging enough to revive even a corpse. Moreover, my hair was orange.

"Please, take a seat," said the lad, pointing to a stool next to the counter.

He placed a gun on top of the glass counter, the sort used by people who play Russian roulette in films. It had a moveable section where the bullets went.

"This is a revolver," he said. "What did you want to know?"

"Is this weapon chambered for 9mm-calibre bullets?" I asked, afterwards realizing that might have sounded a bit funny. A bit too technical perhaps. The young man scratched the back of his neck and smiled. He was clearly trying not to be rude but could barely stop himself laughing.

"Madam, why do you..." he waved his hand in the air.

"I'm reading a book. A detective story. Something happens that... Your shop was on my way... I was just curious so I came in. If you don't have the time, I can come back later," I said. If I'd prepared myself beforehand, I might have managed to utter a single whole sentence.

"I'm a big fan of detective stories, but I don't have time to read. I'm more into films. I've seen all the James Bond films. Loads of times. Others go to football matches at the weekend, but I go to the cinema. Every week."

"In that case, you'll understand me," I said, almost warbling with pleasure.

"You'd be hard pressed to find anyone who understands you better than me," he said. "Would you like a tea? Or a coffee?"

"Tea would be great," I said.


By the time I left the gun shop, it was almost four o'clock. I had to meet İsmet Akkan at five and I didn't want to be late. I ate an unbelievably greasy pastry at a stall on the street corner. It was something I would spend a week hating myself for, but there was no alternative. I couldn't spend the whole day wandering around on an empty stomach. I collected my car from the car park, turned on some Tanita Tikaram and headed for Mecidiyeköy.

I generally avoided that part of Istanbul unless absolutely necessary, but I found my way without too much difficulty. By ten to five, I was parked and checking the address. It was apartment number twenty-three in a dark-fronted block that had peeling paint and air-conditioning pipes sticking out of the windows. I pressed the bell for Akkan Imports and Exports. The door didn't open. I waited a bit and rang the bell again. This time for longer.

I heard a window being opened noisily.

A woman leant out of the window and called down, "Who's that?"

I stepped back into the street so that the woman could see me.

"I have an appointment at five. My name's Kati Hirschel."

Without a word, the woman withdrew inside and shut the window. I continued to wait. The door still didn't open. I pressed the bell again. Still nothing happened, so I used my mobile to call the number Lale had given me.

"Akkan Imports and Exports," said a woman's voice.

"I've been pressing your doorbell down here. The door doesn't open and I have an appointment at five."

"The automatic door-opener's broken, so I have to come down to open it. But I couldn't because the phone rang. I'm on my own here. Why don't you press a bell for one of the lower floors?"

"Me? I don't want to disturb anyone. I'll wait for you to come down," I said.

"İsmet Bey will arrive soon anyway. He has a key. I'm really sorry. But I'm on my own and the phone keeps ringing."

"Why don't you throw the key down to me?" I said. That was one solution.

"Ha, I didn't think of that. Wait there."

She put the phone down. A second later, her head appeared at the window again and she threw the key down.

The building had no lift. Poor woman, she couldn't be blamed for not wanting to climb all those stairs.

She showed me to one of the smelly velvet armchairs opposite her desk in the entrance hall that served as a secretary's office. The accumulated grime of many years made the velvet upholstery appear like suede. The floor was covered in wall-to-wall carpet which looked as if it had once been brown. I tried not to breathe through my nose to avoid the smell of stale cigarette smoke. Even when I breathed through my mouth, I was seized by a feeling that I was swallowing all that filth. I felt sick. But if I threw up, I would be obliged to visit the toilet there. In desperation, I forced myself to concentrate on something else: green fields, grazing cows, lambs, cherry trees, happy Italian families eating spaghetti... For some reason, I always imagine the typical "happy family" to be Italian. Probably because I know Turkish and German families well enough to know that they aren't happy.

I'd never in my life seen anywhere as filthy as that office. The woman was just as strange and dirty as the office. She was no more than forty kilos for one thing. Her cheeks were sunken, her hair grey and lank. I felt sick again and forced myself to think of green fields.

However, before the woman could offer me anything, the front door opened.

"İsmet Bey," said the woman, jumping up from her seat.

The poor man had aged a lot since his filming days. He was undoubtedly still handsome, and few men could carry off a moustache so well. His whole demeanour was extremely masculine. Macho, I suppose you'd say. Macho men have never interested me. However, I wasn't planning to spend the rest of my life with him. One hour at this office at most. Maybe two. Not even a night. No, of course not. I had my Selim. Or I did have. No, I still did. Anyway, this İsmet Bey was at the top of my list of suspects. He could be a murderer.

The beautiful specimen looked me up and down with his deep eyes, as big as hearts, and then walked towards me. We shook hands.

"I've kept you waiting. It was the best I could do on a Friday evening in Istanbul traffic. There were roadworks on the bridge..."

"It doesn't matter," I said. What did waiting five minutes matter, even in that dreadful place? Especially if I was waiting for him.

"I needed to pick up some papers, which is why I suggested meeting at the office. If you like we can go out and make the most of this lovely weather. They say it's going to rain again tomorrow.

What do you say? Shall we go somewhere on the Bosphorus? We'd be able to talk more comfortably."

He couldn't have had any idea what we were going to talk about. Otherwise, he would have tried to get rid of me as soon as possible instead of suggesting that.

"That would be great," I said. I didn't want to associate this man with that office. Nor did I want to spend another minute there. "I'll wait for you downstairs by the front door," I said.

By the time İsmet Bey came down, I'd smoked a whole cigarette outside the door. Smoking in the street isn't really appropriate for women in Turkey. I don't do it generally, but that day was an exception. I felt it was justified, having spent a few minutes in that extraordinary office.

"I'd say let's go for dinner, but it's too early," he said, taking hold of my elbow. A bit familiar, wasn't it? But if I'm honest, I didn't have the slightest objection to his familiarity. "If I'd known, I'd have made our appointment for later."

"If you'd known what?" I pounced. Sometimes I can be very quick. Only sometimes.

"If I'd known what a charming young lady you are."

I laughed with feigned politeness, managing to stifle a huge guffaw and producing a sort of whinnying sound.

"Please, get in. We can decide where we're going in the car."

"I have my car here too," I said, thinking how cars always create problems in Istanbul. Not only is it impossible to find anywhere to park, you can't even get into the car of a handsome man without having to think twice.

"Leave yours here. I'll have it picked up later," he said.

This was a real man. Had he been one of my usual educated, house-trained types, the sort who are willing to top and tail beans, he would have said, "Leave your car here and I'll drop you off on the way back." I ask you, have our years of struggle for independence been in order to hear such words?

His hand was still on my elbow.

"That's fine," I said.

He didn't even allow the chauffeur to open the door of the monster black Range Rover, but opened it himself. Never mind the concept, the reality of travelling in the back seat of a chauffeur-driven Range Rover was truly exotic. But I was beyond bothering my head with such details. I'd just discovered that there was a need for such macho-type creatures. Only a few years ago, I'd claimed that such men made me sick, yet here I was, feeling an overwhelming desire to inhale the God-given manly smell of the hunk sitting next to me, to swoon in his muscled arms, to bury my face in his hairy chest, to press his head between my thighs. I had no idea whether this was progress or a step backwards for me. If it was a backward step, so what? I was at the time of life for doing whatever I felt like doing and accepting the consequences.

We went to a bar on the Bosphorus.

"We'll have a couple of drinks here and go on somewhere else for dinner," İsmet Bey said, helping me out of the Range Rover. Naturally, I hadn't expected him to ask if I had any other plans for the evening. Still, there was no need to give the impression that I spent my evenings in front of the television with Pelin.

"I'd love to go out for dinner with you, but I already have a date this evening," I said.

"Cancel it," he said.

I keep saying how wonderfully macho he was, but actually I'd never met anyone so rude or arrogant before. Perhaps that's all part of the equation. Yet strangely, even his rudeness was some-how attractive. If I hadn't found him attractive, who knows what I might have done or where I might have stuck that macho tongue.

"I'll see if I can cancel it," I said, as we sat down at one of the tables next to the waterfront. I called Pelin on my mobile and murmured something into it. I didn't miss the expression on İsmet Bey's face when I took out my mobile. Probably because of the model. As soon as I finished speaking, he took the phone from me.

"What's this? Something from the Stone Age?"

"Will you give it back, please?" I said.

"What kind of phone is this? An antique?" he laughed.

"It soon will be," I said, snatching the phone from him. I switched it off and tossed it into my bag. It was best to switch it off, just in case Selim got it into his head to phone that evening.

He patted my arm to express his pleasure at learning I wanted a whisky with ice. He said that men like women who drink and it had become difficult to find people like me. All the women he knew drank white wine because of its low calories. What's more, they made one glass last the whole evening. God forbid, he'd never go on a diet. He wouldn't have anything to do with needlefish women. Needlefish were all bones with no meat. That's what he called women whose skin clung to their bones. So, what was it I wanted to talk to him about?

Meanwhile, my whisky had arrived, thank goodness. I took my first sip of the evening. My excitement of a short while ago was turning to boredom and I was beginning to think it wasn't going to be easy to tolerate this man if I had a clear head. Perhaps one of the achievements of feminism had been to enable women actually to put up with men like this. My house-trained types were certainly much better company.

"Do you know someone called Osman Karakaş?" I asked.

"I did. Osman was killed," he said, and immediately shouted to the waiter for him to bring over some white cheese.

"So you know he was killed," I said.

"Of course I do. I was at his funeral yesterday. We came from the same town. I was on holiday when he was killed. At a place I go to every year in Kemer. I couldn't do anything to help the family, but I went to his funeral," he said, shaking his head thoughtfully. "He wasn't the eldest member of the family, but he was the wisest. A good kid." He frowned and added, "So, what's your link with Osman?"

"Do you know Osman's office?" I asked, making my question sound so casual that I decided I must be the real actor.

"The one at Kuledibi? I've been there a couple of times. Why?"

"I wanted to buy that apartment, to live in—"

"Why there?" he interrupted. "Find a decent area to live in. I'll get you an apartment on our estate. We have the best views in Istanbul. Watchman on the door, swimming pool, tennis court – everything you could want. Kuledibi is no place for a woman to live."

"It suits my budget. And anyway, I don't like estates," I said. He looked at me as though I were a green-eared alien.

"So, you're a bit of a bohemian then?"

"More than a bit," I said, suddenly feeling that his attitude towards me had gone cold. He seemed to be having difficulty restraining himself from calling for the bill and leaving.

"Fine, so the link between you and Osman is that you wanted to turn his office into a place to live. But where do I come into this?"

"The police think I killed Osman," I said, immediately realizing I'd said the wrong thing. If he'd been at Osman's funeral, he would have known who the police suspects were.

"What, you kill Osman? No way. It was probably that bastard of an uncle who killed him. Do his brothers know that you're a police suspect? Wait..." he said, taking out his mobile phone.

"Just a minute," I said. "The uncle is the number one suspect, I'm number two." I was really making a mess of it this time. Everything I said seemed to be proclaiming "I'm a liar".

"Just tell me everything from the beginning, babe. What exactly happened?"

I told him the story of the ashtray. From the look in his eyes, I could tell I was regaining his respect. He heard me out without saying a word.

"Well, what do you want from me?"

"I thought you might know who Osman did business with and who might have done this."

"Yeah, I get you, but what's it to you? He's dead, whoever killed him. Get on with your own life. The cops haven't carted you off as a murderer, for God's sake!"

"But," I said solemnly, "the problem is that I was at home on my own at the time of the murder. I have no alibi. If it turns out that the uncle didn't do it, then the police..."

"Alibi? Nobody's going to accuse you."

"You have an alibi for that night, don't you? I don't," I said.

"Well yes, I was on holiday. Anyway, I don't need an alibi. What's it got to do with me?" he said, sounding somewhat perturbed.

"Don't you understand?" I said. "If this isn't cleared up, they'll interrogate all of us. Ask us where we were that night."

He shrugged his shoulders. Had I not known this man was an actor, I would certainly have concluded that he had no connection with all this. But can an actor be trusted?

"I was on holiday from 12th August. They can ask anyone at the holiday village. I'd been filming a big summer series and I went there to recuperate. Didn't even set foot outside the holiday village," he said, bristling like a male chicken, I mean cockerel.

"Why the hell should the police question me about any of this? Because I knew the man? Have you any idea how many million people I might know in this country? If one of them gets bumped off, what's it got to do with me?"

"Do you know who Osman did business with?"

İsmet Bey was starting to get suspicious about me.

"Why are you bothering your pretty little head with all this?" he said. "Come on, let's go and eat."

*

We got into the Range Rover with great ceremony. The waiters lined up outside to say goodbye to us, or rather him. It was already clear that the subject of Osman wouldn't be broached again that evening and I would gain nothing from going for a meal with this man. The best thing was to jump in a taxi, collect my car and go straight home. While we were still fairly close. Before it got too late. That is if I was sensible. I could hear Selim's voice in my head saying all this.

But something, which I couldn't quite control, was telling me I should go out for this meal. When I have to choose between a wise and an unwise option, I've never yet chosen the wise one.

The same thing happened this time.

We edged our way slowly through the dreadful traffic towards Ortaköy. The back seat of the Range Rover was so narrow our legs were touching.

"The press mustn't see us together," said İsmet.

"What do you mean?"

"They'll be waiting outside the restaurant now. Why don't you get out here and get a taxi for the rest of the way?"

"Taxi? It's just up there, isn't it?"

"Are you going to walk it then?" he said, laughing.

"Of course I'll walk," I said. The only sport I did was walking. Now that I was using my car so much less, I walked as much as it was possible to walk in Istanbul. One should try to change one's lifestyle as one gets older.

"As you wish," he said, making it clear that he didn't like the idea.

The place we were going to was an Italian restaurant. There were groups of paparazzi outside the door, waiting for anyone worth photographing. They didn't give me a second glance.

"I'm meeting İsmet Akkan," I said to the waiter who blocked my way.

The waiter retreated rapidly.

"Please, madame. This way," he said when he came back.

İsmet Bey kept asking me questions during the meal. By the time we were on our main course, I was beginning to think I had no secrets left in my life. Whether it was because actors are experts at getting people to open up or whether I'd had a bit too much to drink I really didn't know and was in no position to know.

We were nearly at the dessert course, or rather he'd just ordered it, when he suddenly put his hand on my leg. I'm not sure if I mentioned it before, but I was wearing a skirt. A fashionable one: flared, with a hemline that rose from the knee on one side to mid-thigh on the other. His hand was touching my leg on the short side of the skirt. Before feeling his way upwards towards my thigh, he glanced sideways at me, waiting for a reaction. Not knowing how to react, I waited too. To see what reaction I came up with.

At such moments I let myself go with the flow. Whatever that means. I suppose I should say the flow of desire. As far as I'm concerned, you can't use reason once desire comes into it. Anyway, there are so many situations that require reason, why spoil everything for yourself by using reason to control desire? Reason should be used in marriages, or in relationships. Relationships!

Selim! My master of common sense!

Thinking of Selim made me blush all of a sudden. Or if I didn't, I felt as if I did. I could feel my temperature rising.

Events, emotions, desires – whatever they were – I was in no position to allow myself to give free rein to whatever was pulsating inside me. My future might not have been assured, but I was a woman in a relationship. I was the type of woman who needed monogamy. The sort who needed to go out for meals with her lover, her lover's friends and their wives, who needed her lover to accompany her to the cloakroom, who needed to say "cloak-room" when she meant "lavatory".

The irony of fate! A woman sitting next to a man whose hand was wandering up her leg was also a woman who dined with the immaculate wives of lawyers.

If only someone could have appeared with a set of tarot cards to tell me what was going to happen that night if I didn't immediately, without hesitation, push his hand back, or at least pull my leg away.

But you needed to believe in the cards for that, didn't you?

Never mind the rest of that evening then – what about the following day? Would I be having breakfast with this man the next morning? Or would I be trying to scuttle away before he awoke? Or even before dawn? How did I feel?

Did I just claim there was no need for reason? Forgive me. It was an old habit, a principle left over from times when I wasn't in a steady relationship. As you see, my life was now alternating between lurid cloakroom adventures and civilized evenings with respectable men and their perfect women.

I don't want to bore you with the fears I had about losing my identity to middle-class values, but you couldn't lead the double life I was living without fear of losing something. However, it was certainly worth trying to have it all!

I hope I've explained myself sufficiently well.

Anyway, reason surfaces whether you like it or not, whether it's necessary or not. It just keeps whirring away all the time. Not everybody's of course. But mine never stops.

So, what was the situation? Let's recap. Both for me and for you, dear readers:

1. I was a woman in a steady relationship
2. I was fed up with my life
3. Just once wouldn't matter

I started to stroke the hand that was on my leg.

Don't get me wrong, we were still sitting on those uncomfortable chairs, there were waiters and customers coming and going all around us, and the man beside me was as easily recognizable as a multi-coloured dog.

And I was drowning with excitement.

"Let's get out of here," I muttered in a husky tone of voice, almost licking his ear as I said these silly words.

"We can't leave together," he said, almost licking my neck, rather than my ear, as he uttered his equally stupid words, which meant I didn't hear exactly what he said.

"What?"

"The paparazzi are teeming outside. We can't leave together and get into the same car," he said.

Clearly, an evening of passion with a famous person brought its own problems.

If I hadn't been so fed up with my life, I'm not sure I'd have put up with all this.

But why not?

"You go on ahead and take a cab to my house," he said.

"Very well," I said with a meekness that didn't suit me at all. What a pity it wasn't like it is in films and that we hadn't got up to go to the cloakroom one minute apart and then returned to our seats one minute apart. I've never yet worked out how people have sex in the toilets. It can't be very clean. And you don't have to be a hygiene fanatic to think that. What's the best position for sex in a toilet? I can think of several options, all of them equally excruciatingly uncomfortable. It's beyond me how people take pleasure in adopting those gymnastic positions. How on earth do you wrap your leg around your neck? And why, when there are civilized positions you can adopt in bed, on the sofa, kitchen table or hall carpet?

I'm not turned on in the slightest by the fear of discovery, or seeing the feet of some desperate person outside the door who is hammering to get in. If it took that much to get aroused, better not have sex with him at all.

In the end, it was for this reason that I thought it better for us to get up and leave separately rather than go out to the toilet one at a time.

However, to be honest, until I got into the taxi, I had been thinking of nothing except that hand on my leg.

I hope I'm not boring you by my constant changes of mind. I would love to have been able to oblige you, dear reader, with a story of unbridled sex that lasted until morning. The man in question certainly had what it took to arouse a woman. Or at any rate, he had that effect on me.

However, we just have to accept that by the time I got into the taxi, on my own, the whole tone of the evening had changed.

Sitting in the back seat of the taxi gave me time to consider whether I wanted to go to the other side of the Bosphorus, seek out the address I was clutching in my hand, enter a completely strange apartment and spend the night with a man whom I hardly knew and had thought might be a murderer until a few hours ago. What's more, I was no longer particularly aroused. Reason and sense. In short, all my thoughts were of Selim.

The one night of passion I was ever likely to have at my age wasn't supposed to be like this.

Not at all.

"I've changed my mind about going to the other side," I said to the cab driver. "Take me to Mecidiyeköy."

I got out of the taxi and, standing there in the street, I lit a cigarette. Apart from the occasional passing car, the street was empty. I looked at my watch. It was twenty past twelve. I switched on my mobile and called Selim.

"You're drunk," he said to me.

"So what if I am?"

"For God's sake, don't try to drive in that state. I'll come and get you."

"Of course I'm not going to drive. What do you think I am? A Turk? I'll get a cab and come over," I said.

"I know you won't do that because you can't bear to waste money on taxis," he said.

"Don't be silly. What do you think I am? A German?" I said.

"I think I've missed you," said my lover, whose email password was "Kati".

"Only think?" I said.

## 8

I felt my arm suddenly knock against somebody. I jumped in panic. The spring mattress rocked about like crazy. Thinking it must be an earthquake, I tried to open my eyes to look around the room for a desk to hide under. But there was no desk. What would a desk be doing in a bedroom? I was in a bedroom. A bedroom I recognized, but it wasn't mine. My shoulders ached, my head even more. I had no idea where I was until I saw the person my arm had knocked. Seeing Selim's bald head brought back vague images of the previous evening. When I'd arrived, I'd been unable to keep upright and had come up with some sort of tearful explanation. Probably said something disgraceful. The sort of thing one would never say when sober. I did an enormous yawn, knocking his head again. How could he still be asleep? Of course, it was Saturday. That made no difference to me. My responsibilities didn't stop at weekends. There was a murder I needed to solve. If only I knew what time it was!

I propped myself up on an elbow to look at the clock next to Selim, once again rocking the bed. It was a digital clock. Eight thirty-four. What a ridiculous time to wake up on a Saturday morning. I did another huge yawn, without even covering my mouth. Should I get up and make breakfast for us both? Should I go for a shower? A shower wouldn't help. I always feel terrible after drinking too much. Really dreadful.

I prised myself out of the bed, where Selim was still sleeping like a baby. I went into the kitchen and tossed an Alka-Seltzer into a glass of water. It tasted disgusting. I sat down and waited for the kettle to boil for coffee. When the water boiled, I found there was no coffee in the house. Maybe this was some sort of divine intervention. Someone was saying, "Never forget the cellulite, even at moments when the only thing you really need is coffee." That's how I saw it. I might have thought, "I'll ask the corner shop to send up some coffee," or I could have brewed some tea instead.

I went into the bathroom for a shower. I couldn't stand up properly for long enough to take a shower, so I decided to run a bath. There was some raspberry bubble bath on the shelf. Wasn't it a bit odd for my lover to be using fruit-scented products? Other men insist on covering themselves with smells so pungent they burn the back of your throat. I turned on the taps and sprinkled lots of raspberry bubble bath into the water. Closing the toilet lid, I sat on it and waited for the bath to fill, still yawning constantly. I felt wretched. It was all too much for me. Suddenly, I began to howl, as if I'd trapped my finger in a door. As I cried, I squirmed like a worm and fell off the toilet seat. My leg hurt. That made my cries get louder. I was gasping, shrieking, grovelling on the floor and crying my eyes out. Surely Selim couldn't sleep through all that noise. I carried on sobbing my heart out.

It's not a good idea to strain the face muscles too much when crying, or laughing for that matter. Both can cause premature wrinkles. But I only thought of that after my violent crying had subsided. But people need to cry sometimes, and to laugh.

I came out of the bathroom and phoned my mother.

"I'm getting old," I said.

"Are you sleeping properly?" she asked.

"Not really, but I don't have insomnia," I said.

"Are you eating vegetables?" she asked.

"Hmm," I said. I lived on toasted cheese sandwiches most of the time, with the occasional plate of okra. Okra once in a blue moon.

"Do you get enough exercise?" she asked.

"No," I replied.

"Then of course you'll age," she said. Aren't mothers terrible? They make me feel very glad I'm not one. No mother should close the subject with the words, "How old are you? What makes you think you're getting old?" Mothers should ask probing questions and make nonsensical interpretations of the answers.

"When you start the menopause, you'll know what ageing really is," said Mother. My very own birth mother said that. She sounded more like an enemy, don't you think?

"The menopause doesn't start at this age, Mother," I said.

"It does in our family. You only have a year or two left," she said.

"How's your rheumatoid arthritis?" I asked, hoping to change the subject. It worked. For the next five minutes, she told me all about her ailments, how Frau Hellersdorf, her best friend at the German Rest Home in Majorca, had fallen out of bed and broken her arm and how good the weather was. I had to promise to visit her in October. Otherwise, she was even going to risk coming to Istanbul to see me. My mother didn't like Istanbul. She couldn't understand why anyone, meaning me, would live in this city unless they had to. The streets were too crowded, the roads too narrow, the people too friendly. She hated having to be friendly towards people the moment she met them. She would complain continually. About Turkish men spitting in the streets, litter louts, stray animals... She made my life a misery.

I didn't want to put on the top and skirt I'd been wearing the previous day, so I went into the bedroom to look for some clothes that I might have left at Selim's. He was still fast asleep, oblivious to everything. Perhaps I shut the wardrobe door rather loudly, because he stirred and turned over. He finally woke up as I closed a drawer in one of the bedside tables. To make my peace, I squatted down next to him. He stroked my hair.

"This colour is lovely," he said.

"I was very drunk last night," I said.

"I realized that," he said.

"What did I say to you?"

"You mentioned two men: Osman and İsmet. One of them had obviously been killed. Have you been reading Turkish detective stories again?"

What a sweet man. I buried my face in his shoulder – it was just the right shape – and placed my hand on his buttocks.

"What did you do while I wasn't here?"

"I lied to everyone and said, 'Kati's on holiday.' I was afraid you'd bump into one of them."

"And how did you spend your time?"

"Watched TV. Read one of the books you left here."

Had my lover, who prided himself on never reading fiction, actually been reading novels in my absence?

"Which one?"

"It's in German. A book called *Magic Hoffmann*. If you haven't read it, you should. What have you been doing?"

"I'll tell you later," I said. "I have to meet Yılmaz, as you know. I didn't go last week."

"What? Leaving already?"

I kissed his earlobe.

"Lale's got a job. With an advertising company."

"Are we going to see each other this evening?"

"I'll call you. My mobile's switched on. You can call me too. Pelin's staying with me."


I took a taxi from Selim's place to Mecidiyeköy, collected my car and parked in front of my apartment building. It was easier to find parking spaces in the daytime at weekends. I wanted to sing out loud. To salsa with the lad in the corner shop. Oh, if only I could belly dance or play the hand drum. Chisss tak. Tak ta tak tak.

I rang the main doorbell. Pelin leant almost double out of the window.

"Did you forget your key?" she called out.

"No," I said. "I'm going to meet Yılmaz at the café in Firuzağa. Do you want to come?"

She pulled a face. She couldn't stand Yılmaz, but was too polite to say so.

"I've got things to do at home," she said.


After Yılmaz left me to go and see some newly released film, I called Batuhan.

"We've found the uncle," he said. "He'd gone to his village. All that money in his pockets and he couldn't think of anywhere better to hide it than his village. He's being brought back to Istanbul today. So that's it. Case closed, I guess."

"Congratulations," I said. "To both of us." *Ein Glück kommt auch selten allein.* In other words: not only disasters, but good things also come in pairs.

"Let's drink to it," he said.

"I don't think we should be in a hurry to drink to anything," I said. "It all looks far too simple to me."

"I can't help it if real-life murders aren't as complex as they are in your whodunits. That's why working in the murder squad isn't exactly thrilling."

"Yes, but I expected it to be more intellectually challenging than that," I said. "Have you managed to find out who killed the old woman?"

"Do you think there's a link between the two incidents?"

"Why don't we meet in Kuledibi? I want to show you something," I said, not wanting to fall into the trap of withholding information from the police. I knew my responsibilities as a citizen. I was also one very happy citizen.

"I can't. The guys have just left Van. They're bringing the uncle back, as I said. We could meet tomorrow. At twelve o'clock. At that tea place."

"OK," I said. Reluctantly, I got up and went home.


"The uncle says they have an ongoing blood feud with a neighbouring clan and it must be one of them who did it."

I was sitting with Batuhan in the tea garden in Kuledibi. It was Sunday. Not really warm enough to be sitting outside, by Turkish standards.

"It's strange the brothers said nothing about a blood feud, isn't it?" I remarked.

"Yes, it is strange. I wonder why they didn't mention it. But since no one has been killed on either side for thirty years, they probably thought it was all over."

"Is a blood feud ever over?"

"Of course. If they make peace," said Batuhan.

"Well, they certainly should do in this day and age. I don't know what the practice is, but... I read an expert-witness report written by my father on vendetta killings among Turkish migrants in Germany."

"Your father?" said Batuhan.

"Yes, he was a criminal lawyer. He used to be called in as an expert witness for cases involving Turks because he'd lived in Turkey for a long time and knew Turkish."

Batuhan looked at me with curiosity, nodding his head.

"From that report," I continued, "I learnt that reduced sentences are handed out for vendetta killings in Turkey. Just think, you commit premeditated murder but get a light sentence. Very odd."

"What did your father say in his expert-witness report?"

"He wanted reduced sentences for vendetta killings in Germany too."

Batuhan clapped his hand to his mouth and laughed.

"So, if I kill someone in Germany because of a vendetta, I get a light sentence?"

"I don't know if it's always like that, but the judge reduced the sentence in the case where my father was the expert witness."

"You know, they get their kids to carry out the murders because they're given light sentences."

"How does a blood feud start?" I asked.

"It can start with any sort of dispute. Territorial issues, for instance. Someone occupies someone else's land and the owner then kills him. Then someone in the first family kills a member of the second family, and so on."

"And it ends when there's no one left to kill?"

"There's always someone left to kill. They hide their children – pack them off to the big cities to keep them safe. Depending on which family's turn it is, the next in line to be killed runs away and the other side hunts him down."

"So was it the turn for someone in Osman's family to be killed?"

"That's why they came to Istanbul in the first place."

"Did the other family remain in Van?"

"They've migrated all over the place. Some settled in Adana. But others are still in Van."

"What are you going to do?"

"We'll take the uncle in for questioning. And Osman's brothers."

"Doesn't it seem strange to you that the murder weapon was a revolver?"

"A revolver? How do you know that?" he asked, narrowing his eyes as he looked at me.

"You told me," I said.

"I did? I don't remember that at all. So, what about the revolver?"

"Do you think Osman's uncle or a blood-feud killer would use a revolver?"

He patted the pockets of his jacket, looking for cigarettes. As he pulled them out, a photograph fell onto the table.

"This is the uncle," he said, pushing the photo across to me.

He was a dark, spindly man with sunken cheeks, a moustache and large eyes. To the average German, he was a typical Turkish male. I gave the photo back to Batuhan.

"I had also wondered whether these people would use a revolver," he said.

Once again, he narrowed his eyes.

"How do you know about guns?" Batuhan asked.

"I don't really, but I know what a revolver is. They're quite expensive and more of a connoisseur's weapon, and getting hold of bullets for them isn't that easy. That sort of gun is way out of the league of a poor wretch like the uncle."

"You're right. You're definitely right, but where does that get us?"

"To the old woman," I said.

"The old woman? The woman who was stabbed?"

"There's definitely a connection between those two murders. That woman always sat at the window watching the street. If the murder took place before dark, say seven-thirty or eight o'clock, it's extremely likely she saw the killer. He must have realized the woman had seen him leave the building and killed her at the first opportunity. She was a key witness, don't you see?"

He sat thinking and playing with his lighter for a while.

"Your imagination is working overtime," he remarked.

I managed to stop myself from snapping back at him. What is there to say to a police officer who refuses to look beyond the simplest solution in order to close a case?

"I'll show you, if you like. The old woman used to sit on the divan that's in the corner by the window. From that angle, the stairs of the opposite building are visible. The woman could have seen the murderer."

"Fine, but I don't suppose he had 'murderer' written on his forehead. How would she have known that he or she was a murderer?"

"She?" I said, instantly realizing that I'd been focusing too much on the idea that the murderer was a man. "Why did you say 'she'?"

"Figure of speech. But women can be killers too, as you know. Or are murderers always men in fiction?"

Saying "figure of speech" was just a diversion. He undoubtedly thought the killer might be a woman.

Batuhan spoke to someone on his mobile and said he had to go immediately, leaving me wondering what to do with myself.

Hopping into the car and driving from place to place is never the best way of spending a Sunday in Istanbul. In fact, every day is a bad day for doing that in Istanbul, unless your life depends on it.

I walked as far as the street where the two murders had been committed. Kuledibi is unbelievable on Sundays. It's shrouded in silence, like all areas that mainly consist of offices. If only every day were Sunday in Kuledibi.

I went up to the main door of the building where Osman's office was. It was wide open. I hesitated for a moment on the first floor in front of Yücel Bey's door, then pressed the bell. There was no response. I went up to the next floor.

A large yellow notice had been stuck on the door of Osman's apartment and the padlock was secured by some rope with a red seal. I was afraid to touch it, thinking of DNA tests, fingerprints and so on. Anything was possible. I sat down on the stairs and phoned Selim.

"What would happen if I were to break a seal the police had put on a door and go inside?"

"Have you gone crazy? Where are you?"

"What's the penalty for breaking a seal?"

"Kati!" he said, like a father rebuking a child.

"I've no intention of doing anything like that. I'm just asking," I said.

"What's the penalty for breaking a police seal?" he asked someone next to him. "I'm a commercial lawyer, don't forget. How should I know the penalty for breaking a seal? No! Yes, a first offence. Oh, OK then, cheers."

"What is it?" I asked.

"The penalty isn't very harsh – one to three months. Can be converted to a fine, of course. Daily rate starts at seven million lira. You can break it all you like. You have a lawyer ready and waiting. He's sitting right next to me."

He thought I was joking.

"Where are you?" I asked.

"At the office. I have two hearings tomorrow that I'm working on. Come over here if you want and we can leave together," he said. Our relationship was continuing from where we had left off, and at the same pace. People develop certain behavioural patterns with each other that never change, unless something disastrous happens. I think I'm right in saying that.

"I'll call you when I'm on my way. I'm just looking around Kuledibi at the moment," I said.

"You won't touch that seal, will you? I was only joking before."

"I won't touch it. Anyway, what's the good of breaking a seal if I can't open the door?" I said.

There are people who open doors with things like hair-clips. It happens in real life, not just in films and novels. I wanted to be one of those people. If I had been, I wouldn't have thought twice about that daily penalty of seven million lira.

If only I could take a look inside that office. It would undoubtedly provide me with some sort of inspiration about who had committed the murder.

I sat down on the marble stairs and lit a cigarette. Waiting for inspiration. My chin resting on my hand, waiting for inspiration like poets do. I thought it might come if I sat in a place where I had never sat before, by the door of an apartment to which I had formed an emotional attachment.

The inspiration that came to me was of no use in finding out who had committed the murder. But it produced the following poem:

> like russian roulette
> a 9mm bullet
> fires from a revolver
> piercing an artery in the leg
> with pierced artery
> you crawl to the door
> leaving trails of blood
> down the long, long corridor
> down which your cries
> accumulate and hover in the air
> but no one runs to your help

I took care not to throw away my cigarette butt until after I had reached the street. It was important to be careful at all times.

I had parked my car in a street near the Neve Shalom Synagogue. Even in Kuledibi there was no problem finding a parking space on a Sunday. I walked towards the synagogue, playing with my keys. I felt sure that if I could only talk to the family of the old woman, they would give me something to go on. Or that's what I hoped. However, I had no intention of going to that basement for a second time without good reason. Had I been a private detective, I could at least have created the impression of having a valid reason for asking questions. But I had no police officers under my command, no criminal laboratories updating me with reports, and no witnesses to interrogate. I was stuck.

Sighing with frustration, I turned on the ignition.

The prospects didn't look very bright.

Not bright at all.

The killer was the uncle.

Or someone involved in a blood feud.

There was no link between the murder of the old woman and Osman.

......

It just didn't feel right to me.

But that's how it was.

So what?

What did it matter to me?

I wasn't even a private detective.

I was nothing.

No! It wasn't that bad!

I was a woman who sold crime fiction.

I had to take care of my own life.

So what about this property-buying business?


I turned off the engine and called Kasım Bey.

"I was just about to call you. Congratulations. The hearing was on Friday. The judge broke his pencil."

"Broke his pencil?" Isn't that what they say when the judge issues the death penalty? Hadn't the death penalty been abolished? Anyway who was the suspect?

"Oh, it means everything's done and dusted. When that happens, people say 'he broke his pencil'."

I had no intention of trying to teach Turkish to Kasım Bey.

"How did he reach his decision?"

"Since no inheritors could be found, a decision was taken to turn the estate over to the Treasury. The ball's in my court now. I'm going to speed things up and put it on the market immediately. You get your money together and I'll let you know when the auction date has been set. Be happy. There's just one colleague holding things up. I need to talk to him."

He wanted money again. I'd been living there long enough to understand Turkish euphemisms.

"How much?" I said.

"What?"

"How much more do you want?"

"It's for my friend, not me."

"Fine, so how much does your friend want?"

"Let's not discuss it on the phone. I'll call you and we'll meet somewhere."

"Ring me and I'll call you back," I said. That man sickened me. Also I didn't feel at all sure that Osman's brothers would let me have that apartment. Still, there was no point in being pessimistic. One thing was going well and worth living for: my love life.


"You must be joking, pet," said Selim. No one else I knew addressed me as "pet".

"No, I'm not joking," I said, rolling my eyes. "Anyway, why should I joke about something so absurd?"

"I said, 'you must be joking' as a figure of speech. I know you'd never joke about a thing like that, don't worry."

People kept talking about figures of speech for some reason.

"I've bribed Kasım Bey so that he'll get me an apartment. He works in the trustee department at the National Real Estate Bureau."

"You can't really have bribed someone, that's... No, I don't believe it."

"Why not? You hand out bribes to officials in the justice department."

"Not bribes, pet. I hand out baksheesh. Like you tip a waiter who serves you in a restaurant. It's the same sort of thing."

"Don't talk nonsense. You're forever handing out bribes."

"I give people money if they provide a service that's beyond what they would normally do. They do what is required and I reward them. If I handed out money for something they shouldn't do or was illegal, then it would be a bribe."

"Yes, well, I wasn't getting him to do anything illegal. I just gave him a little sweetener to secure me a perfectly lawful prerogative that will enable me to buy an apartment that would otherwise have been impossible. Why should yours be baksheesh and mine a bribe?"

"All right, darling. We'll call yours baksheesh. What can I say? I mean… It seems strange for someone with your principles. I just can't imagine you bribing anyone. How did you give it to him, in a brown envelope?"

"Huh? I gave it in just the same way as you would. And I'm not proud of myself."

My reason for telling Selim about my dealings with Kasım Bey was to get him to find someone to go to the auction for me. It wasn't to boast to my darling man about what I'd been doing.

"Fine, I'll find a lawyer to go with you to the auction," he said eventually.

He was lying on the sofa, twiddling his toes. I sat down next to him and stroked his belly.

"My one and only Selim," I said, with genuine sincerity.

For the first two days of that week, I hardly had time to catch my breath. I paid off the refuse-collection tax in order to escape the nagging phone calls from my landlady. I met my accountant. I accompanied Özlem to collect her belongings from the apartment she had shared with the husband she was about to divorce. I even tried to reconcile Pelin and her boyfriend. I failed miserably there, but sorted out the other matters without any difficulty. The Pelin business had turned into a battle of wills.

On Wednesday, it poured down all day, yet again. Pelin was accusing me of being unsympathetic when Batuhan turned up at the shop. I'd completely forgotten about Osman, vendettas and the uncle. Seeing Batuhan reminded me that I hadn't heard from İnci for days. Not taking my detective work seriously was one thing, but it was sheer disloyalty to ignore a newly established friendship in that way.

Pelin had clearly had enough. She saw Batuhan's arrival as an opportunity to go out, regardless of the rain. I know what she was thinking. She thought I wanted her to make up with the boyfriend in order to get her out of my apartment. But that had nothing to do with it. It was just that I knew how hard it was to find a decent, straight man. I reckon you shouldn't let go of what you have until someone better comes along. If young people would only listen to me, their lives would be much easier. What a shame they can't understand that.

"Am I disturbing you?" asked Batuhan.

"Not at all," I replied.

"Your friend got up and left the moment she saw me."

Turks are like that. They think the world revolves around them. I find it very tiresome sometimes. Life with Germans is easier.

"What's that got to do with you? She had business to see to and was about to go anyway," I said. "What happened about the vendetta people?"

"Nothing. We obtained twenty-four different sets of finger-prints from the office, but none of them correspond to those of the uncle, who says he's never set foot in that office anyway. From the fingerprints, he might be telling the truth. He was still wearing the same clothes as when he ran off with the money. His wife verified that. He was filthy all over but there was no trace of gunpowder on his clothes."

"Was there any gunpowder on his hands?"

"His hands?"

"Don't people use their hands to fire guns?"

"The murder was committed two weeks ago. Is it likely that he'd still have traces of gunpowder on his hands?"

"No?"

"Impossible."

"What about the vendetta people?"

"We took fingerprints from everyone we managed to get hold of and compared them with the ones found at the office. Not one of them matched."

"Have you started to think that maybe there's a link between this murder and the old woman?"

"Sweetheart, I don't know what I think. I've just come from the basement where the old woman was killed. You might be right. I sat on the divan where the woman used to sit. From there you can certainly see everyone who enters the main door of the building opposite. I made one of our lads stand in front of the door while I sat in her place. He was clearly visible and you could make out the people standing on the steps. It's a narrow street anyway. The buildings are practically on top of each other so of course I could see him. I spoke to the forensic pathologist again about the time of death. He says it was between seven-thirty and nine-thirty, but probably closer to seven-thirty. Since the sun would have set at seven-thirty or eight o'clock in Istanbul on 29th August, it is indeed very likely that the old woman saw the murderer leave the building. We're working on the assumption that the murderer left when it was still light. If it had been dark, the woman couldn't have seen him, of course."

"Great," I said. "So you're well and truly convinced."

"It's not a question of being convinced. The uncle and the vendetta theory got us nowhere."

"Then you must find some new suspects," I said, smiling. "Did the old woman have good eyesight?"

"Oh, well done you. That's a very good point. According to the grandson, she couldn't see things close up. That boy's got a good head on his shoulders – studying at university. He says his grandmother had spectacles, but didn't use them for distance because her distance vision was very good. I haven't looked into that yet. I'm taking the woman's spectacles to be analysed. If her eyesight was good, then there's no reason why she shouldn't have seen the murderer come out of the main door. In that case, our job is to find out who saw the woman and why they might be a suspect. Would the woman suspect everyone who left the building at that time? Not Osman's brothers, probably. They're in and out of there every day. There are builders on the top floor. One of your intellectual types has bought the penthouse and he's doing it up. All sorts of people go in and out of that building during the day, from the architect and owner to technicians and labourers. None of them, or anyone like them, would have aroused any suspicion in her mind. That's why I think Osman's killer was someone she knew, someone she was surprised to see in her own street. The woman had just returned to Istanbul where she knew no one apart from her family and neighbours. I'm getting fingerprints taken of everyone in the neighbourhood and all the relatives. Anyone the woman might have known. Let's see what turns up. If none of them match the fingerprints at the office, then I'll carry on with my mental gymnastics."

"How did the killer know the woman had seen him, and why should that terrify him? Do you think the woman called out to him from the window? Or they caught each other's eye? Or that perhaps she said something to him?"

"I also got one of my colleagues to sit on the divan while I stood on the steps. The old woman could easily have seen anyone standing on the steps, but the killer wouldn't have been able to see her through the basement window so easily. That's why I think she probably opened the window and called out. Maybe there's an eyewitness who saw her talking to the killer."

"If anyone else gets killed in the neighbourhood, I suppose we'll know there was."

Batuhan looked annoyed with me.

"At this very moment, the boys are going round all the apartments and shops asking if anyone saw the old woman talking to anyone after seven o'clock on the twenty-ninth of August," he said.

"They should also ask if anyone heard a gunshot that day," I said.

"We asked that a long time ago. Nobody admitted to hearing any shots. It's very noisy around there so it's possible for a gunshot to go unnoticed."

Actually that was true. It wasn't hard to believe that the sound of a gunshot might get lost in the noise of Istanbul.

"I think the killer was someone well enough known for the woman to recognize him," I said.

"What do you mean by that?"

"A film actor, singer, TV presenter or something. I don't know – someone in the media."

"There weren't any famous people in Osman's circle, believe me," he said, with a sideways grin. He looked at me to make sure I appreciated the burst of intelligence in those words.

"Why are you so disparaging about Osman? Anyone can have famous people in their lives."

"Not a car-park attendant," he said.

"But the man certainly had a spark about him. How many people start with nothing and get to own several car parks, a restaurant, café and coach company within fifteen years?"

"Oh, I see you've researched your victim well. So what else did he do? Did you know he held gambling sessions in the café basement? Or that he ran a trade in women? Did you know he had been asked to stand as an MP for UEP at the next election?"

"UEP?" I said. Some cigarette smoke went in my eye and I blinked to stop mascara running into my eyes.

"That's what they wanted. This family belongs to Van's biggest clan and Osman had acquired a bit of a reputation. If a popular clan member is chosen as candidate, it wins votes for the party. There's nothing surprising about that. Osman was keen at first. But later he probably thought his past might catch up with him."

"I think his past was much cleaner than that of the killers, gangsters and fraudsters currently in parliament. What's a bit of gambling and pimping these days?"

"Burning down historical buildings, turning people's land into car parks, providing unlicensed weapons... I'm sure we could find more if we tried."

He lit a cigarette.

"You owe me a meal," he said suddenly, as if it had just occurred to him.

"Yep," I said, "you're right, But we can't go out before Pelin gets back. Anyway it's pouring with rain. I could order some toasted sandwiches if you like."

I wasn't in the mood for going to the fish restaurant in Kadiköy with Batuhan.

"Very well, order me two sandwiches and some buttermilk."

As we ate our sandwiches, my mobile rang once and cut off immediately. I knew without having to look that the caller was Kasım Bey, but felt it might not be quite right to speak to a government employee whom I'd recently bribed when I was with a police officer. I decided to wait until Batuhan had left before calling him.

"You took your time," said Kasım Bey. Turkish men are like that. The moment they feel the slightest bit sure of themselves, they expect people to come running.

"Yes," I hissed, knowing it was impossible to knock manners into every Turkish man I encountered. Selim was enough for me.

"There's a complication with this apartment of yours. I went to see it today to work out a reserve price, something we have to do before the auction. Some squatters had been in there, using it as an office. Apparently one of them was killed there a couple of weeks ago. The door was sealed so we couldn't get in. I'm just about to try and get it unsealed. I thought I should tell you in case you don't want to buy an apartment where someone's been killed."

"Makes no difference to me," I said. I'm not known for being sentimental. "When will the auction date be known?"

"I'll put it up for auction as soon a reserve price has been set. If we'd been able to get in today, the auction would have been next week. But I'm on the case."

"You mentioned a friend of yours the other day. What happened about that?" I asked, wanting to know how much more money he wanted.

"We'll discuss that later. Let's get this sorted first. I'll just say you should be prepared. You need to have twenty per cent of the reserve price at the ready in order to bid at auction. A banker's letter of guarantee would be better. Put your money into a dollar deposit account and get the bank to give you a letter of guarantee. That way, you'll gain on both the interest and the rise in value of the dollar in the meantime."

Clearly, my baksheesh to Kasım Bey had not been for nothing.

"How much is twenty per cent?"

"We'll do our best to keep it reasonable. After all, that's why you're taking care of us, isn't it?"

"Always lick the hand that feeds you, eh?"

"What?" he said.

I wasn't sure if that saying existed in Turkish.

"Nothing," I said.

I couldn't leave the shop until closing time because Pelin had turned off her mobile and disappeared. I started reading a book, but was bored with it after three pages. I made some green tea, which I left untouched. I even stubbed my cigarettes out after smoking them only halfway down. I was sullen to my customers. I had a terrible feeling that I'd missed something or omitted to do something I should have done. A feeling of guilt. A feeling that I'd known since childhood, that was engraved on my identity, that I'd never quite managed to escape as an adult. It burned my insides like a hidden dragon that would raise its head to spout flames at inopportune moments. Like when I entered the forbidden territory of my father's study, read notebooks I wasn't supposed to touch, and learnt things I wasn't supposed to know.

I wondered if I'd omitted to ask someone a particular question, not listened properly to a reply or not evaluated a clue well enough. Why couldn't I shake off this feeling? What could be the link between the old woman and someone in Osman's circle of acquaintances? Or was there in fact no clue there to evaluate, and I was reading too much into mere coincidence? Why shouldn't there be two murders right after one another in the same street? Why not two completely unconnected murders?

But if there was a link between those two murders?

The killer could have been someone local, as Batuhan reckoned. Or somebody famous, as I thought. A famous person that the old woman would recognize. So I was back to where I'd started – İsmet Akkan. After all, his claim to have been in a holiday village on the night of the murder wasn't enough to get him off the hook.

As soon as I realized that this was why I felt uneasy, I went straight to the phone and called Batuhan. The time had come for İsmet Akkan to be questioned by the police. Also Osman's other famous friend, the retired footballer Yalçın Tektaş.

You can't usually solve a crime by just sitting and thinking with your chin resting on your hand. To solve a crime, you have to go out into the street and talk to people. You have to know about the victim's past, even his or her plans for the future. The more a detective knows about the victim, such as acquaintances, occupation and secrets, the closer that detective gets to a solution: the road to murder is paved with the victim's deeds. For instance, in the latest book I read, an old man kills a neighbour who is about to sell his garden to a construction company. The poor man wants to live out his days of retirement in peace but gets his hands bloodied because he can't bear the idea of noisy construction work going on in the garden next door. Thus, if you didn't know the victim was about to sign an agreement with a construction company, you'd never solve that murder. Yet to me, that murderer's motive was obvious, and one I'd sympathize with. Living in Istanbul, I can't understand how I too haven't ended up murdering someone. Perhaps the reason is simply that I lack the murderous gene.

Turks definitely have a poetic gene. God, how this country teems with poets! Even the most ordinary people turn out to be secret, undiscovered, misunderstood poets who thrust their leather-bound notebooks of doggerel in your face. They even take pride in presenting you with these sordid outbursts. I said poetic gene, but anyone who spends long enough in this country of histrionic poets will eventually start to write verse. Take me for instance. Was it not I who, a few days before, sat writing a poem outside the apartment where Osman was killed? Unless it was sheer coincidence that I chose to rest my chin on my hand and write a poem, it meant only one thing: I was turning into a Turk.

Yes, I was definitely turning into a Turk. I no longer spoke the truth, to avoid breaking people's hearts, ending friendships or getting myself into trouble. I would gaze at my girlfriends when they looked as if their heads had been licked by a cow and say, "I love your new hairdo." And I'd stare at their sagging tummies when they sat down and say, "Darling, you don't have an ounce of fat on you."

When I handed back İnci's notebook of squalid verse that she called poetry, I said, "These are wonderful."

After phoning Batuhan, I'd closed up the shop and rushed over to see İnci, since I was never going to solve this crime by staying in.

"Did you really like them? Tell me the truth," she said.

Hearing the truth is enough to break a Turk's heart. But as I said, I'm no longer as tough as Germans are. Or at least Berliners.

"They're lovely. Have you shown them to anyone else?"

"No, you're the first person to read them. I lost contact with all my friends because of Osman. I don't have anyone else to show them to."

"What sort of person was this Osman? He must have been unbearable if he didn't let you see anyone," I said, thinking I was changing the subject rather masterfully. Quite masterfully, in fact.

"He wasn't at all unbearable. Just a bit jealous."

"Only a little?"

"Well, he didn't lock me up when he went out. I could come and go where and when I pleased. He used to say, 'I trust you, but I don't trust other people. If I left you with a battalion of soldiers, I know you'd come back white as white.' He was right of course. You've no idea how evil people can be. After all, look at what's happened. They killed Osman."

İnci had started to miss Osman. She didn't say anything like that the first time we met.

"Yes, but what about him not wanting you to read and so on?"

"Look, I graduated from high school. Osman didn't even have a primary school diploma. He was too poor to go to school. Because he didn't have a diploma, he couldn't get a driving licence. He could read and write of course, and he tried to better himself. 'I'm a graduate of the University of Life,' he used to say. It was true. He was a very knowledgeable person."

"Do you think the reason he didn't accept the proposal from UEP was that he didn't have a primary school diploma?" You needed to have finished primary school to become an MP, as far as I knew.

"Did UEP approach him? He didn't tell me. Oh my God. He'd never have had anything to do with those religious fanatics. Amazing, who told you that?"

"The tea-boy in Kuledibi. He knows all the gossip." What I said was a dreadful lie. But what could I say? Should I have said that I'd heard it from my Chief Inspector friend?

"Actually, Osman never discussed business matters with me. I only knew about things if he spoke about them on the phone when he was with me. But he wasn't how you think he was. He cared a lot about knowledge and culture. He has four children and they all go to private schools. He tried to get Özcan to study, but he ran away from school. Osman had a lot of respect for people who studied. He was a very unusual person. There aren't many like him in this world." İnci was definitely missing him.

"So did you learn anything when you were listening to his phone conversations? What sort of business was Osman involved in?"

"He was burdened with taking care of us all. There was the car-park business. Nothing illegal about that. He respected the law. He had a restaurant somewhere near Aksaray. I think it was in Laleli. I've never been there. 'It's not suitable for respectable women,' he used to say. They had dancers there. And he had a coach company. You remember Özcan told you that the other day? The company operated between Van and Istanbul. I don't know how many coaches were his, because other people who owned coaches were also allowed to operate under his company name. I think they put his name on their vehicles and gave Osman a share of the profits. I'm not quite sure how it worked."

"Is that all? I thought he dabbled in all sorts of things."

"No. Osman was persistent. Once he put his mind to something, he'd see it through. For instance, he was thinking of going into the construction business. He saw it as a way of putting food on the table for everyone. There are loads of relatives, and they're mostly in the building trade. Labourers, you know. He wanted to set up a company that would make money and provide work for his relatives at the same time. But he didn't live to see that happen."

By then, she was really crying. I'm not the sort, like some idiot men, that can't bear to see a woman cry. I do get uneasy if someone is crying right in front of me, but whether it's a man or woman makes no difference to me. I just have no idea what to say or how to console them.

That's how it was then. I felt absolutely useless.

"Poor man. At least he was spared."

"Spared? Why did you say that?" she said. The crying had stopped and she was studying my face carefully.

It was because of my Turkish of course. I'd got my clichés for such situations muddled up.

"What I mean is that he died without too much suffering," I said, again without really understanding the significance of what I was saying.

She started crying again.

"Without too much suffering? He crawled across the floor right up to the door trying to get help. How much more could he suffer? He couldn't even stand up. He died crawling on the floor." Her crying had now turned into real sobbing. I went to the kitchen to fetch a glass of water.

As I opened the refrigerator, I changed my mind and took out a can of beer, pouring it into two glasses. That much alcohol was unlikely to harm a pregnant woman.

She drank the beer and asked for a cigarette. That pleased me because normally she wouldn't allow smoking in the house. I immediately lit one for myself as well.

"How's your financial situation while the inheritance is being sorted out?" I asked, thinking that lack of money might be upsetting her.

171

"He'd already opened a bank account in my name. There's not much money in it, but I can get by for three or four months. And he made this apartment over to me. Özcan said he'd see I didn't have financial difficulties, but he doesn't know that Osman bought this apartment for me. I think there may be a problem when he finds that out."

"So what does he think?"

"He thinks this place is rented."

"Well if you don't tell him otherwise, then there's no problem."

"The running costs here are very high. What if he tells me to move somewhere cheaper?"

"Then you move. You weren't born around here, after all." I hadn't meant to insult her, but I had the feeling I might have offended her. "I mean, there are nicer and more reasonable places you could rent in Istanbul. Then you could rent this place out."

"You don't understand," she said, her eyes filling with tears again.

"What don't I understand?"

"We were very poor. I spent my childhood in poverty. No one knows better than me what it's like to be poor. My mother used to set out in the morning while it was still dark and walk to work because she didn't have money for the bus. Me and my brothers and sisters, we all worked, but it still wasn't enough. I don't want to go back to that life. I know what it's like to have a bit of money now, do you understand? I have a car and someone to clean my apartment. I buy clothes from the best stores where the managers, who used to turn me down for jobs as a sales assistant, now call me 'madam'. There's no going back for me now. I won't go back to live in Bağcılar or Güngören. Also, I take care of my family. Do you have any idea what all that comes to every month? They spend as much as I do."

"Yes, but supposing you win the case and your child gets a share of the inheritance. What are Osman's assets? He certainly didn't own factories and mansions, after all. He made his money from running car parks and coaches. He had to be there on the job in order to make money. There's no way you can continue your old standard of living, even if you get some of the inheritance, or if Özcan gives you money every month."

"That's exactly what I'm saying."

"So?"

"Osman's killer might as well have shot me! And the child in my belly! I'm ruined!" she cried, rocking back and forth. "My life's ruined!" she exclaimed, covering her face with her hands and burying her head between her knees.

Once again, I didn't know what to say or do – which won't surprise you. For a while, I sat like an imbecile watching this woman cry her eyes out in front of me. Finally, I decided that beer wasn't going to be the answer, so I looked in the drinks cabinet for some whisky. I took the bottle to the kitchen and poured a couple of glasses. With ice.

When I returned to the sitting room, her crying suddenly subsided. She sipped the whisky without saying a word.

"I think that officer who's on the case reckons I'm the killer," she said. "He's got it in for me, practically accused me of killing Osman."

"What makes you think you're a suspect?"

"He took my fingerprints. Özcan must have said something to turn him against me. When Osman didn't come home that night, Özcan says he called me to ask his brother something or other. But he's lying! I've no idea why he rang. He's never called me to get hold of Osman. Osman would stay with me at least four nights a week and never let anyone know where he was. Nobody seemed to care. So why were they curious that particular night when he didn't come home? Why were they curious about him on the very night he was killed? He'd been with me two nights before, but nobody phoned. Why check up on a grown man anyway?"

"Probably because his mobile didn't answer," I said, remembering what Özcan had said.

"Even if his mobile had been on, they still wouldn't have called him. OK, maybe there was something urgent. Or maybe it was just coincidence. But that seems a bit too coincidental to me."

"Hmm," I said. *Ein Zufall zuviel.* There were indeed too many of these coincidences, don't you think?

"But what of it, if Özcan called you?"

"It means he found out I wasn't at home that evening, because I didn't answer the phone."

"What do you mean? Weren't you at home that night?"

This time she cried silently, tears rolling down her cheeks.

"Can you keep a secret?" she asked hoarsely.

What can you say to a question like that? Can you really say, "No, I can't"?

"Of course I will," I said.

"I wasn't at home."

I felt a sudden need for someone to massage the back of my neck. I twisted my head from left to right and rubbed the stiff muscles. It didn't really do much good. Massaging yourself is like masturbation. I've never mastered either of them properly. Or rather it's never been effective. An awful lot of effort for very little result.

"Have you got a lover?" I asked.

She started crying loudly again.

"It's not what you think," she said between sobs.

"I'm not thinking anything. Calm down. I don't think you're the killer. Anyway I'm in no position to pass judgement." Which was true of course. I'd cheated on every man in my life until Selim came along. And it was only a question of time before I did the same to him.

"What did you tell the police when they asked where you were that night?"

174

"I said I was at home watching TV." İnci had told me the same thing.

"Was Özcan with you when you told them that?"

"No, but Özcan also asked me where I was."

"And what did you tell him?"

"I told him I was watching TV as well," she said, starting to cry again.

"İnci!" I said in an authoritative voice. I held her by the shoulders and shook her. "Calm down. Pull yourself together and go and wash your face."

She went off to the bathroom, sniffling.

I lit a cigarette.

I really wished I could lose this compulsion for detective work, become like my self-assured, properly behaved, middle-class friends and stick to those lovely bourgeois morals. Nothing at all wrong with bourgeois morals, even if I don't happen to have received my share in that department.

"Özcan didn't tell me he tried to phone me that night. If I'd known, I'd have made up a different story. But when they asked where I was, I said I was at home. That's where I would be normally. Once I'd said it, I couldn't go back on it. I told Özcan I was probably in the bath when he rang and didn't hear the phone. I didn't know he'd kept calling until morning."

"He kept calling you till morning?"

"That's what he said."

"You should have said you don't answer the phone after a certain hour."

"I didn't think of that. I was caught off guard. He pretended not to take much notice, but he was definitely suspicious. Bastard. He informed on me to the police. Otherwise, why would the police take my fingerprints?"

"Didn't they tell you why?"

"They said they were taking everybody's and they'd get a

court order if I didn't consent to having them done. 'Give your consent, then we won't have to resort to such methods,' they said. What could I do? If I'd refused, they'd have been really suspicious, so I let them do it. They said they destroy all fingerprints afterwards."

"I think it's normal to take fingerprints. And nothing will happen if you tell the police you weren't at home that night. Your lover will testify that you were with him. The police are trying to solve a murder; they're not interested in where you were, who you were with or what you did."

"And Özcan?"

"Do you think the police are going to go and tell Özcan that you were cheating on Osman?"

"I don't know. But what if it comes out?"

"The real risk right now is that the fact that you lied might come out. I think you should make up some story for Özcan, but tell the truth to the police and let them call on your lover if they want."

"They can't call on my lover," she said, biting her lips as she tried to hold back her tears.

"Why?"

"Because he'd kill me, that's why."

"Is he married?"

She gave me a horrified look. Dear God! Did I say something so terrible? I'm forty-four years old. Of course I know why people try to keep the identity of their lovers a secret. I mean, you don't have to be a crime-fiction addict to work that out.

"Alp was my childhood sweetheart. We were in the same class at school. His father was a schoolteacher and he saw that Alp got a good education. He graduated as an engineer just last year. He's married to his boss's daughter, but doesn't love her. I've seen his wife – she's very ugly. But, she's the boss's daughter, and the boss is very rich. So if it comes out now... If anyone hears about us..."

The whisky burned the back of my throat.

"Hang on a minute!" I said. İnci fell quiet and looked at me absent-mindedly, still completely engrossed in what she'd been telling me. I drummed my fingernails on the table. Tik, tik, tik, tik... There was nothing complicated about this. A woman in a steady relationship was cheating on her lover with a married man. Well, I know a bit about that sort of thing. If it's evening, men say they have to go out to a dinner. If it's daytime, they say they're going to the bank, a business meeting or to pay the telephone bill. But what can a woman say? A woman who has no contact with the outside world? What can a woman say to get out of the house in the evening when she never has business dinners to go to? Doesn't even have an excuse to go out during the day?

"How did you get round Osman?"

"We used to meet when I knew Osman wouldn't be coming."

"In the evenings?"

"Hardly ever in the evening. For one thing, we never knew where we could go. Six months ago, Alp made an arrangement with a friend who has an apartment near here. Alp paid part of his rent and he gave us a room there. But we can't have met more than half a dozen times in the evening, what with Alp's wife and my Osman. It was too dangerous. But that week, Alp's wife was away on holiday. The family have a summer place and she went there for a month."

"How did you know that Osman wouldn't be coming to you that night?"

"I phoned him."

"Osman?"

"Of course Osman. Who else?"

"What time was that?"

"I don't know. Wait, are you saying I was the last person to speak to Osman?"

I nodded my head. I really wanted to screw up my eyes and examine her face very closely. But screwing up the eyes is bad for you. Bad for wrinkles. The reason crow's feet form around the eyes is that people screw up their eyes. I raised my eyebrows and looked at her.

"Let's see, what time would it have been?" said İnci. "Alp phoned me, and then I phoned Osman straight away. I hadn't seen Alp for a week because he'd been on holiday with his wife. I'd missed him so much."

I was trying not to think about the fact that she was pregnant, but things like that have a way of sticking in the petit bourgeois mind.

"You see, I have a mobile that only Alp knows the number of. I'd keep it turned on if Osman wasn't here. It's like a code between us. If the phone's on, Alp knows I'm alone. Just a minute." She ran off with an energy and excitement that was totally at odds with her sobbing of just a short while ago.

"The time Alp rang is on here," she said, as she came back into the room with a mobile phone in her hands. "I think it was about seven. Maybe a bit earlier. Let's see. I haven't used this phone since that day. There's been no need. I've been using my normal mobile."

We waited patiently for the mobile to start up. Her thumbs flitted rapidly over the keypad. I wondered if I would ever learn to look so professional when using my mobile.

"It was the twenty-ninth of August. We spoke a few times that day. It must have been the last but one call that day. It says the last call was at ten o'clock. Did you know there are mobiles now that take photos? You can take a photo and actually send it over the phone." İnci let out a squeal that made me jump. All this squealing, weeping and howling was getting too much for me.

"Look! Look at this!"

She thrust the mobile right under my nose. I couldn't make out a thing.

"What?" I said impatiently. "What time did you speak to Alp?"

"It says nineteen fourteen. Oh, thank you, dear God!" she said, with a deep sigh of relief. "I'd spoken to Osman before he was killed. Maybe ten or fifteen minutes before. The police asked me where I was between seven-thirty and nine-thirty. So the murder could have been committed at seven-thirty because I called Osman immediately after Alp called me, which would have been at about seven-fifteen."

"Did you call him on his mobile?"

"Yes. Özcan says his brother's phone was switched off, but if I spoke to him at seven-fifteen..."

"He probably switched it off after speaking to you."

"Probably," she said, and paused. "I asked what was happening that evening. He said he had work to do and wouldn't be coming over. He said he had a 'respected brother' with him and they were talking business. He says 'respected brother' when it's someone important. So that means he wasn't alone." She suddenly got excited again and put her hand on my knee. "What do you think? Do you think the man with him was the murderer?"

I just shook my head.

"Think hard. Did he give any clue as to who this man was?"

"We only talked very briefly. If he'd mentioned a name, I would definitely have remembered."

"Do you think this 'respected brother' might have been someone you know?"

"What do you mean?"

"Well, for instance, if he'd had İsmet Akkan with him."

"Do you think he's the killer?"

I shrugged my shoulders.

"I don't know," İnci said. "I think he would have referred to him by name. I'm not sure. He might not have wanted me to know who it was if they were talking about something secret."

"How were you so sure that he wouldn't be coming to you that night?"

"From his tone of voice. He sounded distracted. When he was like that... When he was involved in business, he wouldn't come to me. He used to say coming to me was like going on holiday. And he wouldn't go on holiday if he was doing business or if there was a problem."

"What gave him problems?"

"The construction business gave him problems. He'd been glued to the phone for over two months. He'd be talking on the phone, then suddenly rush out. I think money was tight. He never used to have money problems, but recently he'd even started to grumble about what I spent on myself. He wasn't normally tight-fisted. We were going abroad for a holiday. Last year we went to Paris and London, and I did as much shopping as I wanted. But this summer when I asked for money to go and buy new clothes, his hands were trembling when he gave it to me. We hadn't even gone out for a meal lately."

"Maybe another woman..." I didn't complete my sentence. Even two-timers can't bear to face the fact that they're being strung along.

"I thought of that. But I'd have known if there had been. Also, he was always either at my place or his own. I used to phone Özcan to check up on what Osman was doing on the evenings he wasn't here. Özcan always knew where he was."

I didn't like to say that Özcan might have been lying.

"Also, he hadn't lost interest in me. It was nothing like that. Money was certainly tight. He even regretted getting a new car. I overheard him saying on the telephone once that times were hard because of the economic crisis. He was thinking of selling the car, which he'd paid a lot for. I really wanted a Range Rover, but didn't like to ask. How could I ask him for a Range Rover when he was complaining about me buying a few fake Sisley T-shirts? You have to be reasonable."

"When did the money problems start?"

"At first he used to say he wasn't affected by the crisis. And that was true. We went to Europe only last year, and the crisis had already started then. But later, this year..."

"Is that why he decided to go into the construction business?"

As İnci thought about this she waved her first and middle fingers indicating that she wanted another cigarette.

I passed the packet over.

"I'd never thought about whether the cash-flow problem and the construction business were connected," she said. "But I think you're right. He was having discussions about setting up this business and then... well, I think the money just ran out. He could never hold on to money anyway. There were so many needy relatives. Their family's not like yours or mine. Families are really big in the east. Their village got burned down during the war and lots of the people there came to Istanbul. Where were they going to find jobs? They used to come and see Osman. Even those involved in the blood feud came to him to ask for help. Do blood feuds actually still go on these days? People were hungry. They wanted to move away, but had no money. Can you imagine it? Those who managed to get to Istanbul were the richest. The poor ones only managed to find enough money to get them to Diyarbakir or Adana, where they lived in areas by the refuse dumps and existed by scavenging. There are people living in this country who don't even have the money to get a bus to Istanbul. That's why he went into the construction business. To create work opportunities for relatives and people from his village."

"Were any of these villagers from the other side of the feud?"

"Oh yes. Even they were reduced to asking for work and money. They suggested calling a truce. Osman probably gave them some money because he didn't have work for so many people. They were all peasants – men who worked in the fields or reared animals. What could they do in a city? Even a car-park attendant needs to be able to drive."

"So, the money for the construction business ran out."

"That's what I assume. Yet, come to think of it..."

"Had he bought any land to build on?"

"I don't know. I think he'd found a place in Kasımpaşa. But, as I said, he didn't talk to me about these things. I just picked up odds and ends from his phone conversations. Kasımpaşa was mentioned and there was no other business in Kasımpaşa, unless he was buying a car park there. But no, it was definitely to do with the construction business."

"Did you manage to pick up any other names from his phone conversations?"

"He never used people's names. He addressed everyone as 'my brother'," said İnci. She paused for a moment, then shrugged and added, "Or maybe I just didn't listen."

İnci covered her mouth with her hand and stared at the ceiling, deep in thought, before continuing.

"Wait, there was a Temel. What a strange name that is. I was amazed the first time I heard it. A typical Black Sea name. It's the sort of name I associate with jokes for some reason. I couldn't believe it when I heard Osman talking to someone called Temel on the phone. It stuck in my memory. His name came up a lot recently. I think Osman owed him money and couldn't pay. Sometimes he wouldn't pick up if he saw a call was coming from that number."

"I don't suppose you know the man's surname?"

"No, I don't. But he definitely had interests in the construction business. In car parks too. One day I heard Osman say, 'I'm very stretched at the moment, but I'll get it for you. Give me a bit of time.'"

We both fell silent. I toyed with my empty whisky glass, making the ice tinkle. I shouldn't really drink on an empty stomach, but

I went to the kitchen and poured myself another. I returned to the sitting room, again to the sound of tinkling ice. It was time I drank up and left.

İnci was sitting there, fiddling with her blouse and skirt.

"What is it?" I asked.

"I've just thought of something, but I'm not sure. I was thinking about my phone conversation with Osman. I think somebody knocked at the door while we were talking. Osman hung up very quickly. I couldn't be wrong about that. It was a very short conversation. He was trying to hang up anyway, but the reason he cut off so quickly was because someone was at the door."

"Are you sure?" I said.

"No, I'm not sure. I hadn't really thought about that conversation. In fact I'd forgotten all about it. But now I come to think about it... You know how you suddenly realize something, but have nothing to base it on? I'm worried I might be making it up because I'm trying to find some clue in that call."

"Of course, a knock at the door could mean nothing. It might have been the tea-boy."

İnci thought for a moment.

"Yes, maybe it was the tea-boy," she said.

"Did you know Osman's uncle?"

"I've never met him. According to Osman, he was half crazy. A lazy, useless man."

"The brothers have tried to pin this murder on him, did you know that?"

"Really?"

"It's very obvious to me that he couldn't have done it. Even the gun used to kill Osman wasn't right for the uncle. It was the sort of gun an expert might carry."

"How do you know that?"

"I know a bit about guns," I said. Ha ha, very funny!

"No, I mean how do you know what kind of gun killed Osman?"

183

I rubbed my nose.

"I asked the police officer who was conducting the investigation," I said.

"Was that Batuhan Bey?"

"Mmm."

"He's very good looking, isn't he? I adore dark men. Probably because I'm blonde. You're fair-skinned too. What's your natural hair colour?"

Clearly my orange hair left no room for doubt that it was dyed.

"Light brown."

"Your natural colour would suit you," she commented, looking at the ceiling apparently in a daydream. "But he's a serious man, Batuhan Bey. Keeps you at a distance. If it's true what they say about men with long noses having long whatsits, then his must be as long as my arm." İnci held out her arm to demonstrate.

To be honest, I'd never noticed the length of Batuhan's nose, but I did know things about Batuhan that backed up İnci's theory of the nose–penis ratio. Of course, I said nothing. Instead, I cleared my throat as an indication that I didn't approve of that sort of conversation and wanted to change the subject. Is it the same in other cultures? I don't know, but that's the code Turks have for it. They never say anything completely openly, so they need a host of codes.

"What's wrong with that?" said İnci. It sounded like a reproach.

"Nothing," I said.

We sat in silence again for a while. I downed my whisky in one gulp.

"So, you say they're trying to pin the murder on the uncle!" she said. "Well, they might be right. I hadn't thought of that. Didn't he steal the money?"

Oops! I'd forgotten to ask Batuhan what happened to the money. What a stupid idiot I was. He hadn't mentioned it either. Or had he? My head was hurting. I couldn't even remember what

184

I'd discussed with whom. Should I start recording my conversations perhaps?

"Oh that," I said. "It was just an idea I had. Next time you talk to Özcan, just slip in a question about what happened to the money."

Half drunk, I drove to Selim's apartment. I would never do such a thing normally, but I couldn't bear the idea of having to go back to İnci's place the next morning to pick up my car.

Selim met me in the doorway, smiling broadly. I felt as though we were playing out some gimmicky idea promoted by a women's magazine about how to maintain a relationship by keeping a distance or going on separate holidays. Ten ways to spice up your relationship. The sort of recipe that turns my stomach. What would a woman know about an exciting love life or simultaneous "peaking" if she was such a brainless idiot that she had to resort to magazines like that to spice up her relationship? Do the poor women writing for these magazines have to have all this stuff explained to them? And why don't men's magazines give out the same sort of advice to their readers? Is it purely a woman's responsibility to spice up and prolong a relationship and ensure that simultaneous orgasm is achieved?

Well, if that's what is expected of women in this world, it didn't happen in our relationship. At least, not that night. Selim made a brave attempt at steering us towards simultaneous orgasm by greeting me at the door, placing his hands on my hips, nuzzling my neck and pressing his body against mine. Very gently, so as not to hurt his feelings, I pushed him away. My mind was busy with other things. Sex requires the wholesome attention of mind and body. However, my mind was consumed with matters of murder, at the cost of disregarding my womanly duties.

I went straight to the fridge. Selim had a very imposing fridge. Why, who knows? It probably came from the house he used to share with his ex-wife. I didn't ask. Nor would I. I hate listening to my lovers reminisce about their previous relationships. Who doesn't? But it's always what gets discussed at the beginning of a relationship. Men do it more than women. A woman is more likely to be trying to convince her new lover that he is the only one for her. Men believe that kind of thing. It's what they want to believe. They certainly don't want to hear about what went on with her previous lovers, yet they love to recount their own suffering in that department.

I opened the fridge door. There was nothing inside, or nothing that I wanted. Just a jar of mustard, the French sort that I love with little seeds in it, two eggs that had been there for who knows how long, an open carton of long-life milk, one blackened banana and a lavish selection of alcohol.

"What did you eat?" I called out towards the sitting room.

Selim was clearly walking towards the kitchen as he spoke, because his voice gradually got louder.

"I'm hungry too. Shall I order in a pizza?" he said, running his fingers up and down my spine.

"Pizza?" I said, screwing up my face. "You mean a wodge of pastry."

"Or there are kebab places that deliver."

What a choice! Pizza or kebab. One as bad as the other.

"Pizza," I said.

The worst thing about ordering food over the phone is the unbearable hunger while you wait for it to arrive. I lit a cigarette to suppress the pangs, thinking how I was really going to age before my time if I carried on like this.

"Could you find the name of a company for me if I gave you the name of one of its partners?" I asked.

Selim was watching some stupid film on TV and clearly didn't want to be disturbed.

"Could do," he said. "You ordered Cola as well, didn't you?"

That's just what I'd have expected if we'd been married.

*

186

I called Selim the following afternoon, because he was at court in the morning and had said he wouldn't be able to look up Osman's company until afterwards.

"What happened? Did you find them?" I asked.

"Did I find what?"

"The other partners of the company Osman Karakaş was in," I said irritably.

"Oh, I forgot all about it, pet. A good thing you called. Tell me that man's name again. I'll send someone to find out right away. Look, I'll call you back. The place he has to go to in Eminönü is very close by."

I'd have chewed my nails out of irritation if I'd allowed myself, but made do with chewing the cuticles.

To pass the time, I mulled over the problem of Pelin's lover. She had begun to relent. What else could she do? She didn't want to spend the rest of her life living at my place.

The phone rang and I flew over to it. It was Selim.

"This man isn't a partner in any company, pet. I sent our trainee solicitor to look him up. She's a resourceful girl and would have found anything there was to find. What business did you say he was in?"

I always had to repeat everything I said to Selim because he didn't listen to me.

"He was meant to be in the construction business," I said.

"Hmmm. Have they started any construction work?"

"I don't know. I think he bought a place in Kasımpaşa..."

"Kasımpaşa?"

"Yes."

"Fine, that's Beyoğlu Council. He must have obtained a building permit. You don't need to form a company for construction work, but you must have a building permit. I'll send Asu over to the Council to ask at the Department of Technical Works. I have a man there, so they'll find out if a permit was obtained."

"You mean a man you give baksheesh to?"

He laughed.

"See? The baksheesh I distribute benefits you as well as my clients," he said.

What could I say? It was true.

About half an hour later, my mobile rang. It was a woman's voice.

"Kati Hanım?"

"Yes, that's me," I said.

"I work in Selim Bey's office. I'm Asu Ketenci, the trainee solicitor. Selim Bey asked me to phone you. I've just left the Council offices. I understand that it was on your behalf. Can I come and see you to tell you what I found out?"

"Go to the Kaffeehaus at Tünel. It's closer to the Council offices than my shop is. I'll be there in ten minutes," I said.

I got there as fast as I could.

After London, Tünel is the second oldest metro in the world and was also constructed by the British. Unfortunately it covers a very short distance: just one stop. It runs beneath the steep slope at Kuledibi, linking one end of İstiklal Caddesi, the busy shopping street running from Taksim Square, to the sea. The İstiklal Caddesi entrance to this mini metro is in an area called Tünel. Several bars and cafés had opened up there over the last few years and one of them was called Kaffeehaus.

I identified Asu Hanım the moment I entered. With her neatly bobbed hair and buttoned-up blouse, you couldn't miss her. To me, she looked the over-ambitious sort who might rival Selim as Istanbul's highest-tax-paying lawyer in the future. Asu stood up to shake my hand. She clearly knew how to behave. I was of course the "boss's other half", and she had to act accordingly.

"The Council has granted a land allocation to Osman Karakaş," she said.

Personally, I'd have started with a bit of small talk, but she wasted no time in coming straight to the point.

"What does land allocation mean?" I asked.

"A piece of land that is Council property can be allocated at below market price. This has to be agreed by City Hall. A decision over this allocation was made last June."

"You mean Council land is allocated to an individual?"

"No, madam. Osman Karakaş had set up a residential construction cooperative, or was in the process of doing so. These things can take a long time. You have to wait for approval from the Ministry of Trade and Industry to set up a cooperative. However, the Cooperative Founders' Committee is able to purchase land before the set-up procedures are completed. They can even register members. It's perfectly legal. I don't know the extent of your interest in this, so—"

"How did you find out about this land allocation business?"

"Selim Bey told me to go to the Council's Directorate of Technical Works. We have dealings with that department from time to time because of our clients. That's why we already had connections there. I went to see İrfan Bey. He recognized the name of Osman Karakaş straight away and knew that a land allocation had been granted to a cooperative of which Osman was a member. It's called Neşekent Residential Construction Cooperative. If you want, I could get the file from the Directorate of Trade and Industry."

"This cooperative has an address, I suppose."

"Yes, madam. It's at 3/6 Papağan Street, in Kuledibi."

"Did you find out the names of the other founders?"

"Yes, madam. Just one moment please," she said.

I was getting fed up with her officious manner.

She rummaged in her briefcase and brought out a handwritten list of names. I glanced at it. Seven of the people were surnamed Karakaş, but Özcan's name wasn't there. However, there was a Temel.

Why wasn't Özcan on it if Temel was?

*

I called Selim when I got back to the shop.

"The Council hardly ever hands out land allocations," he said. "And they'd never do it for a bunch of nobodies like them. I've heard of land allocations being granted to cooperatives set up by artisans, lawyers and so on, but not to rogues like these. A great deal of money must have changed hands over this."

"Does the Greater City Council have to arrange this?"

"It can be arranged through the District Council. The Greater City Council has to give its approval, but that's not difficult to sort out. Anyway, the chairman of Beyoğlu District Council and the chairman of Istanbul Greater City Council belong to the same party. They wouldn't scupper each other's business affairs. That kind of thing happens when councils are run by different parties. I don't know much about Council matters because I don't have many cases that involve the Council. Last year, I obtained a building permit for someone, which was how I made the connection with İrfan. But I know someone who's familiar with all the ins and outs of Beyoğlu District Council. You won't find anyone better than him. Baki knows everything: who to go to for what, how much to pay and how to pay it. He owns about ten restaurants in Beyoğlu, and does the best pickled bonito."

"I remember eating pickled bonito. It was at bar called Kios, wasn't it?"

"Oh yes, at Balıkpazarı. I forgot I'd taken you there. Kios is the Greek name for Sakız Island. Baki comes from Sakız. I mean his family, of course. They settled in Istanbul years ago. About one tenth of his earnings comes from his restaurants and bars, the rest he gets from chasing up Council matters. I'll give him a call and get him to talk to you. If he has the time, could you go now?"

"Of course," I said. I wasn't going to miss an opportunity like this, was I?

While I waited helplessly for Selim to call, Pelin went out to eat. A truck was trying to manoeuvre its way down our narrow street, bumping into things right and left. I lit a cigarette and watched the men's efforts through the window. I'd been smoking an extra light brand for a while, with the result that I was smoking more. Either that or I was smoking more because I was feeling edgy. It suddenly occurred to me that I might be feeling edgy because I was about to start the menopause. That scared me. Or rather, startled me. I hadn't a clue when the menopause normally started. I hadn't been created to have children. In fact, never in my life had I looked at a child and thought, "How lovely". Yet the idea of starting the menopause wasn't appealing. Even the word was unattractive. Menopause. It conjured up images of a shrivelled, nervous-looking woman with sunken eyes and purple veins in her neck. I took my powder compact out of my bag. Not to powder my nose, but to look at my face. I looked at myself as if for the first time, carefully examining each feature in turn. Was that the face of a woman about to start the menopause? My skin was radiant. As indeed it should be. I'd spent a fortune on creams and serums containing things like DNA, RNA and salmon eggs. I stuck my tongue out at myself. Only a fool would think I was about to start the menopause. It was all because of Selim that I'd become a bag of nerves, nothing to do with the menopause.

But this conclusion still didn't completely satisfy me. I was now back together with Selim, so why was I still... It was the murders, of course. Those two murders were enough to make your hair curl. It was because I was taking this detective business too seriously, wasn't it? After all, what did it matter to me if a man and a woman got killed?

Indeed, what did it matter?

Ah, if only I could make myself believe what was happening to me!

# 9

An hour later, I found myself in a bar sitting at a table opposite Selim's fixer, Baki, the fattest man still capable of walking that I'd ever seen. Since he couldn't fit on a normal-sized chair, he had an extra-large one. Or rather an armchair. Speaking left him breathless. His shirt must have been at least size 70 – if such a size existed. The buttonholes were strained to the limit, as if two strong hands were pulling at his shirt on either side. In between, his pale pink skin was showing through. And some chest hair. It wasn't disgusting. It was almost interesting, actually. He was more like a curious creature worthy of lengthy examination and study, rather than a human being. He was panting through his mouth like a dog. Every pant left him out of breath, and he would put his tongue out slightly, again like a dog. His head looked small on top of his body, yet it was twice the size of mine. What I mean is that it was small in relation to the size of his body.

He was leaning on the desk with his fingers, which were the size of Chiquita bananas, and seemed to take strength from this support as he spoke.

"Why are you interested in these regulations?"

Waiters were rushing around getting the bar ready for the evening. One of them came up to us.

"Shall I order in some tea, boss?"

"Do you want anything to eat? The meze are fresh. I can get the boys to bring some over?"

"Tea would be nice, but I'm not hungry," I said. In fact, I hadn't eaten anything since the pizza of the previous evening, but sitting opposite such a fat man makes you lose your appetite.

He said he would just have tea as well.

"I've started a diet. Doctor's orders. Lost three kilos," he said.

I smiled, shaking my head and thinking it must be like an ocean losing a spoonful of water.

"Kilos are so easy to gain, so difficult to lose," he said, pointing to his belly.

I tried not to look at the pink skin between the buttonholes and smiled again.

"So, what are you to Selim Bey?"

"I'm his girlfriend," I said.

"He's a good client of mine. An honourable person. He was very helpful to me at one time. My brother was a real menace. Good head on his shoulders, but got himself involved in party politics."

"If he had a good mind, he was probably involved in left-wing politics," I said.

Baki Bey made no response to this comment, but merely raised his hand from his belly, with some difficulty, to stroke his cheek.

"Selim Bey doesn't get involved in political matters," he remarked.

"True, he deals with commercial cases," I said.

"Take me, I never touch meat or kebabs. My expertise is in fish, so we do fish. Everyone should do what they're best at. That's the way to success. I can tell the freshness of fish from twenty metres away. I only serve fish at my restaurants. What would be the point of opening a kebab shop just because they do good business, eh?"

He leant forward over his belly and put a couple of sweeteners in his tea.

"Why are you interested in these council regulations?" he repeated.

193

I'd thought up an answer to this question before I came.

"I have a bookshop, in Kuledibi. Business isn't too bad, but..."

"Things will get better, God willing," he said.

"Well, a friend of mine suggested opening a bar around here. We haven't actually found anywhere yet, but when Selim mentioned you I thought I should find out how to establish connections with the council."

"It's good you came to me before finding a place. You have to take certain things into consideration. For instance, the premises you choose should be no closer than a hundred metres to a place of worship, school or training centre. By place of worship, I mean all of them: mosques, churches and synagogues. They're adamant about applying this rule. When you find a place, check that it'll be approved before you sign a lease. Once you've signed, it's expensive to get out of it."

"There's nowhere in Beyoğlu without a nearby place of worship or school, so it must be impossible to open a bar here."

"It's difficult, of course. That's why people usually take over a place that already has a licence. But of course that pushes the price up. We're talking about hundreds of thousands of dollars here. That's how it is. It's difficult to get started. There's the council, the police, the mafia, it's never-ending. Night work is difficult. Even harder for a woman. You'd be starting work just as Selim was coming home. Bar work doesn't go with family life."

I sipped my tea.

"So, licences aren't often granted," I said, "if it's all so tightly controlled."

"It's not as bad as it was. Some people run places illegally, without a licence. There are bars in unimaginable places, where youngsters listen to their strange loud music, drink beer and take all kinds of drugs. If the police turn up to check them out, the owners push a few notes their way and the police turn a blind eye. That's how it works: you scratch my back and I'll scratch yours.

194

I have an apartment here on İstiklal Caddesi. Someone opened one of those illegal bars in the basement and the music goes on all night – boom boom boom... I'm sorry, but it does your head in. I spent a year trying to get it closed down. In the end, I took them to court. But they'd made sure the police were kept onside. And if you went to the council, they just said, 'We don't have the authority to do anything.' It was dreadful. Who else could you go to? I rent the apartment out now. It has a wonderful view of the Bosphorus, and I did the inside up really well. But tenants never stay more than a month. Nobody can bear to stay with that din going on. They sell beer at that bar for a couple of cents a time. How do they make it pay? They're obviously selling something else. But you can't prove it. And if you do, what then? The police are already mixed up in it. If they weren't, do you think the drugs merry-go-round would keep going? They all just fill their pockets and look on. They're shameless, the lot of them."

"So if you're not involved with licences any more, what is it that you do with the council?"

"Oh, miss, there's plenty of work all right. For instance, if a shop is penalized for playing loud music and told to close down, then the owner comes to me to have the order lifted. I also have connections at the Fire Department. I can help with getting permits from there. Oh, all sorts of things crop up..."

"How does the council land allocation business work?"

"Ah, now you're talking about the big stuff. That's out of my reach. You have to go very high up for that."

"Council Chairman?"

"You can't do it at District Council level. My guess is you need contacts on the Greater City Council. They never make land allocations to the people who present the applications. Lots of money changes hands and you need lots of contacts. Getting a land allocation for, say, a sports club or a nice peaceful house isn't at all easy, especially for residential buildings."

"What about cooperatives?"

"I can't say it never happens, because it does. For instance, Şişli Council made a land allocation to a cooperative called Baro Cooperative. But because it was an area with a lot of illegal housing, it was so expensive to clear that they never managed to start the building work. I'm talking about six or seven years ago, when the land allocation was made. I don't mean that land allocations aren't profitable. But if a council gives an allocation for a place that's certain to be good for business, then it always goes to someone in their own circles. It would never be to Baro Cooperative or the Chamber of Physicians, and certainly not to the likes of you and me."

"For a council land allocation in the Beyoğlu area, who would I—" I didn't manage to finish my question.

"So have you given up on the idea of opening a bar?"

"No, I'm asking because I'm curious."

"These things take a lot of work. I don't know what the procedure is. But I'll stick my neck out and say that I think it's all down to the chairman or the vice-chairman. Beyoğlu is in the hands of the religious lot at the moment. It was different before, when the social democrats were in. You could sit down with your man and come to an arrangement. He told you what his cut should be and you paid him in cash, finished. The religious lot are different. They don't accept money themselves. Part of any bribe goes into party funds and part goes into their pockets. Have the social democrats ever got anywhere? No. Why? Because all they think about is lining their own pockets. The religious lot aren't like that. They prop up the party. Every time they gain something for themselves, they gain something for the party. When I say party, I don't mean directly to the party. For instance, the party has a sports club that's possibly the richest one in Turkey. It brings in huge amounts of money. They say, 'Go and make a donation for so much to the Haliç Sports Club, and then come back.' That's their method. Not one of them actually handles any money. But if you go to them with a donation receipt from the Sports Club and lay it down on the table, the job's done. That's the procedure. You can't get anywhere without doing that. And if you get on the wrong side of these men or start arguing with them about anything, then forget it. It's not something that's open to just anyone, because they don't take money from just anyone. They only say 'Go and make your donation, then come back' to people they trust. Otherwise, I'd be making donations. So would every Hasan, Ahmet and Mehmet. No, they don't tell everyone how it's done, because they don't want everyone getting in on it. My man trusts me, but he wouldn't trust anyone else. That's why people who have business with the council come to me. Not to get it done free. I wouldn't do it for nothing, nobody would..."

"So it's Haliç Sports Club," I said. It didn't take me long to remember where I'd heard that name recently.

"All that money, and their football team is still rubbish. No better than a local team. I've been there and seen the place. They have separate facilities like swimming pools and tennis courts for men and women. That's what they're like. They're into everything. Sports and education. They want the girls to go to university in headscarves. You might ask, 'Aren't your women supposed to stay at home and raise children?' But they have a ready answer. They say, 'If mothers are to raise children, they must be cultured.' See? They have it all planned. They're now grooming future mothers who will raise the next generation. This generation hasn't produced anyone anyway. They're all just local tough guys. They get votes from the lowest social levels. Only ignorant peasants fresh from the villages vote for them. Why? Because they think, 'I've got nothing in this world, so I'll try for more in the next.' These men buy votes by giving people work, money, gold or title deeds for paradise. I've actually seen it with my own eyes. I've seen them hand out title deeds for paradise.

They give you a certificate and make you swear on the Koran to give them your vote. My missus is as pure as they come, a true Muslim. Even she was going to give them her vote, but I managed to change her mind, with some difficulty. Our family are traditionally Atatürk supporters. My dear father, God bless his soul, was always talking about what the Greek infidels did. We're from Sakız Island where we used to live among them. Atatürk saved us from the hands of those infidels, so why would I vote for his enemies now? No way."

"How do you manage to do business with the council, when you talk like that?"

"Everyone knows what I am. I sell alcohol in my bars and restaurants, and I'm an evening drinker myself. I've nothing to hide, thank God. Hide from what, anyway? They're the ones that conceal their true faces. They're hypocrites. I'm an honest man, a better Muslim than the lot of them. That's what I tell the missus. On the Day of Judgement, when I'm playing with nymphs in paradise, they'll be burning in hell. Those men aren't going to decide who goes to paradise. Being a Muslim is all about being straight and honest, isn't it? You don't become a Muslim by growing a beard and winding a piece of cloth around your head."

"So you manage to deal with them because they trust you, is that right?"

"Of course it is. They don't trust each other, but they need somebody they can trust. They're not going to trust anyone they know to be exactly like themselves, are they? They all know what their colleagues are up to. Every one of them is just after a few bucks. A decent man wouldn't last a day with them. Things go on that not even the Devil would dream up. I've no documentation, otherwise I wouldn't hesitate for a moment. I'm not interested in money or anything. I'd expose the lot of them, but I've no documentation. Who was it who said, 'Is there any such thing as a bribe document?' That's how it is. I've channelled billions into Haliç Sports."

With some difficulty, he reached over his belly to clasp his tea glass with his chubby fingers. "I've talked so much my tea's gone cold. I'm like the loudmouth whose cigarette burns away to nothing. Waiter," he called out to no one in particular. "This tea tastes like dishwater, bring us two more. Or would you prefer coffee?"

"No, I'm fine," I said.

"Selim Bey is a man I really trust. I'll do whatever I can for you. If Selim Bey asked me for a million dollars, I'd give it to him without any kind of receipt. You must excuse me, but when I'm angry, I get carried away. I have high blood pressure, diabetes, the lot. My doctor says I have to lose weight. 'Those baklava and pastries are poison,' he says. But it's what we put down our throats that keeps us alive. I know I shouldn't eat that stuff, but I can't help it. A kilo of baklava at one sitting has no effect on me. They never rot my teeth. I've banned my missus from making desserts and pastries at home. My missus is Albanian. The naughty girl makes leek pastries so good you want to eat your fingers too. And they have this dessert. Do you know it? It's called *kaymaç*. Of course you don't. Why would you? Like crème caramel, only better. Oh my God, it's delicious! The wife doesn't make it at home. But what happens? The kids go out and buy it, so I still eat it. Tch!" he said, pretending to spit at his belly. "The fatter I get, the more I swell up. My doctor worked out a diet for me. I'm supposed to eat two pieces of cheese the size of a matchbox in the morning, but I eat a kilo of the stuff at one sitting. So what am I supposed to do with those little bits? Am I supposed to measure out cheese in little pieces as if I lived in an orphanage? But I must have cut down on what I eat and drink because I've lost three kilos in three weeks."

My brain sometimes goes numb when I'm talking to Turks.

"Can we get back to the business of land allocations?" I said.

"Yes, sorry about that. As I said, you have to talk to one of the party elders and get him to deal with the District Council. In Beyoğlu, they have a majority in the District Council so it's no problem. That can be sorted. The Council meets twice a year – in October and June. It would be difficult to get anything done in time for the meeting next month. There isn't time. But if you're interested, I'll find out where the council plots are and who can sort it out. Let's see if we can get something done by June. But as I said, these men won't allocate anything to us that might be profitable for them. They keep that for themselves."

"Are you going to talk to the Council Chairman?"

"No, I wouldn't go directly to the Chairman. He doesn't get involved in things like this."

"What kind of things does he get involved in?" I asked, just out of curiosity.

"They say he's set up a team. There's Fevzi Bey who is head of the Historical Works Foundation, our Chairman and a building-contractor friend of theirs. The three of them work together. They select buildings in high-rent areas. For instance, here on İstiklal Caddesi, there's a big Islamic charitable centre dating back to Ottoman times, which the Historical Works Foundation has decided to turn into a hotel and our Council Chairman has approved the plan. Is it right to turn a great Islamic charity centre like that into a hotel? But it's happening. And who do you think is going to build the hotel? Tarık, the building contractor of course. They'll divide the money they make from it three ways. That's how this business works. They're going to plunder something that was built and maintained by the Ottomans for seven hundred years. It makes me furious. The poor orphans have rights too. These men are such crooks."

"Who are you presently in contact with?" I asked, congratulating myself on my subtle tone.

"The Council Chairman has a right hand man, his Vice-Chairman, by the name of Temel. We call him Chief because that's what Temel means. He's from the Black Sea region. I talk to him."

I think the colour of my face must have turned yellow, red or something in between – maybe orange.

"Temel?" I said, with a gasp as if I'd just run 1500 metres in under four minutes.

"Temel Ekşi. He's the Council Chairman's number one man. Everything ends up with him. The Chairman wouldn't get involved personally, anyway. This Temel used to be a building contractor. That's why I say, whenever there's land for allocation in a good area, it gets earmarked for them. I'll ask my boys if any allocations are due to come up."

"Actually, I was just asking. I'm really thinking more of the bar business. I don't understand much about the construction business," I said. "What's this Temel like?"

"Before the twelfth of September coup in 1980, he was into all sorts of things. He and his mates used to go out hunting leftists, but they stopped after the coup. He's still more of a nationalist than an Islamist. His relationship with me is even better. Temel's the only one there worth talking about."

"Does he go around armed?"

"Those people never go around empty-handed. The worst is when they carry a sawn-off shotgun. They cut it down so that it fits easily into a pocket. The ammunition's cheap. The Islamists use that type of weapon. But Temel isn't like that. He's interested in firearms. It's his hobby and he has a collection at home. He carries a gold-butted magnum. It's a fantastic tool. A fight broke out at our restaurant once when he was there and he let them see it. Just let them see it, didn't draw it. He said, 'If I draw this, I won't put it back without firing.' That's the kind of man he is. Likes a drink too. He's different from the others. 'How come drinking is forbidden when it's in all the literature?' he says. 'The Prophet banned drink for people who don't know how to handle it.' I think he's right."

My back had begun to ache. It must have been psychological. I looked at my watch.

"I have to go now," I said. "I'll get back to you when I decide whether to pursue this bar business or not."

"You should have had something to eat. We didn't offer you anything," he said. Another example of traditional Turkish charm! I ask you, what German would insist on trying to make a guest have something to eat? Merely offering a coffee brings them out in a cold sweat.

"Thank you, but I ate before I came," I said.

"Give my best regards to Selim Bey. He hasn't called me for ages. We must go out for a drink one evening," he called out after me.

# 10

I didn't go back to the shop, but bought a spicy sausage döner kebab, the latest Turkish delicacy, and went home. By the time I got there, the grilled sausage inside the bread was stone cold and the fat had congealed. The bread was saturated with orange-coloured fat. I tossed it into the bin without even tasting it, made some green tea and sat down at my desk to make a list of the things on my mind. At the top, I wrote down the question that intrigued me most, even though the answer appeared to have nothing to do with everything else that had happened:

*Who is the father of İnci's child?*

I had a few more questions about İnci that were waiting for answers. For instance, Hafize Hanım. The woman who was supposed to be helping İnci with the housework. For some reason I felt uneasy about her.

*The shared past of Habibe Büyüktuna and İnci.* This was also bothering me. One of the women was lying about how the relationship between Osman and İnci had started. Why? Which one of them was it? I thought about it for a while and then decided the answer to that question was not going to help me solve the murder. After all, I was looking for a murderer, not a liar. I crossed out that question.

*İnci's married lover.* I was pretty sure his name had three letters, but couldn't remember exactly what it was. Never mind. I had a vision in my head of how a scenario with him might have played out. Osman found out about this lover and summoned him to his office. In the fight that ensued, Osman ended up getting shot. However, this didn't make a lot of sense, because the picture İnci had drawn of her childhood sweetheart, the engineer and teacher's son, just didn't fit – a bit of sociology was required here. And something else: if even engineers and teachers' sons couldn't venture out into the street without a Magnum in their pockets, then this country had become a place I shouldn't remain in a moment longer than necessary. If I'd known such things went on here, I'd have pursued my career as an amateur detective and bookshop proprietor in America. It would have made no difference to me.

Another factor that spoiled this scenario was the old woman. I had simply no idea how she fitted into the picture. Even if the married lover was aware that the old woman had recognized him, what could she have said that necessitated her being killed?

Furthermore, what was the point of doing away with a man whom İnci only saw intermittently? Surely he'd realize what harm it might cause her. The pathologist had admitted to being unconvinced that the bullet was intended to kill Osman. In which case... Yes, in which case the teacher's son had just wanted to send a message like, "Watch your step or your life won't be worth living." He couldn't have known the bullet would exceed his intentions in the way it did.

*Osman's brother Özcan.* Why wasn't his name on the list of cooperative partners? Could this have rocked his relationship with Osman? Maybe they had a big row and Özcan reached for his gun. After all, if Özcan was to take over running the business after Osman's death, it meant he had something to gain. It was certainly a mighty motive.

Something else not to be ignored was that the old woman probably knew Özcan. If she'd seen him leave the building looking dazed with a gun in his hand, it would have meant she'd signed her own death warrant. It was quite possible Özcan would have rushed out into the street with the gun in his hand if he'd shot his brother, because he would have been terrified. For the old woman to think he was the murderer, she must have seen him throw the gun down. I could think of no other alternative.

*Council Vice-Chairman Temel Ekşi.* He'd arranged for a land allocation to be made to Osman's cooperative, but hadn't managed to access party funds for the money to pay for it. The party leaders were giving him a hard time, and he'd kept phoning Osman to pester him for money. He'd even been round to Osman's office. That day when Osman had half-suffocated me at the door of his office, the mysterious voice I'd heard calling out could well have belonged to Vice-Chairman Temel. The reason he hadn't come out to see what was going on was that he thought I might recognize him.

He would also have been uneasy about the old woman if she'd seen him from her window on the day of the murder and he wouldn't have been able to get her out of his mind. But I'd failed to find a motive for Temel. What would he have hoped to achieve by wounding (not killing!) Osman? He would have wanted Osman to have two good legs so that he could earn money to pay off his debts. Then I remembered that Turkish men don't think logically like me. If it was Temel, he would have fired in a moment of rage, because having drawn his gun he couldn't put it back without shooting. Why? Because he was a man's man. A prime specimen of a man. A Turkish man.

*İsmet Akkan.* I'd delegated my questions concerning this once-famous film actor to Batuhan, so I just wrote his name down and nothing more.

*The former footballer.* I didn't even write down his name. Sometimes it's best to trust one's instincts. Actually my instincts about murderers, as distinct from my instincts about men in general, had proved to be somewhat wanting in the Kurt Müller murder case (see my previous adventure). Nevertheless, I decided to follow them again. I'd sensed he had nothing to do with the murder right from the start.

I lit a cigarette and read through my notes. They weren't very long.

Then I went for a shower. My stomach had shrunk from hunger. I decided to stop off at the Bambi Büfe before going to see the concierge at İnci's apartment building.

I ate a *kumru* sandwich. I think it would have been better if I hadn't. Not my thing. Certainly didn't take the place of a couple of well-browned toasted cheese sandwiches. Still, I was trying to eat a balanced diet. That's why I stuck it out with the *kumru*, consisting of salami and different types of sausage, all for the sake of the Vitamin B12 that's found only in meat. There are so many varieties of Vitamin B, each with its own number. Very confusing. If they have to put different numbers after the B, why not call one Vitamin T and another Vitamin Z? I don't understand it. We're expected to have a balanced diet, but everything is so complicated.

I got stuck at the countdown traffic lights at Taksim Square. But there was no rush. I waited calmly for the forty seconds it took for the lights to turn green. I had no idea of the best time to go chatting to a concierge. We didn't have one where I lived. This was considered disastrous by my middle-class Turkish friends. Yılmaz, for instance, thought it extremely odd. "So who puts the rubbish out?" he asked once, biting his lips in amazement when I replied, "I do. There's a rubbish bin at the end of the street." Recently he asked, "Still no concierge?" and looked at me in disbelief when I replied, "Do you have to employ someone just to throw out the rubbish and wipe the steps down once a week, for God's sake?"

Actually, I do have a cleaner once a week. But that's not quite the same thing, is it? In my fervent left-wing days, I was opposed to paying anyone to clean up my mess. But my mother always had a cleaner, so it was inevitable that I would as well. At one time,

I even went as far as getting friends to give me haircuts, like my mother did. It was amazing that I ever managed to get a lover.

I didn't want to park in the grounds of İnci's apartment block, so I drove round the streets of Etiler looking for a parking place. I needed to be careful because I didn't want İnci to look down from her balcony and see me getting out of the car. Like a spy. Since I was going to interrogate the concierge.

I'd noticed on my previous visit that it said CONCIERGE next to the bottom bell. Did this poor man have no name? Ahmet or Mehmet, for instance? I pressed the concierge bell at the main door. The door opened immediately. Almost before I'd taken my finger off the bell. Of course pressing the buzzer to open doors is one of the basic functions of a concierge. Nobody opens a door faster than a concierge.

My heart was pounding as I went down the steps. Concierges always live in the basement. Everyone knows that, whether they have a concierge or not. I wasn't sure if his family would know Hafize Hanım. Nor was I sure how I was going to play this scene.

I knocked on the basement door. No one was waiting to open the door for me, so clearly it hadn't occurred to whoever let me into the building that the person who rang the bell upstairs would actually be coming down to see them.

As the door opened, a smell of poverty pervaded the air: fried onions, suet, over-brewed tarry tea, socks with holes in, nylon slippers, print skirts with elasticated waists, winceyette under-pants from the market... I tried not to inhale through my nose, which was impossible, of course.

The door was opened by a young man. He had a dark complexion and brilliant blue eyes.

"Are you the concierge?" I asked. Didn't this poor man have a name?

"Yes, miss," he said, bowing his head in greeting.

"I'm looking for Hafize Hanım. She used to work for someone in this building, but I think she left."

"Kadriye, come here," he called out. "Someone's asking about your sister-in-law Hafize." He pronounced his wife's name with a 'G' instead of 'K', but that's irrelevant.

Kadriye came towards me, rearranging her headscarf. They had still not invited me inside which, for Turks, was not normal behaviour at all. Standards decline when people migrate from their villages to the cities.

"Were you asking about my sister-in-law?" said the girl. She was still no more than a young girl. Her skin had a radiance which, after a certain age, can only be achieved by using very expensive creams.

"Yes," I said.

"They don't live here," she said.

"I know. I wanted to know how I could find her," I said.

"She left her job," she said.

This time, I said nothing and just looked at her.

"I can give you her phone number, miss," said her husband.

"Yes, we can do that," said the girl.

Great, just what I wanted!

"Why are you asking for Hafize?" said the girl.

"I'm looking for someone to work for me," I said.

"I saw her go to number thirteen a few times," said the husband. As expected, number thirteen was the apartment where İnci lived.

"Are you a relative of Miss İnci?" asked the girl, her face lighting up as she mentioned İnci's name. İnci probably gave them her barely worn Escadas.

"No, I'm not," I said, offering no further explanation.

The man wrote a number down on a piece of paper and gave it to me.

"Hafize lives nearby. They also take care of an apartment block," he said.

"Thank you," I said.

I let myself out into the street.

Obviously in Etiler, like Cihangir where I lived, all the concierges and their families were related in some way and from the same village. The system worked like this: one concierge and his family start working in a district, then gradually their relatives fill up the basements of neighbouring apartment blocks. People who live in Turkish villages are almost always related to one another. Even if they aren't relatives, they are *hemşeri*, which has no equivalent in Germany. People born in the same village, district or even the same city call each other *hemşeri*. They provide each other with support when they migrate to big cities. A number of associations have been formed in Istanbul for this purpose. For instance, the people of Malatya, Sivas and Erzurum each have their Solidarity Association. There is also the İğdir Enhancement and Conservation Association and the Azeri Cultural Promotion Community. This concept of *hemşeri* has clearly rubbed off on Germans as well. I hear that an association of German women married to Turks has been formed. I've no idea what sort of activities they get up to – I haven't been married to a Turk, so far. Actually, I haven't been married to anyone.

After seeing Hafize Hanım, my mobile rang as I was returning home. It was Selim. He wanted to tell me that it was his mother's birthday the next day and thought I might get cross if he left it any later. Actually, I get cross when I'm called on my mobile while I'm driving. Whatever the reason, I was feeling cross.

There was, of course, the problem of finding a present for Selim's mother. It's hard enough choosing a present for a close girlfriend, let alone a fussy old woman. Actually, the poor woman wasn't fussy at all. My mother was the fussy one. She'd turn up her nose at anything I bought unless it was a diamond ring, as if my life overflowed with diamonds that I concealed from her.

Selim's mother appeared to be a woman who was happy to receive a bunch of flowers. I say "appeared" because I'd never actually bought her anything before, so I had no idea about her attitude to presents. As for me, I'm polite enough to feign pleasure, even if I'm given a CD of ethnic music. And that's the sort of behaviour I expect from others.

Buying a present for a lover's mother is a sensitive matter. If you buy something valuable, you're suspected of trying to ensnare their boy. Get something trashy, and they think you're saying, "Who do you think you are, you old bag? Your son loves me now, you're nothing to us." You therefore have to find something good but not too good, so as not to upset the balance.

I spent all evening thinking about this. At such times, I wish I were a painter. Then I wouldn't have to buy any presents. I'd just dash off an ink drawing of an owl and wrap it up. Of course, it would have to be like Picasso's owl. An owl that had a profound effect on mankind. But I couldn't even draw a straight line. Whatever I drew would come out cockeyed.

Maybe if I were a composer it would be better. I'd jot down a little ditty, say a birthday song. But no, better to be a painter. Because the recipient could hang the present on the wall. A composition would only be a birthday present when performed. At other times, it would simply be a piece of paper sitting on top of the piano.

I'm sure I'd find some creative solution if I were a jewellery designer or a potter. But I had to accept that I was merely the proprietor of a bookshop selling crime fiction, and there was no way I could ever come up with a creative marvel to give as a present.

In the end, I decided to take a book from my own bookshelves: a selection of Lord Byron, published in 1946. This ticked various boxes. It was:

1. Not too valuable, because it was neither a gravure nor a first edition.
2. Not without value: a hardback and a good edition.
3. Appropriate as a present from a woman who runs a bookshop.
4. A present with meaning, because at our previous meeting we had discussed Lord Byron and the reasons for his hostility towards Turks.

When I awoke the next morning and saw the book by my bed, I felt pleased with myself. At least I wouldn't be spending the day searching for a present. I woke Pelin and packed her off to the shop. If I hadn't had so much to do, I'd have gone to the shop myself instead of struggling to wake her up. I was finding her very wearisome. Since breaking up with her lover, Pelin was no longer the diligent person of happier days. It needed a winch to get her out of bed.

Without wasting any time, I went to the telephone and called Batuhan. I wanted to learn what he'd found out about İsmet Akkan, and also to pass on my new information. Goodness knows why, at my age, I was still trying to work with the police. People who knew me found it incredible. But life blows people in different directions, and their obsessions know no bounds. I'd developed a passion for detective work. I couldn't help it.

Batuhan answered after the first ring.

"Have you got time to meet?" I asked.

"Yes, but not until later this afternoon. I'll come and pick you up. Shall we have dinner together?"

I didn't want to say that it was my lover's mother's birthday dinner that evening. It's always better to keep people's hopes alive, especially if they're in a position to help with the things you're obsessed about.

"I have a date this evening. I'm going to the cinema with a girlfriend," I said.

In men's eyes, going to the cinema is the most harmless social act two women can do together. Even if you say you're going to watch television with a cup of hot chocolate, men imagine that you're arranging an orgy.

"What time are you going?" he asked.

"We're going to the seven-forty-five performance," I said. I wasn't sure if there was a showing at that time, but I was certain that Batuhan knew no more than I did about such matters.

"In that case, I'll come to your shop at five," he said.

It wasn't even nine o'clock in the morning yet, so I still had hours ahead of me to devote to my research. Before going out, I planned what I would wear that evening. You can't leave these important matters until the last moment.

An hour after my phone call to Batuhan, I was standing outside the door of the basement where the old woman had been killed ten days before. On the way, I'd made up some new excuses for being there. I rang the bell. It didn't work, so I knocked on the door.

The woman who opened the door was obviously Figen's mother. They were as alike as two halves of an apple. I hoped this similarity was only physical. I didn't have the stomach for another woman with the ability to dissolve into floods of tears at will.

"Who do you want?" asked the woman. What a nice reception! Had "hospitality" become just a slogan used on advertisements for drawing tourists in to Turkey?

"We're neighbours. I have a bookshop near here. I'm so sorry for your loss," I said.

"May she rest in peace," she said, still not inviting me inside.

"I lent Figen a book," I said.

The woman straightened her spectacles, twisted the ends of her headscarf and tied them behind her ears. She was clearly surprised that I knew her daughter.

"Figen's at school. I know nothing about a book of yours. Come inside and look for yourself," she said.

I wasn't going to miss that opportunity! I tossed my shoes off inside the door and went inside. The woman looked slightly uneasy, as if she might change her mind about letting me in. I entered and, remembering the room from my previous visit, walked over to sit by the window where the old woman was supposed to have always sat. This divan was higher than the other two. When I sat on it, my head was level with the window, which meant I could easily see out into the street.

"My mother-in-law always used to sit there," said Figen's mother, following me into the room.

"You can see the street from here, so you'd never get bored," I said.

"Not even Süleyman the Magnificent managed to remain in this world. Now she too is gone, turned to dust. Happens to us all in the end," she said, staring vacantly. "Shall I make some tea? Or I have Nescafé if you'd prefer it."

"I don't want to put you to any trouble," I said, like a good Turk. In coded Turkish conversation, this means that you would like something to drink.

"No trouble, my dear. Tea or Nescafé?"

"Tea, if it's not too much trouble," I replied.

She went into the kitchen and I followed her.

There had been no change to the kitchen decor since my last visit. The same posters adorned the walls.

"Do you work for the party?" I asked, obviously referring to UEP.

"Not at the moment, actually. I took some time off. What with my mother-in-law dying. She was sick, so it was expected.

213

But not like that. God give us strength. It's been very hard on all of us. She suffered terribly. But if it's God's will, what can you do?" she said, shaking her head. "Come through and have a look at Figen's books, if you like. Take whichever one's yours."

"The book's not important," I said. "Figen can call in at the shop one day and drop it off."

The woman looked at me questioningly. She was obviously wondering why I was there. Still, there's no need to respond to unarticulated questions.

We returned to the sitting room and I went back to the old woman's place.

As I turned to ask Figen's mother a question, I noticed a picture on the wall. It was hanging next to a party poster showing the little girl praying with tears in her eyes – like the one in the kitchen. It showed four men posing in front of the beautiful pink Beyoğlu Council building. Beneath the picture, in large letters, was written: *Council Chairman and Senior Engineer Hayri Tokçan and advisors – United Endeavour*. My eyes began to twitch. Probably from excitement.

"Who are those people in the photo?"

"The Council Chairman and his advisors," said the woman. I'd seen that much myself.

"Is Temel Bey among them?"

"Yes," she said, pointing to one of them. "Do you know Temel Bey? He's a very good man. He got my husband a job at the Council. Thanks be to God," she said, handing me a framed picture that was standing on top of the television. "That's him with Temel Bey. He really likes my husband. 'There's always a need for an honest man,' he says."

I was speechless. I looked at the photo for some time without saying a word.

"Do you know him too?" I asked.

"We arrange home visits in order to promote the aims of the party. We go to local households where the mistress invites other local Muslim women. We all sit down together to talk and discuss matters. The women ask questions about our party and we answer them, and we tell them what we're going to do if our party gets into power. We meet with the women in the daytime, and the men's meetings happen in the evenings. Temel Bey does the evening ones, of course, but if any of his *hemşeri* are present at ours, he sometimes comes and gives a talk to the women."

"Has he been here? Or has he been to a meeting attended by your mother-in-law?" I blurted out. The woman frowned. I probably shouldn't have asked this, but I was very excited. "I know he's a very good speaker and I was wondering if your family has benefited from his wisdom," I asked.

However stupid that sounded, she was convinced. People never think you're waffling if you say something complimentary.

"Of course. We organize meetings at our house and Temel Bey has honoured us with his presence. No one helped us more than he did when my mother-in-law was ill. Thanks be to God. We know his wife too. Temel Bey is knowledgeable about lots of things. He's very well informed on religious matters. Dear God, if only everybody could be like him."

She paused and looked at me. "Aren't you religious?" she asked, probably because of what I was wearing, even though I'd put on a high-necked T-shirt with my jeans especially to visit her.

"I'm not religious," I replied.

"God forbid. That's impossible. Doesn't everyone have a religion?" she said.

I wasn't going to get into an argument.

"Actually, I'm not Turkish," I said.

"What difference does that make? You get Muslims in every country. There's no race or language discrimination in Islam," she said.

Having learnt what I had come for, I couldn't wait to get out. I might even have allowed myself to appear ever so slightly Muslim in order to close the conversation since, unlike men, there was no need for me to be circumcised.

But naturally, I did no such thing. I wasn't going to give this woman the satisfaction – she was too good a politician.

"I'm not religious and I intend to stay that way," I said, in what I thought was a firm tone of voice.

The woman shook her head, indicating that I wasn't worth making an effort over. Her lips moved as if in prayer. Of course there was no point bothering with someone like me. You can argue for hours with a Christian or Jew about which religion is best, but what can you say to an atheist? That it's better to be religious than an atheist?

Despite the fact that we really had nothing to say to each other, she still offered me tea. After thinking for a long while, she made her last statement to me as I was tying up my shoes by the front door:

"If you don't believe in God, you could commit a murder, robbery or adultery. There's nothing to stop you! Just let me talk to you. Get to know about Islam, and then make up your mind."

"Thank you for the tea," I said.

"Islam is a tolerant religion. Everyone has a place in Islam," she called out after me.

"Lazy woman," I hissed, as I went down the stairs. At least Christian missionaries trek across continents for their beliefs. Didn't they go out and convert half the Buddhists in South Korea to Christianity? And they work damned hard. What do Muslims do? They visit other Muslim brothers to collect votes, yet they know nothing about atheists living two streets away unless they come and knock at the door. Even I could churn out propaganda to people who came visiting me. The Muslims do nothing except wait for an atheist to turn up. Useless.

I just made it for five o'clock. If I hadn't felt I had to go to the hairdresser's, I would have called Batuhan to suggest meeting earlier. Still, I was able to calm down a bit at the hairdresser's, which was in the newly opened Tower Hotel in Kuledibi. It was all so exciting. I'd solved another murder case! I could leave the task of proving my claims to the Turkish police. After all, they were the ones with access to forensic laboratories and pathologists.

However, there were still a few unexplained points. One in particular was still bugging me, even preventing me from enjoying the euphoria of success. Why wasn't Özcan on the list of cooperative founders? Especially since he was the most talented and competent of the brothers.

I left the shop in the capable hands of Pelin and went to the tea garden with Batuhan. I felt like a really mean boss because I was continually complaining about her being lazy, yet it was thanks to her that I could go out wherever and whenever I pleased. On the other hand, she was using my home like a hotel. There aren't many bosses who would let you turn up on their doorstep with all your belongings, are there? True?

I had no time for small talk if I wanted to be looking radiant at Selim's mother's house in Nişantaşı by eight-thirty. I got straight to the point, without even waiting for the tea to arrive.

"I know who the murderer is."

Batuhan covered his mouth and laughed out loud.

"Oh, yes! So who is it?"

He thought it was all a joke. Would punching him in the face have made me feel any better? Perhaps not, since the guy whose brains I wanted to smash was a police officer. I took three deep breaths in an attempt to dispel my irritation at his stupid laughter.

"The Vice-Chairman of Beyoğlu Council, Temel Ekşi," I said.

His face trembled and he clicked his tongue.

"Babe," he said. Ugh! What a disgusting word, but I swallowed it. God knows why. "What does the Council Vice-Chairman have to do with it?"

If the cretin sitting opposite me were ever to earn a police medal for extraordinary service, if there was such a thing, then it would be because of me. He might even get a salary rise. Or promotion. Become Chief Commissioner.

No, that was going too far!

"Tell me, what's the connection, pet?" he said this time.

I decided to contain myself and be polite.

"Look," I said. "I address you as 'Batuhan'. There's no need to use epithets when talking to me, my name is sufficient."

"Pardon?" he said, seeming not to have understood me. Not that I'd said anything complicated, but the brainless idiot's mind was on other things.

It's always best to be blunt. That way, everybody understands what you're trying to say.

"Just call me Kati," I said, "There's no need for 'babe' or 'pet'."

He strained his neck from side to side, with a clicking noise.

"OK, Kati. Please, would you explain to me the connection between the Council Vice-Chairman and the murder?"

"Firstly it's not the murder, it's murders," I said.

"Very well, but please explain."

I did.

He listened to me without saying a word.

"That's a theory, of course," he said when I'd finished. "A sound theory, in fact."

"If I only had all your officers and laboratories at my disposal."

"I understand," he said. "You don't fancy me today."

Ugh!

"Darling, I always fancy you," I said. I was being sarcastic as you no doubt realize.

"What else have you found out?"

What a question to be asked by the officer in charge of a murder investigation!

"Who do you suspect, tell me that first," I said. "Did you look into İsmet Akkan?"

"That man has at least four reliable witnesses, not counting the people working at the holiday village."

"Was he with them on the night of the murder?"

Batuhan nodded.

"So, who do you suspect?"

He laughed.

"I've suspected everyone at some point. There's nobody else left," he said.

"Osman's lover?"

"İnci Hanım," he said with a sneering smile.

"Hmm."

"Let me explain a few things to you about how the world works," he said, indicating to the waiter that he wanted two more teas brought over.

"This İnci Hanım had a lover who was the son-in-law of someone well known, and Osman found out about it. Fifteen days before he was killed, he got one of his brothers to follow her. Musa, the one who looks after the car park here. He followed her day and night. What these men get up to! Who would think they'd play at being detectives among themselves? The woman didn't suspect a thing. They'd also been tracking the man she was meeting and found out who he was. But Osman was killed before he could take action."

"Who told you this?" I asked.

"The young one, Özcan."

"Why didn't he say so right from the start?"

"Never mind him now. İnci wasn't at home on the night of the murder."

"And it just so happened that Musa had stopped following her," I said with some irritation, "because he thought there was

219

no point in carrying on now that everyone knew she'd been deceiving Osman."

"Yep! That's exactly what happened."

"So how did you know İnci wasn't at home that evening?" I asked.

"She admitted it herself. We took her in for questioning this morning and she told us everything. The only thing she wouldn't tell us was the name of her lover. She thinks we don't know. She doesn't care about being accused of murder, but she won't give away her lover's name. We told her to prove that she didn't go to Osman's office that evening, but she wouldn't. She might at least have tried. She doesn't realize."

"Doesn't realize what?"

"That she called Osman's mobile on her landline at fourteen minutes past seven, which was just before Osman was killed."

"Aha! If you've got hold of the phone records then you also know if Osman spoke to Temel Ekşi."

"Wait, I'm coming to that. Be patient."

I couldn't be patient – it was my lover's mother's birthday.

"Tell me quickly. I have to leave for the cinema," I said.

"Oh, for God's sake, cancel the cinema," he said, taking out his mobile and handing it to me.

"Impossible. I can't get hold of Lale. She's coming to the cinema straight from a meeting."

"We could have gone out for a nice dinner."

"Sorry, I just can't."

"I've found a really good kebab house. The cooks there remove every bit of sinew from the meat. It's very special. And the turnip juice comes all the way from Adana. Their kebabs are so good you want to eat your fingers too."

"Impossible," I said yet again. "Anyway, forget about dinner. You were talking about telephone records."

He took hold of my hand. I didn't pull it away.

220

"I want to talk to you," he said.

"Here we go again," I thought to myself.

"What are we going to do about us?" he asked.

"What about us?" I replied.

He looked straight into my eyes.

"Very well, you mustn't be late for the cinema. Let's go," he said, sounding offended. This was always happening to me. It was always the sensitive ones who became infatuated with me. There never seemed to be any of the tough ones around. If only one of those would fall for me, it wouldn't be such hard work.

He was already on his feet.

"Will you sit down?" I said.

He sat down immediately because, despite being sensitive, he didn't have the courage to play hard to get. He knew me very well, of course. I don't pander to anyone.

"Are you married?" I asked.

"Where did that come from all of a sudden? Is our problem that I might be married? Anyway, what makes you think I'm married?"

"If you weren't married, you wouldn't be insisting we went out for dinner this evening. We could go tomorrow," I said.

"It can't be tomorrow," he said.

I nodded, thinking he must have told his wife he was working that evening, and you can't tell the same lie two nights running.

"Well then, let's make it next week," I said.

"Fine," he said, lowering his head.

"Do you really suspect İnci?"

"I'm just curious," he said, raising his head again.

"What?"

"Whose is the child?"

I laughed so loud that people at the other tables turned round to look at us.

"It's not Osman's," I said.

"What!" he said. "Wait, how do you know this?"

221

"I spoke to the maid that İnci sacked. I'll give you her address and you can speak to her yourself. The woman's very keen to explain everything."

"What does she know and what does she say?"

"All about İnci's private life. It turns out the teacher's son wasn't her only lover."

"What!" he said again. "How on earth did she manage the logistics of it all?"

"By buying a different mobile for each lover," I said.

"What do you mean?"

"İnci had a different mobile for each lover. One particular lover would have the number for each mobile. Supposing she wanted to meet X that day, then she would turn on the mobile whose number only X knew, and switch off all the others. The next day, she'd turn on the mobile whose number Y knew. She had the same number of mobiles as she had men. Or maybe it was SIM cards. I don't really understand these things. Anyway, she was exploiting the blessings of technology."

"Just a moment. If Musa was following İnci, he must have known about the other lovers."

"I agree," I said.

"So what's your theory about that?"

"That Musa didn't follow İnci," I said.

"And?"

"Osman's brothers threatened her and got her to talk. Either that or they offered her money. I don't really know, but it was something like that. She was afraid that if any one of her lovers was exposed she'd be ruined. Push her a little and she's sure to give you the name and address of the teacher's son. After all, he won't go to jail for murder," I said and stopped suddenly. "Hang on, you're not torturing this woman, are you?" I asked.

"Are you joking? What torture? We live in a constitutional state and we're currently preparing to go into the European

Union. Do you think we still use torture? Is that what you think?"

"No, I don't," I said, but I still scrutinized his face carefully. I didn't trust this police state.

"So, what about the child's father?" asked Batuhan.

"The maid says it's not Osman's. I don't know. Nobody knows. How are you going to find out something like that?"

"What makes you say it's not Osman's?"

"İnci has given up the idea of pursuing a paternity suit. She went to see a lawyer a few times, but in the end did nothing. The maid must have known what was going on from İnci's telephone conversations," I said, shrugging my shoulders.

"Phew! What bastards. And she's pregnant, too. Tuh!" he exclaimed, pretending to spit in the face of İnci and her different lovers.

"I spoke to Temel Ekşi," he said, pulling a face as if he had just eaten a whole lemon.

"Why?" I asked.

"His number appeared frequently on Osman's telephone records. I went to the Council to see him. He said nothing about this land allocation business. He just said, 'I know Osman. He has a car park in Beyoğlu and wanted another place for a car park in Kasımpaşa. We spoke several times recently.' It all sounded reasonable to me, so I left. What else could I do?" he said, putting his head between his hands. Then he looked up at me and said, "We're getting close to the end, aren't we?"

"I don't know. Are we? Were there any fingerprints on the knife that killed the old woman?"

"You've touched on a very good point. Very good. Bravo!"

"Why?"

"There were no fingerprints," he said in a way that made me think there was something else.

"So what was there?"

"A strand of hair in the woman's hand. As the knife was going in, she must have grabbed at the murderer's head and plucked out a hair."

"Whose was it?" I asked, excitedly.

"We're looking into it. Samples have been taken and they're looking for a match."

"Who did you take samples from?"

"Everyone. As I said, everyone's still a suspect."

"Temel Ekşi?"

"No, we didn't take a sample from him. Until talking to you, I... I don't think he would consent anyway. We'd have to have a very good reason. Other than the phone conversations, there's no evidence against him, so it would be difficult to persuade the prosecutor. We'll see what happens."

I looked at my watch. Time was flying and I needed to leave immediately.

"One other thing," I said. "They're all cooperative founder members apart from Özcan. Osman made everyone else in the family a partner, so why not Özcan? Don't you think that's odd?"

"It is odd," he said, cracking his knuckles. "Very odd."

"Also, the family ganged up to pin it on different people, starting with the uncle, then İnci and even me. They're just trying their luck."

"But they didn't get anywhere with you," said Batuhan.

"What do you mean? They took my statement at the police station, didn't they?"

"OK. Let's clear this up. You told those men your father was Minister of the Interior, didn't you?"

"My father's dead," I said.

"But they didn't know that. You must have scared the wits out of them."

I crossed my legs, swaying the upper leg back and forth. It

224

always pleased me to think that there were people who were afraid of me.

"What are you going to do now?" I asked.

"I'm going to seek consolation in my wife's arms," he said.

I stared at him wide-eyed, couldn't help it. I was no longer swaying my leg, as you can imagine.

"I have no wife," he said. "I mean it! I'll show you my ID card, if you want."

What did it matter to me if Batuhan had a wife? What do I care about people's marriages? Or whether they are married or not?

"Show me," I said.

He emptied the contents of his pockets onto the table. Wallet, keys, a half-empty packet of tissues, a ballpoint pen and notepad with curled-up edges. His mobile, cigarettes and lighter were already on the table.

"What is it?" I said.

"I don't have my ID on me," he said.

"I don't believe you," I said. "Look inside your wallet."

He opened each pocket of his wallet. Unfortunately, there were only a few coins in it. Life's tough for state employees in Turkey.

"Fine, you can bring it next time we meet," I said.

The dinner that evening was a great success. Firstly, Belkis Hanım, Selim's mother, loved the present. Secondly, all Selim's relatives were there and nobody expected me to say a thing. I even scored a few points by not speaking unless spoken to. That way, I created the impression of being a serious, respectable and enigmatic woman. Turks love that sort of thing.

Selim, of course, suspected something. As soon as we were in the lift, he asked why I was like "a nightingale that's eaten a mulberry". "What do you mean by that?" I asked. I'd never heard that saying before. It was an interesting metaphor. Apparently it's used when a normally talkative person, like me, remains silent.

"My head's in chaos," I said. "*Tohu va vohu*."

"What does that mean?" he asked.

"It means 'chaos'," I said. "It's in the Torah. Book of Genesis, second sentence. In the original Hebrew text, it's used to describe the state of the world before God began to create order. When the Torah is translated into other languages, all sorts of adjectives are used for *tohu va vohu*. For instance, the earth was 'desolate and void', 'formless and void', 'disorderly and void', the earth was 'void and its surface formless'. But what it really means is that the world was in chaos."

"My chaotic Torah-quoting darling," he said. "What was it? Tohutu what?..."

"*Tohu va vohu*. It's not me that's chaotic, it's your country."

He drew back my hair and kissed my neck. Why don't men take women's intellectual and political concerns seriously?

"So, Frau Hirschel, what is it that's so chaotic about our country?" he asked, putting his arm around my waist and pulling me towards him.

"This murder for a start," I said.

He was playing with my hair.

"True," he said.

We reached the car park level and got out of the lift.

As we drove to Selim's apartment, I told him some of what had been happening. He listened to me without saying a word. I told him the rest while we were sitting on the sofa having a brandy.

"So what's the problem now?" he asked when I'd finished.

"What's the problem? What do you mean?"

"What's bugging you?"

"I'm wondering if in fact the murder had nothing to do with Temel Ekşi and if Osman's family planned the whole thing. They may have got Özcan to commit the murder because he was still a minor and would get off with a short sentence. The old woman's murder was then unavoidable because she would have seen who Osman's murderer was. Or there's another possibility: Özcan was angry because he wasn't a founder member of the cooperative, so he went to discuss it with his brother and a fight broke out. The family know that Özcan is the killer but won't hand him over to the police. That seems more logical."

"Not really," he said. "It's not logical at all unless there was another reason for hostility between Özcan and his brother, other than the fact that he wasn't a member of the cooperative."

"What do you mean?"

"If, as you say, Özcan is a minor, he can't be a founder member. Founder members have to be over eighteen. He could be a shareholder through a guardian, but not a founder."

My eyes were burning, as if I'd rubbed pepper into them.

"Say all that again," I said.

He repeated what he had just said.

What a wonderful thing it is to have a lawyer as a lover. Such useful people, lawyers. And what a good lawyer he was to have his girlfriend's name as his email password. Lovely man. The solution to some things is so easy. Love a lawyer and learn how many little things get overlooked by ordinary people. So Özcan wasn't hostile towards his older brother. Or if he was, there was nothing in the information at my disposal to tell me that. So who did the hair found in the old woman's hand belong to? Temel?

When I woke up, Saturday morning had come round again. I left the house without waking Selim. I could never understand how a person who woke up at seven o'clock every weekday without fail could stay in bed until noon at the weekend. I didn't have a single outfit at Selim's place that was suitable for going to meet Yılmaz at Firuzağa, so I had to go home first to get changed.

Pelin was asleep. I went into the study and looked to see if there were any voicemails. The light was blinking. My landlady had called to remind me about the refuse-collection tax. That woman was a serious head case. I'd already paid it, together with all the previous years' bills.

No one else had called.

As I was putting on my trousers, my mobile rang. I knew who it was without looking. It was Batuhan.

"The pathologist's results have come through," he said.

I swallowed hard.

"Who?" was all I could say.

I heard the sound of a lighter down the phone.

"It doesn't match any of the samples we have," he said.

"Did you take a sample from Özcan?"

"We did. I stayed awake all last night thinking about your theory. It certainly seemed plausible. But as you know, these things are never cut and dried. We're having to go back to trial and error methods. There's not a shred of substantial evidence. Let's see if Temel Bey will consent to giving us a sample. I've spoken to his colleagues in Beyoğlu. Your Temel is a very colourful figure. They say he always goes around loaded. Has a gold-handled Magnum that he's very proud of. Apparently he struts up and down İstiklal Caddesi like a cowboy and has previous form for wounding a policeman outside the French Cultural Association."

"Is his gun unlicensed?"

"I had a check done and he certainly has a licence for one gun, probably the gold-handled one. But that wasn't the gun used to shoot Osman. However, guys from the Black Sea region are mad on guns and he's bound to have others. I just called to let you know. Let's see if anything comes of it this time. If it does, I'll owe you a big thank you."

"My pleasure," I said. "It's my duty as a citizen." Before putting down the phone, I couldn't help asking, "Did you find out who the father of İnci's child is?"

"We'll talk over dinner," he said.

# 11

I told Selim a lie on Wednesday evening as I was leaving to meet Batuhan. I wasn't going to tell the world I was having dinner with a police officer, let alone someone in the murder squad. Especially not my lover!

We went in Batuhan's red car to his newly discovered kebab house. After passing through the strange back streets of Aksaray, we suddenly came out at the waterfront. Istanbul is so big, even the people who live here can't be expected to know every district, especially someone like me who became an *İstanbullu* late in life. Moreover, what would anyone interested in the beauties of Istanbul look for in that district? Its single item of beauty is the Aksaray mosque, which also bears the name of a woman called Pertevniyal Valide Sultan. Actually, looked at closely, this mosque is indeed beautiful. It's the most decorated of all Istanbul's mosques. However, if I had to pick a mosque whose beauty made me tremble inside, my vote would always go to the Sülemaniye Mosque. Designed by the architect Sinan on one of the seven hills of Istanbul, for me it remains without equal on account of the way it harmonizes with nearby edifices such as that centre of human sciences and scholarship – Istanbul University – and the way it dominates the city's historic peninsula.

Batuhan's kebab house was in a district close to Aksaray called Samatya, where I had spent several Sundays strolling through the streets during my fifteen or so years of living in Istanbul. Samatya is one of Istanbul's lovely old neighbourhoods. The delicious meze and pitta bread covered with well-seasoned mincemeat, known as *lahmacun*, certainly matched the beauty of the surroundings. However, by the time the kebabs arrived, I found our topic of conversation had made me lose my appetite.

It had been established that Temel Ekşi was the murderer of the old woman. The hair found in her hand matched the sample taken from Temel, who had at first denied everything, but in the end admitted to killing the old woman.

I obviously needed a little time to digest this. It meant I had indeed solved the murder! There was no need for modesty. It was definitely me who had solved it. I looked at the man sitting opposite. He was busy spreading some spicy dip on a piece of bread. Did he really think there was nothing to connect two murders that had been committed in two buildings opposite each other? Was he never going to reach the same conclusion as me?

Maybe he would.

But what difference would that make?

Would it diminish the righteous pride I felt?

Should it?

No!

I was the one who had solved this murder case!

"Osman," said Batuhan, stuffing the slice of bread into his mouth.

Yes, back to Osman. Apparently, Temel Ekşi was claiming that he got into a fight with Osman and, when things turned nasty, shot at him in self-defence, wounding him in the leg. After that, Temel had left. He learnt of Osman's death from the newspapers.

"You mean," I said, "that he's going to be charged with killing the old woman and causing grievous bodily harm to Osman?"

"Most probably, because of the pernicious circumstances leading to the cause of death," said Batuhan.

"Hmm," I said, not quite understanding his last sentence. "But Osman was still killed by a bullet from that man's gun."

"No, you don't understand," said Batuhan, putting his head between his hands. His mouth was moving as he chewed some bread. I watched a lump of it go down his throat.

"What don't I understand?" I said.

Clearly he was disturbed by what he was about to say.

"Osman wouldn't have died if he'd been able to summon help. He would have survived with proper medical treatment."

I shrugged my shoulders.

"Fine, but he didn't. Maybe he didn't know the number to call an ambulance. Or he fell down, bumped his head and fainted. Who knows? Maybe he couldn't get to the phone."

I fell silent.

"There was no phone in the room."

I took a sip of white wine. White wine may not be the most appropriate drink to have at a kebab house, but I'm a German. Nobody can expect me to conform to Turkish patterns of behaviour. Not when it doesn't suit me, anyway.

"You mean there was no landline?"

To be honest, I hadn't paid much attention to this detail before.

"Does Temel say that Osman could have opened the window and called out?"

"Temel? Why would Temel say that?" said Batuhan, with an expression that suggested he found my question strange.

"To save himself," I said.

"Forget about Temel," he said, as if he thought I was enjoying thinking about Temel.

"Fine, but he is the murderer, isn't he?"

Batuhan took a large gulp of rakı.

"Look. Temel and Osman had a fight... But something happened before that, which I need to explain," he said, as if to himself. "Osman's mobile rings. It's obviously İnci. İnci says she called him at that time, and Temel says Osman had a short conversation with someone. Then there's a knock at the door. İnci, who is on the telephone, verifies this."

This much I knew.

"And?" I said.

"Osman hangs up and goes to the door. Temel hears him talking to a woman, or rather hears them shouting at each other."

"And?" I say again, suddenly sitting bolt upright. "Does the woman see Temel? If so, why hasn't she been to the police yet?"

"No, the woman doesn't see Temel. But that's not the point. Just let me speak, please. If you stop interrupting for a moment, I'll explain."

I made a sign with my hand telling him to get to the point.

"OK, get on with it," I said.

Osman doesn't ask the woman inside. He talks to her at the front door and sends her away. However, from the shouting, Temel realizes the woman is angry about something. She insults Osman, he shouts at her and then she goes away."

I swear I still hadn't got it.

"Did the fight between Osman and Temel start after that?" I asked very calmly.

He nodded. "You know the rest. They fight, Temel fires the gun and leaves. When he leaves, Osman's mobile is on the desk."

"Wasn't there a landline at the office?" I asked again.

"There was an unused telephone which had been cut off for some time because the bill hadn't been paid. Osman did all his business on the mobile."

"So someone took his mobile?"

Batuhan nodded.

"Someone who wanted to prevent Osman calling for help. Someone who guessed that if Osman didn't get help, he might not pull through. Someone intelligent enough to work that out."

He said this as though he was paying me a compliment.

He was staring at me leeringly.

Almost flirtatiously.

I still didn't understand.

Then finally, I understood. I clapped my hand to my chest as though taking my last breath and gasped, "Me? You mean me?" Did Batuhan really think I'd taken Osman's phone and prevented him from calling for help?

Batuhan didn't appear to be at all amused. He looked even more serious than the day my statement was taken.

"The woman who knocked on the door when Temel was at the office," he said, nodding at me.

"Wait," I said. My brain was beginning to work.

"Couldn't Temel have taken the mobile with him when he left the office?"

"He could have done. Of course he could."

"Couldn't this story about a woman coming to the door be fabricated?"

"It could be."

"In which case?"

"Temel thinks he killed Osman anyway. He says, 'I didn't shoot to kill, but my hand slipped.' Temel wasn't the one who drew my attention to the matter of the telephone."

"Even better. If he'd taken the telephone, he'd hardly draw your attention to the fact, would he?"

"Temel admits he shot Osman. We're not yet certain about the time, but let's say it's seven-thirty. It's not yet dark when he leaves. Somebody calls out to him in the street – the old woman. She opens the window and invites Temel in for a meal. Temel is forced to exchange a few words with her, but he refuses the invitation and walks down to Karaköy."

"The gun?" I said.

"What about the gun?"

"Does he throw the gun into the sea at Karaköy?"

"No. The gun he shot Osman with is something special. A Magnum. He wouldn't throw that away! He changes the barrel and has the serial number erased. We found the gun at his house. If we hadn't had any other evidence apart from the gun, say if his fingerprints hadn't been found in Osman's office, it would have been difficult to prove he was the killer. However, he admitted the crime without much effort on our part."

"Is it normal practice to change the barrel?"

"That's what people do if an expensive gun like that gets soiled and the owner can't bear to throw it away."

"Gets soiled?"

"A gun used for a murder is said to be 'soiled'," Batuhan said, with a laugh that revealed his gleaming white teeth. "See what you learn from me?"

"Oh yes. Really useful things. But why did he kill the old woman? Did he say?"

"It was as you suggested right from the start," he said, looking at me admiringly. "He was afraid that we'd go to the old woman once the investigation got under way."

"A groundless fear," I remarked. "You didn't have time to interrogate the neighbours, except for an eccentric bookshop proprietor."

He scratched the back of his head and then stretched his neck from side to side, making a clicking sound.

"There's another thing, of course," he said, pausing for a moment and studying my face.

"What's that?" I asked.

"The apartment that Osman used as an office was about to be put up for sale. That's the place you want to buy, isn't it?"

234

"So what?"

"Nothing," he said. "Nothing at all."

"I told you in my statement that I wanted to buy that apartment, which was the reason I wanted to see inside and why I argued with Osman."

He nodded.

I had to admit that things didn't appear to be going very well for me. I could see the case against me:

One day before the murder, I'd argued with Osman at the door of his office and had a scuffle with him. On the day of the murder, he'd come to my shop and had an ashtray hurled at his head. Then, unable to contain myself, I'd gone back to his office that evening for another argument. I'd refused to leave when the door was shut in my face, but waited outside on the stairs, during which time I heard the sound of gunshot. Then, after Temel left, I went inside to prevent Osman from calling for help.

It was all plausible. There was even a motive. I wanted to buy the apartment, didn't I? Would I have been able to buy it if Osman was still alive? Actually, I still didn't know if it was going to be possible. Would the brothers let me?

"Did Temel leave the office door open?" I asked.

"He doesn't remember. He may have done."

"The next morning... Who found the body? I know it was one of the brothers, but I forget his name."

"Musa."

"Yes, Musa. When Musa arrived, was the door shut?"

"Yes, it was."

"So, you think that between the times that Temel left the office and Musa arrived, a woman came and took the mobile from the desk, and that this woman was Osman's real murderer."

"That's what I think."

"Osman could have opened the window and called out," I said. I'd said this before but hadn't received a satisfactory reply.

Batuhan took a deep breath and exhaled loudly.

"If he'd opened the window and called out, who would he call out to? You could shout your head off all night across the Bosphorus, not a single fisherman would come from Karaköy to help you. And there was no one else in the building."

"So, Osman's office wasn't on the side overlooking the street," I said.

Batuhan narrowed his eyes and looked at me carefully.

"What are you trying to say? That you never saw the apartment?"

"I don't need to prove that. I didn't see the apartment. I'd only seen the workshop on the floor below where I sat in a room overlooking the street," I said.

Batuhan leant back in his chair.

"Wait a minute," I said. "What did you just say?"

"I don't know, what did I say?"

"You said there was no one in the building. What about the building workers upstairs?"

"The illegal workers?" he said. What difference did it make if they were working illegally?

"Didn't they hear anything?"

"It so happens that on that very day, the council sealed up the penthouse apartment, because they didn't have a building permit. That block has been declared a historic building, so the slightest modification requires a permit and they hadn't obtained one. If we could prove that Temel Ekşi had had the building work stopped in order to ensure the building was empty, then we could claim that he intended to kill Osman. However, I doubt if that's the case."

"Would you be able to prove that? Did Temel say anything about having the work stopped?"

"It looks as though Temel had nothing to do with the fact that the work was stopped. The council was merely responding to a complaint by one of the neighbours. One of the nutty intellectuals living in Kuledibi had made a complaint about the building work."

"Who was that?"

"Someone who's obsessed with Kuledibi. An amateur architect," chuckled Batuhan. "We have so many nutcases in this country."

"Have you spoken to this man?"

"Of course. He really did hand in a petition to the council and refused to leave the building. Anyone who tried to talk him round just got handed one of his petitions. It's not the first time it's happened."

"I think he's right," I said.

Please don't think I approve of informers. But not all informers are the same. People trying to protect their district and city from villains are hardly the same as those who informed on Jewish families hiding in basements during the period of German fascism, are they?

Anyone who has been to Kuledibi will understand why I chose the word "villains". In the 1970s and 1980s, extra floors were added to the wonderful buildings surrounding Kuledibi Square, with the result that the load-bearing walls of many of the buildings collapsed to the ground, as though cocking a snook at centuries of Istanbul earthquakes. But since so much had been paid out in bribes for these hideous, illegal rooftop extensions, nothing could be done about them.

"So you're saying the workers weren't in the building at the time of the murder?"

"When the penthouse was sealed up, they took their belongings and left."

"What belongings?"

"Migrant workers like that live in the apartments they're working on so that they don't have to pay for accommodation."

"Have you found these workers?"

"Do you have any idea how many illegal workers there are in this country?"

"No, I don't," I said.

"We think there are over a million. Turkey has over a million illegal workers with no place to live and no identity papers – most of them in Istanbul."

That sort of thing didn't bother me at all, to be honest. I've worked pretty hard in my time for people's right to freedom of movement.

"So you haven't been able to find them."

"I haven't found them, nor have I looked for them. When we searched the scene on the morning after the murder, the seal on the door of the penthouse was intact and we have no reason to suspect that any of them got in that night."

I wrinkled my nose at what he said.

"Nor do you have a good reason to suspect that a woman took his mobile," I said.

I hadn't been in such a situation before. Nor would I ever have expected to be. Sitting next to me at the wheel was a man who thought I was a murderer, or, at any rate, an accessory to murder, and he was trying to squeeze his hand between my legs as he drove. I drew them away from him towards the door, out of harm's way.

"I'm a suspect again, aren't I?" I said.

He banged the steering wheel with his fist and said nothing.

We went past Valide Sultan Mosque towards Unkapanı.

"Was the mobile ever used again after that evening?" I asked.

Again, he said nothing.

"Was the mobile—" I started to repeat, but he interrupted me.

238

"I live apart from my wife," he said. "We're getting divorced."

I looked up at the roof of the car. What was there to say?

"Sorry to hear that," I said.

"Sorry?"

"It's sad when people separate. Do you have any children?"

He lit a cigarette and nodded thoughtfully.

"I understand," I said. "I understand you very well."

A bit later, just as I was beginning to think I could bear the silence in the car no longer, he replied to my question, saying, "The mobile wasn't used again. It's probably lying at the bottom of the Bosphorus."

"Hadn't you noticed before that the mobile was missing?"

He seemed to pull himself together.

"Yes, I had noticed. But the gun that Osman was supposed to always carry with him was also missing, so I assumed the murderer must have taken both of them. Later we realized that Osman's brothers had disposed of his gun before the police arrived at the crime scene. Because it was unlicensed. But we still don't know what happened to the mobile."

"Who's to say that Temel wasn't lying when he said he didn't take it? Maybe it was him, in fact."

"Yes," he said, making a tutting noise between his teeth. "If you saw him, you'd understand why I don't think that's the case."

"Why?" I said.

"He's an odd character. A real shyster type who goes around with wads of money in his pockets. Not the type to think, 'I'll take his mobile so he can't call for help and dies.' If he'd really wanted to kill Osman, he'd have put another bullet in him, not wasted his time over a mobile."

"You mean he's so rich he wouldn't steal a telephone to sell it on," I said.

"Yes. Temel taking that mobile just doesn't fit the jigsaw."

"What?" I said.

239

"It just doesn't fit," he said.

"But it's possible that a passer-by went inside and took the mobile from the desk. They could have thrown away the SIM card and sold the phone." I was thinking of the workers on the floor above as I said this.

"It's possible, but not at all likely. Osman's body was very close to the front door when it was found. He must have crawled there. If the mobile had been on the desk, he'd have crawled towards the desk instead of the door. But he headed for the door, which was the only place where he could ask for help. Which means that Osman was still alive when the person left with the telephone."

"What do you conclude from that?" I asked.

"Firstly, if Osman had phoned for help, he wouldn't have crawled towards the door. Secondly, nobody would enter a place and jump over a corpse to steal a mobile. Not just a phone anyway. Osman still had his wallet in his pocket and his watch was on his wrist, plus his gun was in the desk drawer. A thief would have taken those too."

# 12

When Batuhan dropped me in front of my apartment building, I saw that all the lights were on in my sitting room. Pelin was obviously at home. Out of politeness, I rang the front-doorbell downstairs, instead of letting myself in with my keys.

A young man I'd never seen before, wearing enormous boots, was stretched out on the sofa in my living room. It's a bit strange to bring your guests home if you're a guest yourself. And there's only one word to describe guests who create infant-sized pits on the owner's designer sofa with their feet: abominable.

I gave a cool greeting to Pelin, who opened the door for me with very red cheeks, and headed straight for my study, I heard the idiot bloke lying on my sofa remark, "Your landlady's pretty fit."

I'd reached that age when young guys fancied me. The worst thing about it was that I didn't find it pleasant at all.

Before changing my clothes, I sat at my desk and looked at the list I'd made the previous week. I'd crossed out one of the items that day:

*Is Habibe lying, or İnci?*

I got up and shut the door so as not to hear the sounds coming from the sitting room. But as soon as I sat down again, I realized I was thirsty, so I went to the kitchen for a glass of water. I returned to my study with a large glass of water, a bowl of ice and a bottle of whisky. After all, the apartment was big enough for three people to roam about without bumping into each other.

241

I sat down at my desk again.

With my eyes fixed on the shelves of books, I sat there smoking and drinking whisky.

I didn't feel like removing my make-up and massaging night cream into my face in tiny circles that night, with the result that when I awoke the next morning I lost a few eyelashes as I tried to prise apart the upper and lower lashes of my right eye. And I hadn't brushed my teeth before going to bed the night before. I felt really dreadful.

I went into the bathroom and felt even worse when I saw my blood-shot eyes in the mirror. I filled the bath. Having a bath in the morning is a strange experience. The good thing is that it makes you feel like someone who doesn't have to work and is lucky enough to be able to set aside any hour of the day for such pleasures. The bad thing is that a bath of still water just doesn't have the refreshing effect of a shower, and you lie there feeling sleepier than ever.

I put on my bathrobe, wound a towel around my head and went into the study. I hadn't aired the room the previous night, and it smelled disgustingly of cigarettes. Pelin had woken up and was obviously alone. She put her head round the door.

"Good morning," she said with a radiant smile.

"Are you going to open up the shop?" I asked.

She was in such a happy state that even this didn't affect her mood.

"Just about to go," she said.

I opened the balcony window to air the room, stubbed out my cigarette and went to get dressed.

I returned to my study, armed with a cup of green tea, and sat down to ring Habibe, but it was still too early for people who didn't have to work.

The phone rang for a long time before anyone picked up. Finally, I heard a sleepy voice say, "Hello."

"Hello, it's Kati," I said, then remained silent as I tried to find a suitable way of explaining who I was.

"Hello, how are you?" said the woman, still sounding sleepy.

"Do you remember me?" I asked.

"How could I forget you?" she said.

We both laughed. Habibe was obviously one of those rare people who can laugh the moment they wake up.

"So, you haven't gone back to Mount Ida yet," I said.

"The guest house doesn't have many clients at this time of year. My partner's taking care of things," she said.

"Did I wake you?"

"No, I was awake, but still in bed. It's good you rang."

"I'd like to see you. To ask you about something," I said.

"You're on the European side, aren't you?" she said.

"Yes," I replied.

"I have to meet someone at Teşvikiye today, anyway. If you like, we could meet around there late afternoon," she said. "What's happened? Are you still one of the suspects?"

"You might say that," I said.

"Is five o'clock all right for you?"

"Yes," I said. "Where?"

"You decide," she said. "You know that area better than me."

I can't claim to be very enterprising when it comes to choosing meeting places.

"Why don't you come to my place?" I said, and gave her my address.

I didn't go out all day, but spent the day pacing round the apartment, smoking and thinking. Unlike Batuhan's, everything fitted perfectly into my jigsaw. In fact, almost too perfectly. But what if I was wrong?

243

It frightens me when everything is going well, when my relationships have no problems and business is running smoothly. I have a tendency to think that I'm unworthy of happiness, triumph or love, and that behind everything good lies something bad waiting to make me grovel. My life is better if things aren't perfect. Only then can I be really happy. For instance, if the shop is doing well and I'm having a wonderful love affair, I still find things to fret about. I insist on wearing shoes that pinch my toes. Or I give up smoking and embark on a programme of intense workouts three days a week. I don't drink coffee. Not even tea. And I even cut out toasted cheese sandwiches.

As I said, one of the worst things that can happen to me is for everything to be going well.

It was an incredible triumph to have solved a murder like that, without a hitch. An outstanding success for an amateur detective, don't you think?

But I never want to accuse anyone of murder just for the sake of it. After all, I'm not a predatory police officer, just a bookshop owner doing her own thing. It's not my job to solve crimes, catch murderers and hand them over to the justice system. I'm not one to point the finger at someone and shout, "Murderer!" I wasn't going to further my career, get a pay rise and more holiday leave, or even a medal for extraordinary service as a result of solving this crime.

It didn't concern me. It might in fact have been a woman who left Osman in agony and walked away with his mobile. That woman might have been Habibe. She might have done it out of revenge. For her, maybe it was the best thing to do. Or maybe the worst.

It didn't concern me.

I wasn't going to say anything to Habibe about the murder when she arrived.

I would make no claims or accusations whatsoever.

What I was going to say wouldn't really count as an accusation.

It was up to Habibe to say if it was true or untrue. If she didn't want to talk to me about it, she could get up and leave. That would be the end of it. I wasn't going to force her to listen to my speculations.

I curled up on the sofa and went to sleep.

When I awoke, a bell was ringing. I ran to the door and pressed the entry buzzer. The bell carried on ringing. I rushed to the phone in my study. The ringing sound was moving further away. I ran back towards the sitting room. To my mobile. The ringing stopped.

I threw myself onto the sofa, mobile in hand, and pressed the keys to find out who had rung me. An undisclosed number, which meant: Selim.

I didn't have the energy to talk.

By the time the doorbell rang at exactly five o'clock, I'd pulled myself together. I never expect Turks to be punctual. To be honest, it's difficult even for a German to be punctual in Istanbul. There are constant traffic hold-ups and it's impossible to gauge how much time to allow for getting from one place to another, so you're invariably late.

I pressed the automatic entry buzzer.

Habibe ascended the stairs in a long black billowing tunic. She looked much more elegant than when we first met. Her hairstyle was different too.

"Your hair suits you," I said, as we touched cheeks lightly.

"I've come straight from the hairdresser's. Just had it cut," she said, handing me a package.

"I brought you some gateau, so I hope you're not on a diet."

I made a noise that could mean either yes or no.

We sat in the sitting room at first. Then I realized that curling up in fluffy armchairs is not conducive to getting people to talk about what's on their minds. We could have sat there for days eating chocolate gateau and talking about winter fashions, cake shops in Nişantaşı, hairdressers in Etiler, or Yamamoto's newly opened boutique. The murder, Osman, his mobile or İnci might never have entered our minds.

"Shall we sit on the balcony? We should make the most of the last warm days of the year," I said.

My balcony overlooked the back gardens of my block and several others behind it. It wasn't a view of the Bosphorus, but I could see several of Istanbul's last remaining trees and it felt far away from the noise of the street.

We went through my study onto the balcony.

"It's nice here," said Habibe.

I put the tea and gateau on a side table and stretched my legs out onto the balcony railings.

"I wanted to talk to you about something," I said.

"Yes," she said. "That's what you said on the phone this morning."

I bit my lips.

"So?" she said.

"Well, it's this. On the night Osman was killed, or rather, evening..." I said, stopping for an intake of breath to contain my excitement. "On the evening Osman was killed, might you have called in at Osman's office?"

She scrutinized me with her beautiful grass-green eyes for a moment and then lowered her head slightly.

"What makes you ask that?"

I took my feet off the railings and crossed my legs.

"Look," I said. "I'm not the police, nor do I collaborate with the police." After my first murder case, I'd learnt that when accusing a person of murder it's best to begin by saying I'm just a curious amateur detective.

"What do you mean by that?" she said, still gazing at me cautiously.

"Well," I said, "I have a theory which I thought you might be able to verify. It's just a theory and, even if you say it's true, it will remain a theory."

She pushed away her plate of gateau.

"You mean, you're saying you wouldn't go to the police?"

I nodded.

She ran her tongue over her teeth.

"Why?" she asked.

"Why what?"

"Why wouldn't you go to the police?"

"Why should I?" I said. Not a very explicit answer, I know.

"In that case, what would happen if I confirmed what you're thinking?"

How do you explain your interest in solving a murder to someone who doesn't read detective stories? Would you be able to do it, dear reader? Still, it was worth trying.

"As you know, I sell crime fiction," I said.

"In Kuledibi," she said.

"Not only do I sell crime fiction, I read it too."

"I've never read a detective story," she said. "Our İnci used to read a lot of them. Ever since she was a child."

I cleared my throat. Better to get straight to the point.

"İnci is your cousin," I said, thinking I should have started by establishing that I'd obtained this piece of information from İnci's former maid Hafize Hanım.

"My maternal aunt's daughter," she said. In Turkish, there's a different term for every relative you can possibly think of, but "cousin" isn't often used. Turks prefer to say "my aunt's daughter", "my uncle's son" and so on.

"Your aunt's daughter," I repeated.

"But she was like a sister to me. I loved her more than my own sister."

"Until she was with Osman."

"Until she took Osman away from me," she said, narrowing her lovely eyes and looking at me. "She doesn't accept that she did it, does she? Denies it. I know. She says it's not her fault."

"I haven't spoken to İnci about this," I said. This wasn't quite a lie because we hadn't spoken about it at length.

She looked at her pink varnished nails.

"In that case, how do you know she's my aunt's daughter?"

"I spoke to İnci's maid," I said.

"The famous maid," said Habibe, shaking her head as if finally realizing the significance of previous observations. "Of course, that woman got to know everything that went on in our family. I said to İnci, 'Don't keep her on, she listens too much.' Whenever we sat out on the balcony, she'd be there cleaning the windows. If we moved into the kitchen, she'd be washing up. Wherever we were, she'd be hanging around."

"Did you go to İnci's apartment a lot?"

Habibe smiled wryly. "Didn't the maid tell you? I did at first, of course. When there still seemed some hope of getting İnci sorted out."

"Why did you insist on her leaving Osman?"

Habibe frowned, as if I'd asked a very strange question and looked at me through narrowed eyes.

"I loved Osman and I was pregnant by him. I wanted to make a life with him and have his children." She leant her head on her hand. "Why else?" she said.

"So it wasn't because you were thinking of İnci."

"I was thinking of her, too, of course. She had a future ahead of her. She could have studied. I'd have paid for her education. There was no need for her to become a man's mistress at such a young age. She had such a lively mind, that girl."

I lit a cigarette.

"Were you pregnant when you split up with Osman?"

She stared at the windows of the building opposite.

"What happened to the child?" I asked, with a slight break in my voice.

"It died in my belly," she said. "I committed suicide by taking pills. They couldn't save the child."

"You mean you tried to commit suicide? If you'd committed suicide, you wouldn't be here." Was it really my duty to correct the Turkish of Turks? She ignored what I said and just looked at me absent-mindedly.

"Osman came to the hospital and..." she said, taking a deep breath, "İnci was attracted by his money and Osman to her youth and beauty."

"And in the end, you gave up trying to change İnci and you stopped seeing her."

"I had no choice. The family would have come down on me like a ton of bricks. İnci had done what I'd been unable to do. She got Osman to buy an apartment in her name and was taking care of the whole family. Osman was like a golden goose. İnci had everyone on her side – my mother, aunt, brothers, all of them. She'd go to them every month with fistfuls of money. She bought them all. They didn't even want to lay eyes on me. Even my own mother turned her back on me. So did İnci's mother, who'd been like a mother to me when İnci and I were growing up together."

"But in the end you gave up on the whole business."

"What else could I do? Give it a bit of time, I thought. People won't stick by her after what she's done. So I brought out a CD."

"Eftalya," I said.

"It didn't sell, and nobody wanted to make another CD with me. In the end, I decided to leave Istanbul. I couldn't bear it here any more, being in places Osman and I used to go to together."

"One city, one person," I said, with quiet empathy. My eyes had filled with tears. Habibe was indeed a real woman.

"You can never turn the clock back. If only none of this had happened. My life would have been completely different. We were very poor. Poorer than you can ever imagine. But we always hoped we'd be saved somehow. We all went to school. İnci even graduated from high school. I didn't because I had to leave early."

"Yes, I've seen this in Turks," I said. "Ambitious deprived youngsters who see education as their way out."

"Not any more. Nowadays, all the poor kids want to be singers or footballers."

"You ended up being a singer, actually."

She made a sound that was something between a sob and laughter.

"Anyway, it's not necessary for everybody to study," I said.

She asked me for a cigarette. Her own were finished.

"How did you know I'd been to Osman's office on the evening he died?" she asked.

"I didn't know. I was just guessing," I said.

"There's plenty of time to think about things when I'm out in the mountains," said Habibe.

"Are you talking about the guest house?"

She blinked to indicate "yes".

"But the more I thought about it, the more I realized I wasn't going to be able to bear it," she said, pointing to her heart. "It's as if someone bored a hole in here. I could no longer look at children, lovers, or even pregnant women. Just couldn't bear it. Everything became intolerable for me."

"But why suddenly, after so many years? What happened?"

"What happened? What happened?" cried Habibe. A tear splashed onto the table, followed by more. "I phoned my mother, even though we hardly ever speak. My father left us when we were kids. He went off to Germany as a worker and never came back. At first he'd send money and stuff, but that stopped after a while. Then we heard he was living with another woman in Germany, even though he and my mother weren't even divorced."

This story sounded a familiar one to me.

"My father and this woman had a daughter who wanted to look us up. She'd been to the Turkish Consulate in Germany and managed to get hold of my number from them."

"And your father?"

"My father died," Habibe said abruptly. "When I was talking to his daughter, she said she wanted to come to Turkey and get to know us. That was why I phoned my mother. I couldn't just let this girl turn up without warning anyone."

"And?" I said.

"Well, I phoned my mother and that was when I learnt that İnci was pregnant. I didn't sleep for a week."

"İnci was about to snatch the happiness that should have been yours."

"It wasn't that. I didn't think, 'Why should İnci have something I don't have?' I just felt sad. So very sad!" Another tear landed on the table.

I'd learnt the knack of dealing with weeping women.

"Would you like a drink?" I said.

She nodded.

# A Pedestal Bath, a Stove and a New Neighbour

Autumn in Istanbul is barely noticeable. Spring is the same. We *İstanbullu* have two seasons in our lives: winter and summer. But this year has been an exception. Autumn just went on and on. In fact, so did winter. It was endless. But at least, if the spring, too, goes on for a long time...

Fashions change whatever the weather, of course. I've been in no mood to make do with last year's clothes, so shopping for outfits in the latest colours and styles has been an absolute must. No time to lose! Workers' overalls, oriental dresses with high collars, ripped T-shirts...

But I'm so poor! Buying this splendid apartment has completely drained my bank account. I have to say, it seems strange to be taking out loans all over the place just to invest in a pair of shoes and a few clothes, especially at my age. What a predicament to be in, just for the sake of having a place to call my own.

You will, of course, understand that the splendid apartment in Papağan Street is now registered as my property. I've done my calculations and I'm starting to do it up. I've had to make some concessions, of course. But nothing was going to stop me installing a pedestal bath.

I don't actually have any money left to put in central heating, but Selim says he'll foot that one as a house-warming present. We'll see. Anyway, having lived in Berlin, I can handle lighting

252

a stove. I'm even quite an expert at it. Lighting a stove is a bit like riding a bike or swimming – once learnt, never forgotten.

Pelin didn't go back to her lover, but has spent the whole winter with me. It hasn't been as much fun as being with Fofo, my previous housemate. Still, I've got used to her being around. We were a bit squashed when Mother and her friend Frau Hellersdorf came to stay, because I never did get to Majorca. But we managed. Anyway, I'd rather be surrounded by people than go off on my own to stay with Mother.

I'm moving into my new home in May. Pelin claims she'll have found somewhere to live by then. I think she's having a relationship with the boy who lay on my sofa in his boots, but she tries to keep it a secret from me. She'll probably move into his place.

Lale complains a lot about her new job, but won't pack it in as long as she still remembers what it's like to be unemployed. However, once her days of unemployment become a distant memory, she'll probably quit. Lale has dreams of settling in a village, preferably not in an earthquake zone, and earning a living doing translation work. To me, that's no more likely than her previous idea of settling in Cuba. I haven't said that to her, of course.

In the meantime, something unbelievable has happened. Özlem has made up with her husband, despite having divorced him. She says they're happier now than they've ever been and won't remarry because marriage kills love. If you ask me, all types of love die eventually. Yet that doesn't stop us falling in love over and over again.

Speaking of which, last week I met the mystery person who bought the apartment above mine. He's a gorgeous, bearded guy. We went to choose tiles together for my kitchen. He's really knowledgeable about things like that. I shall definitely invite him to my house-warming party.

# HOTEL BOSPHORUS

## *Esmahan Aykol*

Kati Hirschel is a foreigner and the proud owner of the only
crime bookshop in Istanbul. When the director of a film starring her old
school friend is found murdered in his hotel room, Kati cannot resist the
temptation to start her own maverick investigation. After all,
her friend Petra is the police's principal suspect, and reading all those
detective novels must have taught Kati something.

This suspenseful tale of murder features a heroine who is funny, feisty and
undresses men in her mind more often than she would actually admit,
even to herself. The men are too hot to handle, but is she too cool to resist?
Sharp observation and wry, sexy humour expose Western prejudices about
Turkey as well as Turkish stereotyping of Europeans.

### PRAISE FOR *HOTEL BOSPHORUS*

"A wonderful novel about Istanbul. The Turkish way of life, prejudices,
men, politics, corruption – Esmahan Aykol writes about all these with a
light and humorous touch."

Petros Markaris, author *of Che Committed Suicide* and *Zone Defence*

"Told in a light, chatty style that is likeable and best compared to
the contents of a personal diary we get a varied slice of personal life
that includes pathos, bathos and sexual revelation. As a portrait of a
fascinating city, *Hotel Bosphorus* paints an intriguing and humorous
picture. The further exploits of this feisty heroine suggest a promising
future for what is intended to be an ongoing series. I look forward to
more tales of strong Turkish coffee and cigarettes." *Crime Time*

£8.99/$14.95
**Crime Paperback Original**
ISBN 978-1908524-041
**eBook**
ISBN 978-1908524-058

**www.bitterlemonpress.com**